**FROM ~~DARKNESS~~ TO LIGHT. . . .**

As Preston lifted the ladder into place, the top rung, along with most of his forearm, disappeared into nothingness. Cautiously, he hoisted himself high enough up the ladder to stick his head into the nebulous area. His heart pounded with excitement. He didn't dare to hope.

But it happened. His ghostly head came out into a sunfilled field of golden wheat.

Such light! Nothing existed like it in Duende Meadow, and the utter vastness of the plain shook him with its spaciousness and uncontrollable beauty. . . .

A heavy, rhythmic sound came from nearby, a decidedly unnatural sound no wheat field could create on its own. It was a crimson harvester combine two stories tall, chopping a wide path through the wheat. On the rear of the giant harvester was a bright orange hammer and sickle and the initials CCCP.

The Soviets had won World War III.

# DUENDE MEADOW

## Paul Cook

BANTAM BOOKS
TORONTO · NEW YORK · LONDON · SYDNEY · AUCKLAND

DUENDE MEADOW
*A Bantam Spectra Book / November 1985*

**ISBN 0-553-25374-3**

*Published simultaneously in the United States and Canada*

*Bantam Books are published by Bantam Books, Inc. Its trademark,*
*consisting of the words "Bantam Books" and the portrayal of a*
*rooster, is Registered in U.S. Patent and Trademark Office and in*
*other countries. Marca Registrada. Bantam Books, Inc., 666 Fifth*
*Avenue, New York, New York 10103.*

PRINTED IN THE UNITED STATES OF AMERICA

O    0 9 8 7 6 5 4 3 2 1

*—This is for my mother*

# AUTHOR'S ACKNOWLEDGMENT

In this book I have made free use—and rather fantastic use at that—of Rupert Sheldrake's recent studies and speculations on the theory of evolution. For a more detailed and certainly less libelous discussion of morphogenetic fields, beyond what I have provided herein, I refer the reader to Sheldrake's work, *A New Science of Life: The Hypothesis of Formative Causation* (Los Angeles: J. P. Tarcher, Inc., 1981).

*To the strong,*
*it is the weak who are wrong.*

—Nineteenth-century Russian proverb

# 1

*We move from darkness to light. . . .*

The words came like a poetic refrain into Preston Kitteridge's mind as he carefully gazed down into the darkness that yawned nearly thirteen hundred feet below him. The ladder upon which he was making his Climb did not shake, for there were no winds this high above Duende Meadow, but the danger in the darkness was there.

However, it was as his brother, Jay, had once told him: Pierce the darkness and the light will shine forth.

But Jay Kitteridge was not risking his life making the Climb this year, nor was Jay interested in adding another section to the ladder's topmost limit of their world. Darkness or light notwithstanding, it was still frightening.

Preston Kitteridge, guided by the tiny crystal beacons at his shoulders, looked up at the ladder which stretched forbiddingly upward into the dark, drawing him on by its netherial challenge. Darkness. Sheer darkness. No stars. No moon. Nothing but the rungs attached by those daredevils in years past crazy enough to jeopardize their well-being by climbing the ladder in celebration of the Gathering.

Beneath him like a starry constellation glittered the Meadow of Ghosts. Duende Meadow. A small city of its own, it seemed to ignore him, but he knew that scores of other *duendes* such as himself were also, in their own peculiar manner, enjoying the Gathering Day. He was simply too far above them to see or hear any such activity.

Still, if the automated "runners" which trundled up along

1

the outer rungs of the ladder ahead of Preston lost their mechanical grip and the nylon safety lines snapped, a fall from such a height would definitely make this one of the more memorable Gathering Day celebrations. And it would certainly be his last act upon the earth.

Or, more properly said, his last act *within* the earth.

For Preston Kitteridge was climbing inside solid rock, and this was a notion from which he could never escape. Each rung he mounted as he towed his scaffold tent beneath him, which also included another ten feet of attachable rungs for the ladder at the top, took him up through the lazy sediment of Kansas topsoil. Just how far above the present apex of the ladder Kansas lay, nobody down in the Meadow knew. Neither the main computer in Saxifrage Mall, the civilian side of the Meadow, nor the one in the Hive, which was the military adjunct to the Meadow, had any reliable estimates of just how far beneath the true surface of the earth the Meadow existed. All they knew was that most of the country above them was probably still trapped underneath the ice sheets left over from the devastating nuclear winter which had set in centuries ago after mankind's last war.

However, as all Gathering Day climbers secretly hoped, Preston Kitteridge yearned for that moment—that unique Climb—when some lucky hero would finally pierce the surface of the earth, even if it would only be to enter the Ice. Besides, he was getting too old for this sort of thing. He had made the Climb five times in the past and he was now thirty-three years old. In all likelihood, this was his last Climb.

Yet he couldn't help but anticipate the Ice. He knew that it would be there, the gray remnant of that terrible conflagration which followed the Last War when billions of tons of soot, ash, and dust blocked out the sun's vital light. Though the Meadow had escaped such destruction, the *duendes* all knew that a new Ice Age, with ice sheets a mile or more in depth, had settled in after a nuclear exchange in which a known sixty thousand warheads were traded between the Soviet Union and the United States.

But as Preston understood all too well, it would be much better to see the Ice than to see the destruction itself—even after six hundred years. That part of Kansas, from which the original Meadow had been derived, had sustained a great many air- and ground-bursts from Soviet missiles, given the number of Minuteman silos and MX trailers that had once roamed the Wichita-Topeka area.

Indeed, Preston Kitteridge could not ignore his heritage even as he climbed. It was literally an act of moving from darkness toward the light, for the "light" above—should he happen to reach it on the Climb—would reveal the truth to them all of what really happened six hundred years ago.

And if he should arrive to witness such a thing, he would arrive on the scene as a ghost, a *duende*.

He touched the wafer-mike at his collar. "How's the Field registering, Travis?" he called out in the spectral darkness.

A sturdy, almost grandfatherly voice came back to him instantly. Travis Wainwright, down in the Games Room of the military Hive, spoke out. "It's quite strong. Holding well. How are *you* doing, Preston? There was a tremor in the ghost-lights far to the east last night. Can you see anything?"

Preston paused momentarily on the ladder, letting the runners above him shinny up another three yards, drawing the safety lines taut. "I don't see anything from here. If they were active, I missed them. I was probably asleep in the scaffold tent by then."

Even though most of the Meadow's *duendes* were presently celebrating the Gathering, there were many others not inclined to indulge in their various intoxicants. These *duendes* were watching Preston's progress up the ladder. Dr. Travis Wainwright, the head Appleseed of Saxifrage Mall, was a longtime friend of the Kitteridge clan. The chief botanist of the Meadow had become something of a father to both Preston and his older brother, Jay, when their own parents vanished years ago. And it was good to hear his voice, as it was also good to know that the Field was maintaining itself with its free-flow aura of atmosphere at such a distance from the Meadow.

The Climb, and further construction of the ladder, was a ritual only twenty years old in the six-hundred-year history of the Meadow. That no one had thought of it before was a mystery to them, for there was not all that much to do in the compound. The Arks and the military Hives virtually maintained themselves, and the *duendes* were always looking for one excuse or another to make their ghostly lives more interesting than they were as they waited out the long healing of the earth far above them. And the idea of building a ladder, one rung at a time, seemed to be a good one, something a bit more special to do on Gathering Day.

However, there were dangers involved, and the fact that the one-hundred-and-sixty-plus inhabitants of the Meadow might be the only surviving humans left after World War Three made many of the Meadow elders—Travis Wainwright was not among them—fearful of an accident which might rob the gene pool of another precious representative.

Dr. Wainwright's voice chimed out. "We're reading you at one thousand, three hundred and twenty-two feet. Are you double-checking all of the rung-joints?"

Preston smiled to himself as he climbed. "Travis, I might be crazy, but I'm not stupid. Of course I'm checking them."

The modulated voice of the chief Appleseed came back to him through the wafer. "Well, I just don't trust that Sebastian Monaco. He might have sabotaged them when he was up there last year."

Preston continued to mount the rungs. He said, "Monaco wouldn't do anything like that. Besides, he'd have no way of knowing who'd make the Climb this year."

"Still," the chief Appleseed continued, "we wouldn't want Holly to become a widow, would we?" The botanist's voice resonated with a touch of humor. Travis knew that their marriage wasn't even scheduled for another year, but already the "married man" jokes and the expected ribbing were quick in coming from the older folks of Saxifrage. It was perhaps a father's role to say such things.

"I have no plans to make Holly a widow, but I do plan on breaking Monaco's record," he reported.

He felt embarrassed in speaking about Holly this way, but his enmity for Lieutenant Sebastian Monaco was well known. Marriages or other procreative arrangements were done through the Meadow computers in order to enhance the best possible genetic combinations for the *duendes'* survival. He had personally considered it a matter of luck, or divine intervention, that the computers had chosen Holly Ressler and himself for a coupling.

Sebastian Monaco had lost out in that winnowing process, at least as far as getting permission from the computer. But that didn't stop him from trying whenever he could to persuade Holly that it might be in her best interest to devote her affections elsewhere. In fact, as Preston continued to climb the ladder further, staring up into the pitch darkness overhead, he realized that Monaco was somewhere below him in the Meadow, perhaps at the Saxifrage Bacchanalia, with Holly.

And while the Ark computer's decisions were never carved in stone, it was true that women of the Meadow, regardless of their scientific station, had to start bearing children as young as possible. And Holly Ressler, all of seventeen, was a pretty hot ticket, as Travis Wainwright once put it rather evocatively. The fact that Holly was young enough to be their baby sister didn't appear to bother either suitor, particularly Preston, who had had a substantial crush on her even before he had been aware of it. He wasn't, however, too thrilled about having the six children the Ark computer wanted them to have. He didn't know if his condominium in the Salina Ark could contain all those little people. He was having a hard enough time, such as it was, containing his two cats, Ike and Tina.

But if six more Kitteridges improved the chances that *Homo sapiens sapiens* might recover from the Armageddon several centuries in their past, then six more Kitteridges it would be.

Besides that, with the Meadow's advanced techniques in reconstructive surgery, Holly Ressler-Kitteridge would always have the body of a seventeen-year-old girl, even as she approached grandmotherhood.

Preston continued upward, rising in the foggy ghost-light that was perpetually drifting on out ahead of him.

"What's the reading now, Travis?" he called out, wiping a glaze of sweat from his brow.

Dr. Wainwright's voice returned. "We gauge you at one thousand, three hundred and ninety feet. If everything's the same as before, you've got a ways to go yet."

Kitteridge had been taking the Climb slowly, allowing the rung-runners to move up, pulling the safety lines ahead of him. Thoughts of Holly at the Bacchanalia below, thoughts of the darkness of solid rock above, kept impinging upon his mind, distracting him heavily.

But that was the danger, letting your mind slip. Ten years ago one of the first record-holders, a Native American of Cheyenne origin, Bill Laughing by name, perished when the rung-runners accidentally broke loose. You had to watch where you were going, making sure that all the rung-sections were sealed and sturdy when you got to the top.

But then, living in eternal darkness was something of a distraction itself. No one knew for sure if Bill Laughing died by accident, or if he had committed a kind of grisly suicide. Perhaps old Bill had yearned for the days when his Cheyenne ancestors wandered the Plains, and realizing that he would never have them, he simply let go. To their whole generation, phenomena such as stars, the sun, clouds, and the moon were almost myths, relegated to pictures surviving in the tens of thousands of hours of stored videos in the computer libraries. They were part of a world wrenched from them when the Soviet Union and the United States—and several dozen other trigger-happy nations in Europe and the Middle East—decided to bring history to an end.

Preston kept on, one rung at a time.

"Fourteen hundred, Preston," Dr. Wainwright said.

All Kitteridge could hear was the rasp and wheeze of his own breathing; all he could see above him were the rung-runners riding up the outside edges of the ladder, hauling the safety lines after it.

"Fourteen hundred thirty," the chief Appleseed said after a few minutes. "How are you feeling now?"

Kitteridge paused and hugged the ladder. "Tired, now," he said. "Really tired. It's got to be the excitement. Atmosphere seems to be fine, though."

The wafer-mike rattled. "Your bio-function readings are normal, and the Field generator in your belt is at optimum. Why don't you stop and rest? There's no hurry, you know."

"I know," Preston said, gaining his breath. "Just complaining out loud. That's all."

"We've got some well-wishers on the line," Dr. Wainwright then announced. "Want me to patch them in?"

"All depends on who they are," Kitteridge muttered. "Go ahead anyway." He began climbing again.

"Hi, baby!" Holly Ressler's cheery voice resounded from the wafer-mike at his shoulder. "How're you doing way up there?"

Then she sneezed.

Preston smiled. He couldn't hear the Bacchanalia in the background wherever she was calling from. "Fine, just fine. I'm almost to the top. Going to break Monaco's record for sure this time."

The rung-runners silently eased upward as he slowed his pace. The shoulder-beacons danced phantasmagorically, and he seemed as if he were at the bottom of a well of light.

"You see any of the ghost-lights?" Holly called out. "We saw a bunch in the Lute and some in the Butterfly constellation last night. That's real close to the top of the ladder where you are."

"Well, I didn't see anything," he reported.

For a seventeen-year-old girl, Holly had a rather husky voice, a throaty quality that separated her from the other girls of the seven Arks in the Meadow. What also separated Holly Ressler from the other girls her age was her rank. She was already a supervisor of the Sonoran Ark, the self-contained desert biosphere that was located at the southern end of Saxifrage Mall. Being a supervisor was no petty ranking given to a precocious youngster by condescending adults; it came with responsibilities, and she was easily capable of handling them.

Sudden static could be heard over the wafer-mike and Holly was cut off. Instead, the sounds of the Meadow-wide celebration could be heard.

Then over the communicator came the voice of Sebastian Monaco.

"I understand that you're about to break my record, son," he said with a touch of bravado. Something fragile, perhaps made of glass or china, broke within the mike's range. Laughter followed boisterously.

But Kitteridge was quick to respond. "If I'm lucky," he snorted, "I'll break more than one record."

"Yes, but you're missing all the fun, chum," responded the distant and jubilant Monaco, wherever he was in the Meadow.

"I'm not missing a thing," Preston said with obvious disdain, and immediately proceeded to climb even further—and faster.

The one quality which they could do without in the Meadow was hatred. It was just this sort of minor-level antagonism which had brought the world its long-anticipated nuclear holocaust, although on a much larger scale. But Preston couldn't help it. Sebastian Monaco belonged to the military Hive half of the Meadow and was not an Appleseed at all. He didn't even have the temperament to be such. More important, Sebastian Monaco was also a lazarus, one of five awakened from their 'combs in the Hive complex in order to facilitate the breeding capacities of the whole Meadow. A man still lodged in a twenty-first-century consciousness, Monaco had an aggressiveness and combativeness that was slightly out of sync with the rest of the compound. Perhaps six hundred years of inbreeding had driven that quality out of them, but even so, Monaco was a reminder of the way their forebears used to be.

But the fact that Monaco was clearly not in the Hive Games Room along with Dr. Wainwright and the other Meadow authorities only meant that he might run into Holly, or even worse try to track her down. Indeed, the tone in his mocking voice seemed to suggest the possibility.

Preston tried to push the thought of Holly and Monaco together out of his mind. He had other things to think about.

"Look," he announced to anyone who might be listening at that point. "I've got a few more feet to go yet, and I need to do this in silence. I don't want to hear anything about what I'm missing or what the Butterfly or the Lute did last night while I was asleep."

"Temper, temper . . ." Monaco said from somewhere far away.

"We'll keep it down, Preston," Dr. Wainwright said solemnly, cutting Monaco off. "We just wanted to stay in touch, that's all. Let us know when you reach the top rung."

With a deft flick of his wrist, Kitteridge switched off his wafer communicator and concentrated on his careful climbing.

In the ghostly silence all he could see above him were the rungs of the ladder, the rung-runners, and . . . *blackness*. The blackness he had known all of his thirty-three years. The blackness they had all known.

Slowly, carefully, and more determined than ever before, he climbed.

Far below, hardly visible at that altitude, was Duende Meadow and all that it meant. Toward the close of the twentieth century a British botanist, named Sheldrake, discovered the existence of what he called "morphogenetic fields" while working in India. According to his research, morphogenetic fields imbued literally everything in existence. He was never able to describe what the fields themselves actually *were*, but others pursuing their own investigations likened them to genuine auras. Every living creature had them.

A Sheldrake Field, or m-field as they were later termed, was the energy structure which gave an individual accretion of matter—living or otherwise—its particular form. Everything in nature, from people to trees, from algae to thunderclouds, even the lint in a mean man's navel, had its own attendant m-field. Everything which had *form*, had such at the behest of a preexisting morphogenetic field. There were no exceptions.

However radical and controversial this metaphysical intrusion into the science of evolution had been, it was soon confirmed experimentally. It wasn't long after that when the government of the United States, which had been underwriting most of the research into m-fields, hushed everything up. The military, apparently, had found some unusual applications of Sheldrake's theories.

With special covert CIA and Pentagon funding, a group of technicians began working on a way to destabilize matter in a Sheldrake field, while at the same time maintaining the integrity of the field itself. The assembled technicians likened the process to the already known, but little understood, Kirlian photography which could record imagistically the presence of pieces cut from maple leaves or fingers shorn from a gecko lizard's hand. The "field" stayed whole even though the leaf part or finger was missing. The leaf and the lizard palm remained pure, in the photograph, *because they were supposed to*. Their respective m-fields, or auras, were still operative. The scientists eventually made the discovery that the m-field of an object, though decidedly present in real time, was nonetheless invisible, intangible, and otherwise totally removed from any kind of physical relationship with the world of men and machines.

But that was not all they found. Even the earth itself had an elusive m-field. Indeed, it had many, depending upon where you looked within the layers of the planet. The two main m-fields which the scientists discovered centered around the m-field which constituted the surface of the earth, and the m-field which maintained itself worldwide at sea level. This was very important to the military planners of the time.

All this took place at a moment in history when the great nations of the earth were preparing themselves for the catastrophe which would culminate in the fires of World War Three. All of the experts—both hawk and dove—knew that a nuclear war using even a tenth of the available weaponry would eradicate all human life and most all of the higher forms of flora and fauna in the northern hemisphere. Their modest projections suggested that once the nuclear fallout of radioactive dust and ash obscured the sun, all life in both hemispheres would be imperiled. An Ice Age lasting centuries would be ushered in, preventing any kind of agriculture above the equator—should anyone possibly survive to till what was left of the soil. But once the bilious clouds of the nuclear winter dissipated, there would come weeks, perhaps months, of very intense bombardment by shortwave ultraviolet radiation. Lamaseries in Tibet and island communities in the South Pacific, isolated though they might be, would also be touched by the cataclysm. Perhaps the only living creatures that would survive would only be found scavenging the depths of the continental shelves. It would be a very primitive life indeed.

So using Sheldrake morphogenetic-field technology, the concept of Duende Meadow took shape in the minds of America's desperate planners. But to build it, they would have to be circumspect and clandestine, lest the diligent Russians in their orbiting sky-city suspect.

Locating themselves in Salina, Kansas, in the abandoned offices and shops of a recently bankrupt shopping mall on the outskirts of town, the scientists converted seven of the largest stores of Saxifrage Mall into biospheres, or Arks. Each Ark contained representative samples of plant and animal life belonging to all of the climatic zones of America from the Gulf-Bayou region to the Colorado-Alpine area. The emptied J. C. Penney store became the Sonoran Ark, the vacant Broadway store became the Orleans Ark, and so on, until the scientists felt that they might be able to restore—if on a desperate and threadbare level—much of the life of North America should the survivors be able to return.

However, so little was then known about the effects of gamma or ultraviolet radiation on m-fields that the technicians opted for lowering the Mall, once it was "destabilized," to the second shell of the earth's morphogenetic field that resided at sea level. In Salina, Kansas, this would place the Mall—now dubbed Duende Meadow, from the Spanish word *duende,* meaning "ghost" or "goblin"—over a thousand feet inside solid rock, far underneath the screaming terrors of that horrible war and long, cold winter.

But the scientists and their families had almost been

caught sleeping—literally. World War Three occurred, Kansas-time, at 3:30 A.M. on Christmas Day in those early years of the new century, when America was asleep. The great Field engines beneath the Mall were engaged at midnight when the Pentagon and NORAD confirmed the advent of a possible nuclear strike, and under the cover of thick clouds, which cut them off from orbiting Russian eyes, Saxifrage Mall, like the saxifrage flower folding up its petals for the harsh Rocky Mountain winter, "deopaqued" itself and slowly sank to the safety of the earth's sea-level m-field.

Three hours after that, thirty direct-impact craters appeared in and around the Salina area, with another ten or so touching down near Topeka, Lawrence, and Wichita. The new *duendes* recorded explosions—and subsequent Minuteman and MX liftoffs in retaliation—throughout the morning. Thirty thousand in all.

Then followed a silence above them that would last them six hundred years.

The new *duendes*, numbering in those days around eighty-five souls, never ventured back up. As their computer profiles told them, there would be nothing to see.

The new *duendes*, under the guidance of their mayor, Alberto Tito Ríos, were now Appleseeds, and they went about their business of keeping the Arks sustained and keeping themselves mentally fit in their world of constantly illuminated darkness. They knew that their wait would be a long one, but as long as their fusion generator kept them in their protective ghostly state, there was a chance that men and women would once again walk the forests and meadows of the earth.

Preston Kitteridge's own life was interesting enough, in this, the sixth century of their wait. He was the supervisor of the Salina Ark. While most of the flora and fauna indigenous to the Midwest was contained there—the original building belonged to the Sears in the former shopping center—it was also mostly held in cryogenic stasis or simple storage. He was an excellent administrator, but he had little to do. The Ark took care of itself. Thus, when the yearly drawing for the Climb came around, he usually put his name in for it. It gave him something exciting to look forward to.

But even though Preston harbored the desire, as did all participants of the Climb, to be the first to make it into the lower reaches of the Ice, he knew that such an event would be a shock to his *duende*-engendered world-view. There was a computer scenario which had suggested that there might not even be an atmosphere blanketing the earth anymore; that it might have been blown off into space. All of that depended upon how much hydrogen necessary for oxygen-nitrogen generation had been lost through ozone depletion. There was a grave possibility that their centuries of waiting out the darkness would all be in vain—that they would have to remain *duendes* forever.

So despite his desire to make it to the Ice, he didn't want to be the bearer of bad tidings.

Still, that didn't prevent him from placing his name in the hat each year of the Gathering Day for the Climb up the ladder. Just the fact that Sebastian Monaco had made the Climb three times already, and each time making it to the top of the ladder to add on another ten feet, was enough to goad him on. The rivalry seemed even more intense now that Holly Ressler was approaching her eighteenth birthday. Monaco was always there in the shadows, somehow, and thinking about Holly in this way made Preston's loins ache.

But he wasn't about to let the Climb record—or Holly—fall into Monaco's waiting hands. He didn't care that the Meadow might lose his potential genes if he fell. There was enough of his sperm and chromosome samples in cold storage to ensure that something of the Kitteridge strain would persist, assuming that his brother Jay didn't disappear as well. He was more immediately concerned at the moment about pain. Ghost he might be to the real world, but a fall of a thousand or more feet to the surface of the sea-level m-field which held up the Meadow would make just about anything go *splat*!

However, the top of the ladder was finally in sight as his shoulder lamps threw their shivering cones of crystalline light up into the preternatural darkness which surrounded him.

"I see it," he announced into his wafer-mike, quickly switching it back on. "I made it!"

"We read you, Preston," Dr. Wainwright swiftly returned.

Preston could hear shouts of exuberant joy over the channel as the other *duendes* in the Games Room cheered him on.

But then Dr. Wainwright's concerned voice came back with something he did not want to hear.

"Preston, we're picking up ghost-light disturbances to the southeast."

The rung-runners eased to a halt, locking into place, as Preston gained the top of the ladder. He hooked his arm through the topmost rung for support. His safety lines dangled to either side of him. He dimmed his shoulder lamps and glanced around searchingly.

"Where are they?" he called out. "In the Butterfly? I don't see them from here."

"No," Dr. Wainwright returned. "In the Spider's Lair."

Kitteridge couldn't see the Lair from where he was perched in the high darkness of the earth's crust. But that in itself didn't mean anything. Even though the Meadow was deep below the surface, there was some unexplainable phenomenon generated by the Sheldrake Field process which none of the best *duendes* could account for.

The ghost-lights were among them. Part of the underside of the upper m-field—that which paralleled the earth's surface—the ghost-lights appeared very much like stars in a constellation. Indeed, the phenomenon had only begun appearing a scant twenty years previously, and for the inhabitants of Saxifrage Mall and the Hive they passed for authentic constellations. The Lute and the Butterfly were closest to him, relatively speaking, but the Spider's Lair, a complex of scintillating coruscations, seemed the most sinister to them all. It, however, was at some distance from the pinnacle of the ladder.

Dr. Wainwright came back. "We've been recording brief flare-ups during your Climb, Preston, but we didn't want to alarm you."

Still, he couldn't see them. He could make out the pale green stars and glitterings of the Three Bells and the Scythe, but they too were far off in the distance.

"Let's just hope they don't begin wandering around," he told them down in the Games Room.

"They haven't so far," Dr. Wainwright responded.

The previous night, halfway in his Climb, he had unlimbered his scaffold tent and slept, thus not seeing the outbreaks of the ghost-lights. He probably shouldn't have made the Climb in his condition anyway. He'd spent much of the day carousing with his friends in the Portland Ark and was rather exhausted when he had set out on his Climb.

Yet, what the *duendes* did not know *could* hurt them.

Since so little was truly understood about the m-field process, the ghost-lights were always a cause for alarm. If anything, they might be harbingers of possible disruptions in the m-field which sustained them. And that's what all the *duendes* feared the most. Should the m-field break down, they would suddenly find themselves occupying the same space as solid Kansas crustal rock. The ghost-lights were simple reminders of just how complex and mysterious was the world they had been forced to inherit.

"Where's Jay?" Preston then asked. "What's he have to say about the activity in the Lair?"

Dr. Wainwright said, "The last we heard from him, he was in his observatory. He said he was meditating. We'd have probably heard from him by now if he'd been using his scope, because the Lair's really acting up. He's sure a strange one, that boy."

Preston said nothing, acknowledging with silence the truth to the chief Appleseed's words. Jay was a strange one, indeed.

Instead, he began tying down the scaffold tent so that it wouldn't interfere with his work. He then drew up the ten feet of links for the top of the ladder.

The ladder itself did not sway or bend with his weight at that height, nor did its own mass affect it. Every one hundred yards there were "anchors" which locked the ladder into the m-field of the particular layer of sediment through which it ghosted upward. On this Climb, Preston did not need to bring a rung with an anchor in it, which would have doubled his weight load. Still, he couldn't help but recall just how high he was.

He concentrated instead on setting the first section of the ladder. Each rung was a single H shape, and like pieces of a puzzle, each section was designed to fit snugly into the one below it. Ferroplastic seals sizzled when snapped apart around the linkages, and Preston tested each one to make sure that it was secure. As he noticed, Sebastian Monaco had done a good job last year in attaching his own linkages. It bore his weight well.

And now he had the record for this year.

"How is the Spider's Lair doing?" he then called out as he hefted another rung into place.

There was a pause before Dr. Wainwright returned to

the microphone. "The Lair seems stable. There's some movement in the Butterfly, but not much."

"If the Butterfly starts flying in this direction," he said as he wrestled with the rungs, "let me know."

Dr. Wainwright invisibly far below seemed pleased by his jocularity. He returned with some of it, saying, "I'd worry more if the Spider came after you. Butterflies are nothing."

Yet, they both knew that something threw Bill Laughing to his death years ago—and it just might have been a shift in the ghost-lights.

The ladder links went easily into place. The ghost-lights stayed in the distance and he knew now that they were of little consequence where he was.

However, he had already decided to return that day rather than spend another dangerous night in the scaffold tent. *Duendes* could be a superstitious lot and Preston wasn't afraid to admit that there were a few things in the dark that frightened him.

Besides, if he managed to get down tonight, he'd be able to spend what was left of the Bacchanalia with Holly.

But then something happened which no one—least of all himself—expected to happen.

As he lifted the eighth linkage into place, the H-shaped rung, along with most of his forearm, disappeared into the nothingness.

"Nemesis!" he gasped, bringing the link and arm back down into the light of his shoulder lamps.

He stared up at the black firmament above the ladder.

"Preston?" came Dr. Wainwright's suddenly concerned voice. "*Preston?*"

Kitteridge's shoulder lights danced nervously as their beams pushed up into the emptiness.

It was an emptiness that seemed to come to an abrupt *end*.

"Preston, what is it?"

"I don't know," he said quickly. "Something's wrong."

"What's going on up there?" Travis Wainwright asked worriedly. "Is it the ghost-lights?"

"No." Preston said soberly. "It's not the lights."

Cautiously he lifted up the link, and again it—along with the hand which held it—disappeared. However, carefully feeling his way, he managed to attach the rung's lower edges into place and engage the ferroplastic strips, connecting it.

Then very slowly he hoisted himself high enough up the ladder to stick his head into the nebulous area. His heart pounded with excitement. He didn't dare hope it or think it, and had not given the matter much thought since their computer projections told him that the likelihood of it happening was remote.

But it happened.

Preston Kitteridge's head—albeit incorporeal and with ghostly astonishment—came out into a sun-filled field of golden wheat.

With a cry of alarm, he fell from the ladder.

# 2

Dangling upside down like an insect snared in a spider's web, Kitteridge grappled with the safety lines as the rung-runners locked onto the outer edges of the ladder. He had fallen approximately thirty feet, but the brakes in the rung-runners had engaged sufficiently to prevent him from plummeting any further.

Twisting about, Kitteridge slammed into the ladder. One of his shoulder beacons snapped off and flashed out into the darkness beneath him. The scaffold tent was also knocked loose, and he watched as it vanished out of sight, bound for the constellation of Duende Meadow far below.

"Dark Nemesis!" he swore as his hands slid along the safety lines. The shadow cast about by the remaining shoulder beacon was also confusing matters because it had been bent inward, blinding him.

With a free right hand he adjusted it as a hundred voices yammered at him from the wafer-mike. Dr. Wainwright was foremost among them.

"Hey, boy! You got a problem up there you want to tell us about?"

"The scaffold tent's on its way down," he said dryly, swinging back and forth. "Look out below."

He righted himself and held onto the hard plastic of the ladder.

"What did you say, Preston?" came Dr. Wainwright's voice. "You had an accident, or what?"

"I fell," he told them. "And the tent got kicked loose."

17

"You want to tell us why?" All was deathly still down below in the Hive Games Room.

Preston peered up at the black fathoms overhead—or what *appeared* to be black fathoms. The remaining shoulder beacon illuminated the crown of the disappearing ladder where it breached the upper m-field of the earth's surface.

"I made it to the top, Travis."

A breath of silence passed between them as the *duendes* down below tried to make sense of what he had said.

"Come again? You want to repeat that?"

"I don't know why, but the surface is a lot closer than we thought it was," he affirmed.

"That's impossible," Dr. Wainwright came back. "The computer says it should be at least three hundred more feet—"

Preston began mounting the rungs as the rung-runners, on his command, slowly eased back up to the very top. They got there before he did, disappearing from the light of his remaining beacon.

*Wheat.*

And crawly things. And sunlight! A veritable ocean of sunlight!

His ghostly head protruded up into the topside world to find itself hovering in a vast field of pure wheat. Amber sunlight canted softly through the brittle brown stalks of durum which crested in the afternoon breeze more than two feet above the surface m-field.

He instantly recognized the wheat to be similar to the several strains which they kept in storage down in the Salina Ark, but there were insects here of an order he'd never seen before.

*Mutations.* But clearly they were of an amicable sort, for they seemed to thrive heartily in their world.

"Okay, Pres," Dr. Wainwright said almost coyly. "How many guesses do we get? Naturally, this isn't going to work if you don't give us any clues—"

Kitteridge could barely comprehend the rapturous vision before him. His mind-set as a *duende* simply had not allowed for the existence of wheat. Or insects. Or even an azure blue Kansas sky.

Ice, yes. Flat, debilitated wastelands, possibly.

But not this.

He said, "Wait a minute. Travis. I want to add on the last section of the ladder. You're not going to believe this."

His collision with the scaffold tent had sent down all of his remaining supplies, including his food and water. He had, however, secured the rungs of the ladder by another nylon cord. He had just two left.

"Fill us in. What do you see?" returned Wainwright's voice with a touch of impatience. Everyone was listening now; they knew that something was up.

"I want to get a clearer view of the surface," Preston told them as he began carefully attaching the last H of the ladder.

He was, at this point, fully contained—if in ghostly form—within the stalks of wheat as he pulled the ferroplastic seals on the ladder rungs. He had to make sure the adhesive took effect before he went up any further, but the gently waving stalks of wheat constituted a great distraction.

"Preston," Dr. Wainwright's voice returned crisply. "We've run another altitude check in the computer and there's no way that—"

The seals hissed into place and Preston hoisted himself up into a sitting position, still attached to the safety lines.

"The computer doesn't know what it's talking about," he said flatly.

"There should be at least thirty feet of ice still on the ground."

He hooked his feet in the rungs underneath him for greater balance. Something that resembled a grouse or a quail fluttered by and he gripped the top rung to prevent himself from falling. This was almost too much! They had a small aviary down in the Meadow, but most of their birds were kept in cold storage. This was the first real bird he'd ever seen in its natural environment.

But there was more to look at than just the bird.

Such light! Nothing existed like it in the Meadow, and the utter vastness of the plain shook him with its spaciousness and uncontrollable beauty. Wheat stretched from horizon to horizon, seemingly endless. Only here and there did an occasional cottonwood protrude. And there were clouds! *Real clouds!*

He was terrified.

"Camera," he gasped, breathing raggedly.

"What?" came Wainwright's stolid voice.

"Should've brought a camera. Something. Anything—"

"What are you babbling about?"

To the far west were the cetacean humps of low hills. The wheat seemed to flourish wildly there as well, almost as if it was the natural ground cover. Bushes huddled near the cottonwoods like little beggar men and the hills were dotted with them as well.

None of their computer projections could have possibly given rise to a vision such as this. Not after a full-exchange thermonuclear war. Not after six hundred years.

Six thousand seemed more likely. But not this. *This* was impossible, the content of dreams.

He touched his wafer-mike, amplifying it. "It's like videos of old Kansas. Wheat. Miles and miles of it," he told them down in the Hive Games Room. "And you should see what the sky looks like. It's the brightest blue I've ever seen. And there are some clouds. . . ."

He seemed to sway upon the ladder, gripped by the hypnotic spell induced by the world around him. He was unused to such enormity.

"Where are the ice sheets? The glaciers that were supposed to reach this far south—"

"No," Preston reported. "It doesn't even look cold."

Although there was a slight breeze outside, he could not feel it. Nor could he perceive the actual topside temperature. But he knew that wheat—or any mutagenic strain—could only survive within a specific range of climatic variations. Clearly, this part of Kansas was not caught in the weir of another Ice Age, even a man-made one.

Other birds frolicked in the sky nearby.

"Nemesis!" he gasped. "It's a White-throated Swift. I swear, it's a White-throated Swift!"

There were other birds as well, but these were too far off to recognize and identify clearly.

"Swearing doesn't become you, son," Dr. Wainwright scolded.

Someone standing close to Dr. Wainwright muttered, "Maybe he's gone crazy—"

"I'm not crazy," Preston retorted. "I do know that we can live up here. We've got to opaque out."

Instantly, almost whispering, Travis Wainwright returned. "Not on your life, Preston. I think you'd better come back down. The height's getting to your head."

"I'm all right," he told them. "I've never been this all right in my entire life."

However, he understood Dr. Wainwright's concern. Every *duende* carried his or her own m-field generator woven into the complex circuitry of their workbelts. So even on a Climb, the m-field stayed with the adventurous *duende*, generating the right kind of accompanying environment in which to live and breathe. Malfunctions, however, were always possible, and people could overexert themselves.

He knew, though, that as much as he wanted to, he couldn't stay there. He needed a chair or a platform floated up, upon which to stand.

But his mind jumped way ahead of thinking about mere observation platforms.

*They were going to have to send up the Meadow itself. Resurrection Day was at hand!*

The implications of what this all meant—and would mean—to the *duendes* staggered him.

"It's almost as if there wasn't a war at all—" He let his thought trail off.

"Come down, Preston," Dr. Wainwright ordered.

Kitteridge could feel the weight of the Appleseed's command, and it took a massive resolve of will to turn from the panorama which surrounded him dizzyingly. He felt as if he were a deep-space voyager having sighted his destination, a destination which took generations to reach. Only in his case, he was a voyager who was traveling in time, not space.

The journey was now over.

Kitteridge began the trip back down to the Meadow. "I'm on my way," he then told the crew in the Games Room. Without food or water, it was going to be a difficult descent, but he knew that the news he was bringing the other *duendes* would be worth the danger and the ordeal.

He reentered the blackness of the underworld's eternal night as Dr. Wainwright spoke out from the wafer-mike. "Colonel Chaney has just arrived, Preston. We've informed him of your . . . discovery."

"Good," Preston said, sliding past the rung-runners.

He could tell from the hesitant nature of the chief botanist's voice that either he wasn't being totally believed, or that the frictions which normally existed between the two co-rulers of the Meadow had already manifested there in the Games Room. Colonel Chaney rarely left the confines of the

Hive since it was his main duty to watch over the 'combs and the sleeping personnel there. But it was almost a matter of status for Chaney to remain separated from the other more convivial Appleseeds, if only to exhibit an air of military aloofness, which implied authority and self-confidence.

However, if Colonel Chaney had been summoned, then it meant trouble. Even if the Gathering Day festivities were still going on.

Preston decided to speed up his descent. The rung-runners were used, on the way down, as safety restraints. Here, he chose to dangle from the nylon safety lines and use his weight to slide down the ladder, with the rung-runners braking his fall. His shoulder beacon bobbed and shook as he plunged, and he was careful to note any signs of overheating in the braking systems of the runners. He placed his feet on the outside of the ladder and simply let himself drop, almost as if he were parachuting to the ground—like in the videos from an older, more archaic hero-infested age.

The Meadow was still far below him, but the closer he got, the easier its ghostly Mall lights came into more distinct view.

The trip back down to the glittering compound of Saxifrage took him an hour and a half. Every five hundred feet the rung-runners began to smoke and he had to stop and wait until they cooled. During those periods, he took the ladder one rung at a time on his own as the rung-runners limped along. When they finally cooled, he began the dangerous process all over again. He had a great deal on his mind, as no doubt did the co-rulers down in the Hive, for he heard very little from them.

He came into full view of the Meadow, with both Saxifrage Mall and the military Hive taking complete shape in the subterranean dark beneath him. Nearly three-quarters of a mile in length, the Mall boasted seven large buildings radiating around one end of the long structure, the Arks. However, at the other end—and the reason for the annual Gathering Day ceremonies—was the Hive with its vital 'combs and its more sinister Armory underneath it. Sinister, that is, to those *duendes* who had been raised for generations as Appleseeds whose only goal was to maintain life, especially as it pertained to the reestablishment of life topside on the surface of the earth.

As was now a well-known legend in the *duende* annals,

the original scientists and technicians thought that the only Sheldrake Field generator in existence had been built beneath Saxifrage Mall outside of Salina, Kansas. But this had not been the case. Leave it to the military to install one redundancy system after another: In a building of rather huge proportions at McConnell Air Force Base near Wichita, the Pentagon had another m-field generator constructed. Since the Soviets in their sky-city would have watched the Base anyway, the American authorities had no problem in revamping the old building inside and out for the singular purpose of seeing to it that something of America's defenses would persist after a nuclear war. The 'combs were built, armament brought in of various kinds, along with computers and tons of spare parts. There was even a small fusion generator installed from which the maintenance crews could keep themselves in energy and raw materials.

Saxifrage Mall knew nothing of this, and six months after the last missiles were fired and the last bombs dropped, the crew of the McConnell Hive—watching over three hundred and fifty sleeping soldiers, pilots, and technicians in their stasis 'combs—made radio contact with the Saxifrage Appleseeds. They, too, had escaped the holocaust, but in even less time than had the Appleseed *duendes*.

However, even though their orders were to lower the Hive to the subsurface m-field of the earth, the militarists hadn't known that the men and women of Saxifrage had done the same. It had only been through the accidental interception of radio-wave experiments from Saxifrage Mall that the maintenance personnel at the McConnell Hive realized that they weren't alone.

Gathering Day ceremonies usually began with a brief narration—or enactment—of how the Hive was literally towed from its location beneath a smoldering Wichita by one of two large machines designed specifically for that purpose for the Arks. The trials and pitfalls of that great engineering feat—and the people involved—were remembered each year on Gathering Day.

But Gathering Day held a great meaning for them all. The original Appleseeds were just over eighty in number, and while they possessed sperm and ova of dozens of human beings in their banks, they themselves did not number enough to perpetuate their own kind, let alone maintain the remnants of a huge shopping mall. The added ranks of the military personnel, who numbered a precious forty-five, helped ensure that at least for the time being Duende Meadow could sustain itself. Only later—centuries in fact—did they decide to awaken one of the sleeping soldiers or technicians in the stasis 'combs in the Hive, a so-called lazarus. As they lost *duende* after *duende*, as the years rolled by, each lazarus became more and more important to their numbers.

Yet none of the Appleseeds ever visited the Hive. They knew what lurked underneath close to the m-field generator housing. There were missile carriers containing satellite killers and tactical nuclear weapons. Five in all. And there was one agile-winged B-10 bomber with fuel enough for a journey to the Soviet Union. Only the ruling Appleseeds could step into the Hive corridors and carry with them the dignity of the station given them by the original founders of the Mall. Duende Meadow contained both the elements of life and death.

As such, theirs was a closed system and required strict cooperation between the two factions. Without that cooperation, anarchy would reign and with it would come the possible deterioration of the Ark maintenance systems. Kitteridge knew this, and he also knew that he would be needed in the Games Room to counter any pressure Dr. Wainwright might receive from Colonel Chaney and the other Hive authorities now that Resurrection Day was upon them.

However, as he neared the bottom of the ladder, he noticed that there were no *duendes* waiting for him, buoyed with the news of his discovery. The ladder itself had been erected at the center of the main concourse of the Meadow, directly midway between Saxifrage Mall and the massive Hive building. But other than a few scattered debauchees falling over themselves in the kudzu on the Mall, he couldn't make anyone else out. The Bacchanalia in the Mall was still going on, and the lights were visible everywhere, but clearly the ruling council had not let word out of what was above the Meadow, beyond the black ceiling of their eternal night.

With two hundred feet left to go, his wafer-mike suddenly hummed alive, but it was not Dr. Wainwright this time. It was his brother, Jay.

"Prometheus descends!" he shouted merrily. "Down and down he comes, with the gift of fire, the gift of light!"

"Where are you?" Preston called out, slowing his eager

descent. "Have you spoken with Travis yet?" He didn't know who might be listening in on the channel, but he had to assume that someone in the Games Room was.

He didn't know what to say, or quite how much to reveal, for Jay Kitteridge, respected as he was among the other *duendes*, particularly those of the Salina Ark, wasn't like the rest of the Appleseeds in the compound. Like most of the Kitteridges who ever lived, Jay was a little *off*.

"There is silence abounding from the Games Room and no words to be had from the good doctor," Jay spoke from the wafer. "But through my erstwhile scope I have seen all I need to know. I have seen the light."

"Then you—"

"Absolutely! The stars in the Spider's Lair shimmered as you rose, then you winkled out of sight. Magnificent!"

"Jay, listen to me," he began quickly. "They're not talking to me down in the Games Room. I don't know if you should tell anyone yet about this."

"Tell them what?" Now he was being coy—despite the bouncy tone in his voice. They knew each other too well. Jay understood perfectly the implications of Preston's discovery topside. It wasn't the mythical Ice up there. Not at all.

But Preston couldn't hold himself back, regardless of who might be eavesdropping.

"The earth has healed itself, Jay!" he virtually exploded. "I saw fields of durum wheat—and birds! The sky was blue and . . ."

He stopped. Silence hissed from the wafer-mike at his collar and he knew immediately that some agency had cut them off. However, those responsible did not come back on line. What was transpiring down there in the Games Room?

He glanced down below. At the far northwest end of Saxifrage, set nearly one hundred yards from the tip of the Appalachian Ark, out in the somber darkness of the subsurface m-field, was Jay's observatory. Egg-shaped and solitary, its silver shell glowed in the perpetual illumination cast off from the Meadow lights. Preston couldn't see Jay coming from it. He knew his brother, though, and he knew that Jay wouldn't put up with an arbitrary communications blackout, particularly during the Gathering Day festival. He'd know that something was up.

On the other hand, it was quite like Jay not to care, if the mood came over him. He might remain out at his isolated observatory for days on end watching the dance and weave of the mysterious ghost-lights until something else caught his fancy.

This, however, was different.

Preston reached the kudzu at eighty-nine feet and halted the rung-runners. Quickly he unstrapped himself from the safety wires and let them dangle into the small cool green leaves of the message-plant.

Removing his glove on his left hand, he let one of the leading tendrils of the kudzu vine slip up his forearm, finding the precise pressure point.

The biotic vibrations came to him: The kudzu, being just about everywhere in the compound, was picking up the riotous sounds of the Bacchanalia in the Mall, but from the stone masonry of the Hive administration building it was absorbing nothing. The hypersynaptical circuits, genetically bred in the ubiquitous plant, relayed in a way no other form of communication they had yet developed could the absolute *sense* of Duende Meadow. Plugged into the kudzu, a *duende* became the whole compound, its three stories above the m-field and the layers of its subbasements below. It felt the constant vibrations of the fusion generator housing and it could even pick up footsteps deep within any of the individual Arks. The kudzu was a living nervous system developed by *duendes* two hundred years ago in the Orleans Ark for no reason other than they thought it was theoretically possible. In fact, it had been some of Travis Wainwright's ancestors who had pioneered its development.

Preston felt the living presence of the Meadow as well as those *duendes* phased out on peyotl juice, who were lying in their kudzu couches lost in the dreams the vine provided. But he could not sense any danger coming from the Hive.

*Odd*, he thought. *Very odd.*

But that didn't imply anything untoward, since the militarists—seemingly derived genetically from the basic paranoid-tactician mold—had constantly fought the kudzu's creeping advance by trimming it here and there, keeping it away from sensitive areas. So far, the kudzu hadn't reached either the 'combs or the Armory subbasement. And it was certainly not allowed to proliferate in the Hive generating stations. It was still a stupid plant, thriving wherever it could gain a tendril-hold.

But wherever it went, it could still transmit secrets. These, Preston wasn't sensing.

That meant trouble was stirring somewhere. Much of it.

Gently he withdrew himself from the kudzu's moist grasp and put his climbing glove back on. He was still perilously high above the Meadow and he would have to be doubly careful on his way down now, particularly when there was a great abundance of kudzu entwined about the rungs at the lower reaches of the ladder.

Down he went, one step at a time, one hand grasping, the other letting go. The kudzu brushed at his legs, getting thicker as he descended. The excitement of his find topside was enough to propel him toward the Meadow, but now he obsessed with curiosity as to the nature of the silence from the Hive. The kudzu had nothing further to say.

The lights of the concourse came up to meet him, enfolding him with its eternal foglike luminence—but it could not compare with the light he'd seen up above.

He jumped away from the kudzu-laced ladder and landed firmly on the green of the kudzu-matted concourse. But instead of being met—as was the usual custom with record-breakers of the Climb—by a crowd of enthusiastic, if inebriated, celebrants of the Gathering, he was greeted by two centurions at the base of the ladder.

Kitteridge knew them both, and had known them since childhood, but the families of the military and those of the Appleseeds hardly got along. Particularly with the military police unit, the centurions.

Clark Busch, a tall, wiry redhead, grabbed Preston by the arm, before he could get his balance, and Brian Busch, younger by a couple of years, though much stockier, held up a stun-pistol.

"Let's do this very quietly, Preston," Clark Busch said with the authority granted to him by the Hive. His centurion's badge and helmet shone in the blue lights overhead. "You're under arrest."

"What?" Preston yanked his arm free. "Are you crazy?"

"I think," Brian Busch said with a sly grin, "it's called 'protective custody.'"

There was no one else about on the concourse, and the uniformed Busch brothers escorted him away, careful to keep him out of the reach of the kudzu.

# 3

The Busch brothers like any other *duendes* on Gathering Day would rather have been enjoying themselves with their own kind in the Hive, playing the festival games preferred by the military personnel there. Yet, their duties as centurions came first, above all else, and they obviously relished their stewardship of the role.

They hustled Preston east across the cement concourse, avoiding where they could any of the other *duendes* who might be about. And they did it roughly.

Preston, however, wasn't taking this without a peep. "Just what the hell do you think you're doing, Clark? I've done nothing wrong, and I'm certainly *not* under arrest."

Clark Busch led them swiftly into the main administrative building of the Hive. The elms planted long ago on the separating concourse shielded them from anyone who might be watching from the east end of Saxifrage Mall. Brian Busch kept an eye out to see if they'd been observed. They hadn't.

"We're to keep you under tight security until Colonel Chaney decides what to do," the elder Busch said as they led Preston forcefully down a hallway to a holding cell. The cell was little more than a lounge, vacant now that its usual inhabitants were elsewhere in the Hive enjoying themselves. They had no prison as such anywhere in Duende Meadow.

"Colonel Chaney? Since when does the Colonel give orders to the whole meadow?" Kitteridge wanted to know.

Brian Busch merely laughed—mirthlessly at that—as they

stepped back to the door. He holstered his weapon. Clark said, "He's only acting on the computer's suggestion."

"Which is what?"

"Which is that you're crazy, or that what you found out is a threat to Meadow security and stability. And that's what we're here for. Meadow security, in case you've forgotten." He seemed both angered and pleased to deliver his little speech. His younger brother's eyes never left their captive, and Kitteridge could feel the generations of antagonisms and innate distrust beginning to sprout. Brian's hand fairly twitched above his stunner.

However, the centurions closed the door and took their posts outside, awaiting further instructions.

Inside, it was absolutely quiet—except for the fevered pounding of the blood vessels within Preston's brain. Never in his life had he been either arrested or tucked away in so-called "protective custody." He was going to lodge an official complaint with the ruling council. Either that or he was going to lodge his fist in Clark Busch's face. He'd let his own brother take on Brian Busch, but Jay was a confirmed pacifist and had chosen to avoid all conflicts which naturally occurred when two different philosophical sensibilities tried to live together. Jay, in effect, chose to mind his own business.

"*Nemesis!*" Preston swore, yanking off his climbing belt and gloves. His remaining shoulder beacon, still functioning, got ripped off with a single tug. He threw everything onto a plant-leather couch.

For several maddening minutes, he stalked the confines of the comfortable lounge. He stabbed alive the compound-wide video unit, but all that was on was a hundred-year-old dream-tale that someone had made depicting an estranged wife's indiscriminate revenge fantasy. He wasn't interested. He then searched the ventilation shafts and other hidden crannies for possible kudzu leads that might provide him with an outside line to allies in the Mall. But the whole place was almost obsessively clean.

In the time it took for him to rage throughout the lounge, though, he realized that his captivity—temporary as he knew it would be—was something of a necessity. He knew that the Appleseeds at the Saxifrage Bacchanalia were probably in no condition to receive the news that their centuries-old confinement was about to end. It was possible that what few Appleseed technicians it took to maintain the functions of the m-field generators might abandon their posts in their excitement. Or worse, they might begin to activate the platform engines underneath the whole Meadow, which were needed to raise the compound. That would be an unparalleled disaster, since over the centuries so much different uncoordinated construction had occurred that it would take some meticulous reworking of the computers to sort out which sections of the Meadow should be separated and how. It was all a grand balancing act.

As Preston knew, the compound could become an asylum. Such things had happened before in the past, and always the results were deleterious to their overall well-being. Indeed, it had only been fifty years into their forced exile—long after the Gathering—when some of the then-ruling militarists decided that the compound would be best served under a martial command. Riots ensued and several *duendes* perished needlessly. The co-ruling council was established after that, but the scars on the old wound still remained.

So, begrudgingly, he admitted to himself the utility of the Colonel's decision to detain him. He just resented its seeming spuriousness, and its being meted out by the likes of the Busch centurions. His only immediate concern was for Jay.

And unknown to the Busch brothers, Preston's wafer-mike had remained on during the whole encounter. If Jay was listening, no doubt he'd have heard. . . .

The lounge doors parted suddenly and Clark Busch stuck his helmeted head in. Preston jumped up from the couch and swept up his climbing materials.

"You can go, now. Colonel Chaney will receive you," the older centurion said evenly.

"Oh, he will, will he?" Preston countered with a sneer. "We'll see about that."

He strode through the doors as the two centurions let him go by, but not without shouldering into Clark Busch somewhat just to let him know who was who. Brian merely stood with his arms crossed, then he and his brother marched at some distance behind Kitteridge as they made for the stairs which would take them to the second floor of the Hive where the Games Room lay.

The Games Room, as every *duende* knew from the histories, was originally the strategy-planning center of the whole

Hive complex. Since the original military planners did not
know how long the Hive would have to sustain itself in its
etheric state in the rock beneath Kansas, it gradually had
become modified to meet other needs. It became the pleasure center for the Hive. There, the dream videos were made
and put into the induction systems for any *duende* who cared
to share another's fiction. Also for easy access were the ancient cinema and television videos.

However, this was the first time in six centuries it was
necessary to alter the Games Room's role. Preston could
sense this in the humming of the many computer banks and
the increased ventilation from the air-conditioners. High energy and excitement filled the air.

In the planning center they had all gathered. Dr. Wainwright got up to greet him. Great relief could be seen on the
features of his face.

Travis Wainwright was about as portly as any *duende*
ever let himself get. But his girth was expansive mostly due
to the room his innate gregariousness needed within which to
knock around. He stood well over six-feet-two and was completely white-haired. His pale blue eyes were always flashing
with life.

"Preston! You made it, boy!" he shouted, rushing over to
shake his hand.

In the background, near the wide row of computer ter-
minals, monitors, and other equipment, was Colonel Victor
Chaney. He and Travis Wainwright were both in their early
sixties, but Chaney's hair was ungraced by any hint of age.
He was somewhat shorter in height, though much more fit.
But his eyes shone with all the power he would need as
co-ruler of the Meadow. He was dressed in standard-issue
military khaki, a tight-fitting tunic besplendored with a medal
of ranking and a belt of weapons and communicators. All of
the Hive personnel dressed in such tunics, having rarely
altered their mode of dress or their basic attitudes regarding
their mission.

Kitteridge, however, immediately fixated upon the Colonel's second-in-command, the lazarus, Sebastian Monaco, who
stood off to one side like a specter of an inquisition. The
Colonel—with Dr. Wainwright's reluctant assent—had no
doubt acted properly in temporarily imprisoning him when
he had arrived back in the Meadow. However, what irked
Kitteridge the most was the Colonel's *enthusiasm* behind the

deed, at least as far as he had sensed it from the centurions. He now knew that not a little encouragement had come from Lieutenant Monaco. He knew that he himself was no threat to any *duende* in the Meadow, regardless of the content of any Promethean message he might have brought them. He was no threat to anyone, that is, except Sebastian Monaco.

But there was little he could do about Monaco's influence on the Colonel. His presence in the Hive—and the Meadow at large—was special. Not only was he a living representative of the pre-War past, he was another vital source of genes for their gene-pool.

Their own computer studies had long ago shown that, if sustained properly, the Meadow could remain on the lower subsurface m-field of the earth for another five to six hundred years without the population of the compound deteriorating significantly. However, the same psychological phenomenon which had given rise to the first revolt fifty years after the War, when the military tried to take control and disavow the scientists of the Arks, had also created a unique class of *duende*. It all had to do with the dark. Both the Ark personnel and the militarists felt it. And as Preston stared into the glassy unfathomable eyes of Sebastian Monaco, he was reminded of the importance of every single lazarus. They were meant to take the place of the Wanderers.

Their eternal night surrounded them as if it were a kind of insensitive punishment delivered upon them by a God who had turned his back upon mankind. Many *duendes* early on began to feel this judgment—real or imagined. So they left. They wandered as far as their individual m-field belts could sustain them, going well beyond the atmosphere envelope the Meadow generators had created around them. Their bodies were rarely found since that envelope had long since extended for dozens and dozens of miles.

Only twenty years ago, after a trawler accident had killed Preston and Jay's father, their mother, still quite young herself, had taken to Wandering. The darkness, the long voyage to wait out the savage centuries, had gotten to her. She simply left one day and was never seen again.

With the loss of a *duende* every few years, the men and women asleep in the 'combs began to be looked upon as their most valuable commodity.

And there stood Sebastian Monaco, staring half-amused at a man who needed him most. Monaco's presence meant that *Homo sapiens sapiens* would continue even if the Kitteridges, now reduced to only two, would not. Monaco knew it; Preston knew it.

Kitteridge turned away from the lieutenant and confronted instead Dr. Wainwright.

"Travis, what's this business all about? You owe me a damn good explanation."

Dr. Wainwright held up a liver-splotched hand. "Now, hold on, son. It was just a precaution, that's all. We had to have a spell of time to talk this thing out. The Colonel and I couldn't have you blabbing the news to every *duende* in the compound."

"You know I'd never 'blab' anything," he rejoined. "And besides that, you cut me off from Jay."

"We had to," Lieutenant Monaco said. "You know how your brother is."

"No," Preston faced him. "How is he?"

Both Monaco and Kitteridge were physical equals of one another. Both were tall and angular, but Monaco was a little more bulky, having the advantage of early-twenty-first-century cuisine and fast-food carbohydrates accumulated within his body. Preston, though, was the more agile of the two, and this was highlighted in the airy, fawn color of his hair. Monaco, true to his military bearing, wore his hair clipped close to the scalp and his blond mustache was terse, true to regulation trim.

Colonel Chaney separated them. "Go easy, men. This isn't going to be a schoolyard fight. Not right now. We've got a problem and we've got to come to some kind of an understanding."

"He's right, Preston," Dr. Wainwright acquiesced. The computer screens and watchdog camera sensors glowed at the wide console behind them. He continued, "We've got most of Saxifrage in one form of hallucination or another. We don't want them breaking into the administration buildings and attempting to raise the Meadow. Not in their condition."

"Don't be absurd," Preston stated. "No one's going to do that. We're a little more disciplined than you think."

"We still have to be careful," the lieutenant said. "There's no telling what might happen."

Dr. Wainwright stepped lightly over to the Games console. One of the Hive technicians, Stu Hagerty, a small man, almost petite in his features, sat before a special screen. He was one of the Meadow's brightest computer experts. The chief Appleseed moored his ponderousness behind him.

"What's the progress, Stu?" he asked.

Preston glanced over at the new television screen and caught a vision of something—a camera mounted on wheels, presumably—husking its way through thick foliage. The sound of leaves tearing as it went came over the audio link.

"We're just about through the kudzu, Doctor. It's slow going, but once it's made it through the vines, it'll only take a few minutes to reach the top." Hagerty's precise fingers danced over the control board, bringing the resolution of the camera's lens in even tighter.

Monaco faced Kitteridge. He indicated the screen. "This is why we detained you."

"What is it?" Preston asked Dr. Wainwright, ignoring Monaco for the moment.

Dr. Wainwright said, not taking his eyes off the screen, "We're sending up a remote climbing camera."

"Up the ladder?"

"Right," the chief Appleseed said. "Once it cuts through the kudzu and gets to the top, we'll know if your story is true."

"It *is* true," he protested. "You think I'd lie about something like this?"

However, he knew that sending up a camera made good sense, even if it meant a deracination of the clinging vines. He wondered how those *duendes* snoozing in their kudzu couches in Saxifrage would take the sudden mowing up the ladder. Plants suffered too, and he imagined that there were a lot of startled *duendes* in their condos right now.

"I still think we should've sent up one of the platforms," Dr. Wainwright then said.

"No," Monaco quickly interjected. "That'd be too easily seen from the Mall."

Preston glared at the lazarus. "What you're saying is that if *your* people saw it, nothing would happen. Right?"

"Your oddball brother's the one with the observatory," Monaco threw at him. "And a platform's engines would light up most of the east end of the Meadow. This way—" And here he pointed to the screen. "This way no one's going to notice."

"Except for those *duendes* attached to kudzu somewhere

in the compound," Preston argued. "They're going to know something's happening."

"They only know *that* something's going on, not *where* or *what*," Monaco said. "Besides, it's not like cutting off fingers and toes."

"How would you know?"

"Okay, men," Dr. Wainwright said as firmly as he could. "We're almost there. The issue's moot anyway."

Apparently Stu Hagerty had already disengaged the rung-runners he had used on the Climb, for the rising camera had crashed right through the rest of the kudzu and kept on going. On the screen, the ladder seemed to stretch out toward infinity into the darkness as if the ladder were the tracks of a train traveling through a tunnel. The camera sped upward, making excellent time.

And then quite suddenly the blackness ended and the screen was flooded with bright blue sky. The camera halted at the top.

"Good heavens," Wainwright breathed, awestruck. "You were right, Preston." He clapped him on the shoulder.

Colonel Chaney, more conservative in his enthusiasm, turned and bent over Hagerty. "Stu, are you getting this on tape? I want everything the camera sees."

In fact, Hagerty had anticipated this, and there were already several videotape cassettes churning away in the console.

Fortunately, the camera had braked just as it penetrated the upper surface; otherwise, it would have shot right off the top of the ladder and come crashing down who knew where.

Hagerty began craning the lens from its vertical position, where they could only see the sky—as if that weren't enough!—to where they were able to view all that Preston had seen on first reaching the surface.

As the robot's eye came level with the wheat field, they all gasped at the beauty displayed unabashedly before them. Everyone, that is, except Lieutenant Monaco, who had seen similar scenes only five years ago—by his time reckoning.

It was essentially the same view that Preston had observed, only it was a bit later in the afternoon.

"Incredible," Stu Hagerty muttered, leaning back.

"It *is* beautiful," Travis Wainwright claimed as well.

Preston eyed them all. "Well, *now* do you believe me?"

However, the question was purely rhetorical. There was no possible way to respond.

The camera's remote-controlled scanner presented them with a serene ocean of virgin wheat, riffling in a wind so gentle that it passed over it like a soothing hand.

And the clouds were still there, tinged amber in the late-afternoon sunlight. They were not rain clouds, but that didn't seem to matter. No *duende* had ever known either clouds or rain except through the expediency of dream-videos and ancient movies.

The camera poised about four feet above the surface m-field of the earth, which put it nearly a foot or so above the fibrous tufts of the wheat. The camera's eye easily made out the same low hills Preston had seen, bringing the trees and stunted bushes closer into view because of its telescopic capacities. Birds, many more of them, were also in evidence.

Travis Wainwright sagged into an empty chair next to Stu Hagerty at the console. He said, "Stu, can we get any sound from up there?"

"Sure," the little technician said. He slowly turned a dial.

Centuries of tinkering with m-field technology had allowed them to make all kinds of modifications in the use of the Sheldrakian phenomenon. The robot camera and ladder were absolutely invisible and intangible to the wide meadow of wheat, but the *duendes* were able to pick up sounds on the outside without the outside knowing that it was doing so. They listened.

The Games Room was instantly filled with the *chirrupings* of birds of myriad descriptions.

Preston, quite beside himself with his own excitement, pointed authoritatively at the screen. "Those birds there are Towhees." A feathered creature, seven inches in length, glided just above the wheat field, disappearing in it. "And those are Juncos. When I was up there, I'm sure I saw a White-throated Swift." Then he ruminated for a second or two. "But I don't know how they're there, though. They would've been the first casualty of a nuclear war, especially in this region."

No one said anything. The audio link in the robot camera picked up the susurrations of the wind over the wheat. Crickets and other chittering beings were hidden deep within the meadow, but the whole field seemed to be thriving with life—life ranging from the most simple to the most complex.

Contrary to what they had been taught to expect, the biosphere was healthy and alive.

Preston stood back away from the thunderstruck *duendes*. "So now what are we going to do? You locked me up because you thought I was either lying or crazy. Well, I'm not. There's your proof."

"We still have a problem that's bigger than just trying to decide what we're going to do," the Colonel told him.

The others looked at him, waiting.

Preston, though, took the lead. "That's relatively simple. We just let the Gathering Day celebrations run their course, then make a general announcement when everyone's in some sort of shape to accept it. We can't sit on something like this for too long, you know."

"I wasn't talking about making an announcement." The Colonel's dark eyes flashed grimly.

Dr. Wainwright considered his co-ruler with sudden coolness.

Preston said, "What do you mean? Are you blind? It's all right here." He gestured at the television screen and the new world above them.

"I know it is," the Colonel said gravely. "But we may yet have a military situation on our hands."

"What?" Preston stood incredulously.

Lieutenant Monaco, though, had followed the Colonel's reasoning. He said, "You know as well as anyone what the effects of a full exchange of nuclear warheads would do to the ecosystems of the earth. You know what it *did* do." With a rather theatrical flourish of his hand he pointed to Stu Hagerty's television screen. "This is totally unexpected, and I would say impossible. Even after six hundred years."

Preston folded his arms across his chest. "I have a little more faith in the earth's ability to heal itself than you do."

"After six hundred years? Don't be ridiculous," the lazarus commented.

Preston had to face it. While the facts were in his favor, the time frame was all wrong. Not in a thousand years could the earth recoup its losses after such a massive onslaught of nuclear warheads. The living entity that was the earth's surface might be able to heal on its own. But the life that would painfully evolve in the company of so much radioactive debris scattered about would not resemble—even in the slightest— anything like what they were faced with on the robot's screen.

Certainly there would be no White-throated Kansas Swifts or their merry songs.

Monaco persisted. "Even in my time we *knew* what even the smallest missile exchange would do to the world. The ozone layer itself would take hundreds of years to restabilize. And we know that at least sixty thousand warheads were detonated worldwide."

"That's why we may have a military situation here before us," the Colonel added.

Preston couldn't follow their reasoning. However, Dr. Wainwright rubbed his chin with a meaty hand, indicating that he was in agreement. He was beginning to understand.

The chief Appleseed nodded his head. "He's right. Wheat grows wild anywhere it can find a suitable environment. But this is different. You'd have to expect severe changes after six hundred years."

"Look, there's no way this could be a military situation," Preston pleaded with them, almost laughing at their somberness. "The past is dead and buried."

Sebastian Monaco and the Colonel stared at Preston as if he were a mere youth, unskilled at the ways of the world.

"You still don't understand, do you?" the Colonel said. "There was a nuclear reactor outside of Wichita. Its radioactive fragments would be all over the region. There'd be particles of uranium 235 and plutonium that would take thousands of years to decay and become harmless. We should be looking at a desert, a wild country ravaged by nuclear explosions, radioactive debris, and erosion from receding ice sheets."

Yet clearly before them were the fields of heaven. *Wheat . . . birds . . . insects . . .*

Preston still didn't see. "All we need to do is to announce the discovery, prepare the Arks, and start up the lift engines—"

That was when the audio remote began picking up a decidedly *unnatural* sound, at least a sound no wheat field could create all on its own.

A heavy, rhythmic *whoosh, whoosh, whoosh!* came from somewhere beyond the range of the camera's ghostly eye.

"What's that?" Stu Hagerty asked.

Sebastian Monaco bent over the screen. "Good Lord," he exclaimed, recognizing it suddenly.

Then something dark enfolded the camera, moving through it and over it.

The *duendes* jumped back, so startled were they by the apparition.

It was a machine. A very *big* machine.

It drifted right through the camera, unaware and uncaring of its presence, and as it receded in the distance the *duendes* could see that it was composed of many rubberized wheels, long blades, and behind it followed a mindless machine of similar manufacture.

Painted a violent crimson, it was a harvester combine two stories tall and perhaps forty feet wide at the tips of the plunging blades. It moved away from the robot camera's watchful eye, chopping a wide path through the wheat, funneling it into a gigantic trailer behind it.

Preston now knew why the military *duendes* thought that they had a military situation on their hands: The earth had had a little help in her recovery.

For on the rear of the giant harvester was a bright orange hammer and sickle, and elsewhere on the sides were the initials CCCP.

The Soviets had won World War Three.

# 4

For the last six hundred years in the Meadow, the *duendes* had considered themselves something like the survivors of a vast shipwreck. Theirs was a community cast adrift, waiting for that time in the impossible future when they should reach harbor and again begin their lives.

In this "lifeboat" of theirs, the *duendes* had spent a great deal of time occupied with their survival. One of the ancillary activities they created for themselves was the Outcome Book. It was a monograph continually being modified as their speculations and computer-analysis profiles kept changing. It was full of ruminations, charts, and statistics as to what America and the world might be like after a nuclear war.

Since the variables were many—which cities were hit, what the climates at the target sites were like, et cetera— there were many chapters. There were studies of hydrogen depletion in the troposphere, estimates on dioxins from burned-out synthetics manufacturing plants, and even the possible effects of enormous islands of floating debris in the oceans on benthic and deep-sea ecospheres. The earliest chapters in the Outcome Book held the bleakest scenarios. What the *duendes* were faced with in the Games Room was a scene taken from the latter, more optimistic chapters. Even this, however, went totally beyond their expectations.

Up and back the harvester went. The farmer inside the machine was hardly visible through the large beveled windows as it passed by once again, its blades fluttering monotonously in the afternoon light. Through the tinted windows the *duendes* got a glimpse of the man within who wore thick-lensed goggles and a radio-headset on his head. The blond-haired farmer seemed quite intent upon his work.

Preston, a descendant of generations of Salina Ark technicians, thought that a scene like this should ring familiar to him. After all, the Salina Ark, when it was to be raised, would spill out all of the life forms indigenous to central Kansas: *Wheat, oats, barley. Trout, whitefish, carp, bream, pike. Hawks, ravens, red-shouldered blackbirds. Monarch butterflies, praying mantises, spiders by the thousands, and bees in the tens of thousands.* Anything which flew, crawled, burrowed, swam, or slithered, they had somewhere in the Salina Ark.

But now there seemed to be no need. Even the plankton, the utter tons of it in cold storage in the Gulf Ark, apparently was no longer needed. Something—obviously *other* plankton—was already working on the oxygen-nitrogen regeneration for the atmosphere.

Not only had the United States been defeated by the Soviets, but so had the Appleseeds.

Colonel Chaney, a man of normally staid character, was visibly shaken.

"This is impossible," he mumbled, moved deeply by the sight of the harvester indifferently going about its business in the sunshine.

Monaco craned closer to the screen. "Son of a bitch if they didn't do it," he said. He pointed at the vehicle, so mountainous in its form, so *alien*. "We had harvesters like that. John Deeres. I used to see them on the way to work all the time."

"But nothing that large," Preston commented blankly.

"Right," Lieutenant Monaco reluctantly agreed. "Nothing like that machine."

Dr. Wainwright had pulled out the large three-ringed notebook which held the finely printed chapters of the Outcome Book, which Jay Kitteridge had once called their Anti-Bible. The chief Appleseed now seemed pale and drawn as he cradled it, yet his eyes were alive with activity, as if the gears and pulleys behind them were grinding away, trying to come up with answers that would soothe his troubled soul.

"There's nothing in here which could account for this," he announced gravely.

Sebastian Monaco, prim in his Hive khaki, pins and

medals agleam in the computer console's light, was the least upset of all of them. He was the only one among them who had what could be called a living memory of topside Kansas. While it had taken him the better part of five years to adjust to his lazarus status as a new *duende*, it was nonetheless easier for him to accept what was before them.

He said, "But we should have expected something like this to happen."

The Colonel looked at him questioningly. "Not after six hundred and nineteen years, Lieutenant. Facts are facts. This whole area was pounded flatter than the head of an idiot."

"Don't you think I know that? I *remember* the night it happened." Monaco's eyes glowed with intensity.

They could all see it and hear it: those thunderous fists of concussions rocking the solid earth overhead as the Hive was in its descent to the lower m-field. . . .

Dr. Wainwright laid the Outcome Book beside Stu Hagerty at the console. Were his hands trembling? Preston glanced at his friend. What nightmares of authority and responsibility were chewing away at him?

The botanist said, "What we see here comes closest to the last three chapters in the Outcome Book."

The huge red harvester, followed by its dutiful bin with its rounded hill of gleaned wheat, passed outside of the robot camera's range. It was unable to swivel or pan horizontally, so they were unable to pursue it. However, what they could see was enough for them.

Hagerty leafed the Outcome Book open to the last of its chapters. He began, "If we take into consideration only a minor disruption in the ozone layer after the war, then according to this scenario," he said, looking up at them, "then something like this is quite possible."

Monaco, who had considerable Intelligence experience, knew from the data in his own time that the predictions had no possible means of verification. Still, as the Colonel had said: facts were facts.

He said, "The war took place after harvest season, before seeds would've been planted for the next year. If the nuclear winter lasted only one hundred days and the ultraviolet bombardment only a couple of weeks, then yes, it's just possible the world may have survived like this."

But there was a ring of uncertainty in his voice. Clearly, he was as startled as they were, and was just as baffled.

However, as Preston pointed out, "Ozone depletion aside, we're talking about major erosion of topsoils from burned-off timber and sage cover. Even soil bacteria would be affected, and there would go your nitrates." His heart pounded as he thought through the ecosystem links and the interconnectedness of all life on the planet. "Our problem has always been how rapidly we could institute topsoil regeneration for crops. Obviously they've got the right insects, the right kinds of earthworms, the right kind of *everything*. Even if undertaken by nature, as we've assumed all along it would have to be, then we're looking at a natural recovery cycle of about five to six *thousand* years. And that's just to begin the process. If a true Ice Age had been created, then the wait would be more along the lines of ten to twelve thousand years."

"But if the change had been ushered in by man—" Dr. Wainwright started in a tremulous voice, all his gregariousness gone.

"If undertaken by man," Lieutenant Monaco took over, "then it would be thirty to fifty years minimum, after ozone-layer regeneration. So we're dealing with a total minimum time frame of seventy years."

Hagerty, who was just as studied as they were in the Outcome Book's futures, looked up at him. "But we do know that an Ice Age of a kind was created. The m-field level here lowered two hundred feet in a century. That means a lot of ice gathered on land somewhere."

There were just too many *if*'s floating around. Preston shook his head. "Forget the Ice Age. The only way the Russians could accomplish this"—he pointed to the television screen—"is if they'd been able to do something about the tons of radioactive debris that'd have been scattered everywhere. All missile silos, storage dumps, even uranium mines were targeted. Striking those sites alone would make a country uninhabitable for years."

"Not unless they avoided those targets," Hagerty interjected.

"Which they didn't," Monaco told him. "And wouldn't. Not with eighty-four on-line nuclear reactors in the U.S. and Europe. The Russians may have been desperate, but they weren't stupid."

Preston considered him in the silence of the Games Room. Silent that is except for the twitterings of spooked grouse from the Kansas fields above and insects hovering near the camera's audio pickup. He turned to Monaco. "So what is it you're saying?" he asked.

"What was their biggest problem toward the end of the twentieth century and on into the twenty-first?" he began. "Feeding themselves. Think about it. They had a climate like Canada's, but they didn't have the mountain ranges or the chinooks to circulate the freezing Arctic air. Their famines of the Nineties document this. It's an utterly inhospitable land for as many people as they had."

Dr. Wainwright, sitting in his spiritual exhaustion, knew as much, if not more, about weather patterns and ecosystem balance. "A war for bread," he said heavily. "Eliminate the opposition and move onto his land."

Monaco nodded, recalling the artificial Soviet-American tensions. "We never suspected that their motives would be based on hunger rather than paranoia. Maybe they just wanted to feed their people—*all* of their people—for the first time since the end of the Pleistocene."

"And now they have all the land they want," the Colonel claimed. His anger was more prompt and to the point: to him, it was a soldier's challenge now. Purely retributive, purely a matter of strategy. Even Monaco's eyes seemed to swirl with the possibilities of retaliation. Preston suddenly realized that despite what was going on above them, these were dangerous men.

The Colonel went on as if transfixed. "With a brief Ice Age, there'd be nothing to stop them. No cement foundations, no highways, no steel structures. The glaciers would have scoured the earth clean, made it ready."

"And they planned it that way," Monaco echoed. "Stu, run back the tape of the harvester."

Hagerty's fingers flew over the console and the replay appeared on the screen. There, the red harvester once again, trundling along, went down the field, its blades dipping and churning, and the huge trailer bin following along stupidly behind.

"No sound coming from the harvester engines," Monaco observed. "It's not running on diesel. They've devised more efficient machinery, just for this purpose."

Then Preston knew. "They planned this. And somewhere they had Arks and Hives," he said. He looked directly at Sebastian Monaco. "All along, the two governments were thinking the same way. Amazing."

Had they developed the m-field process as well? Preston wondered. There was nothing whatsoever in any of the Outcome Book scenarios to account for this development, or any other which could have anticipated the possibility of Soviet survival. They'd just assumed, from the beginning, that there was no way either nation could survive a nuclear war.

"We've got to get out of here," Lieutenant Monaco suddenly said. *Get out there and get them*, was the implication.

Colonel Chaney agreed, adding, "But we have to keep this thing quiet, *real* quiet, until we know more. We can't let news of it get out into the Meadow."

Preston faced the co-ruler of the compound. "How? You went ahead and cut Jay off when I was on the ladder. He knows something's going on. And there's no telling how many times Holly's been trying to get in touch. A lot of folks still think I'm up on the ladder." He glowered at Monaco. "Except for those who were lying in the kudzu. They *know* something's happening."

"We can handle them," Monaco said sternly, sounding now like one of the Busch brothers—and he probably *meant* the Busch brothers.

Dr. Wainwright walked over to a large comfortable couch and dropped himself in it. He resembled a man who had been blasted by lightning eight or nine times and finally figured out that it was bothering him. He said, "We've got to go about this the right way. But I confess I don't know how at the moment."

Preston walked over. "We should get the other Appleseed supervisors in on this. Have a full meeting of the ruling councils, Ark and Hive both."

"No," the Colonel said firmly. His stolidness made him seem like a dark-eyed Titan ready for battle.

Preston considered him carefully. The Colonel stood over beside Stuart Hagerty and the lazarus, all so serious in their military colors.

"What do you mean, 'no'?" Preston demanded. "This is a major decision we've got to make!"

"Kitteridge," Colonel Chaney pronounced. "We're still at war."

The words seemed to fall like an ax. *War*.

"He's right," Dr. Wainwright finally assented. "We have to keep this among ourselves for a while. There are just too many variables, too many unknowns to make an instant decision to raise the Meadow."

Preston, despite his ever-growing hostility toward Monaco and all that he represented from his primitive, self-destructive era, realized that they were correct. They *had* to know more.

"One of us goes out," the Colonel then said. "One of us goes and assesses the situation."

They looked at him. He continued, "We need someone to reconnoiter the immediate m-field above, see what's there."

"Still in *duende* form?" Preston queried.

"Right," the Colonel said quickly. "I wouldn't trust anything else at the moment. That farmer lives somewhere nearby. If Salina is gone, then he's probably living along the Kansas River. Maybe they've even taken Fort Riley. Who knows?"

"Fort Riley," Stu Hagerty said under his breath, eyes glazed before the screen. It was as if he were recalling the fairyland tales his mother once told him when he was a boy in the Hive.

Perhaps in a way they were all children, where all history was nothing more than a series of tales, mostly dark and foreboding, of republics and empires which never truly existed.

On the television screen, late-day winds tussled what was left of the wheat field where the camera's eye ghostly stood. Insects took to wing. Silence came from the speakers.

"I'll go up," Preston then said. "Let me take a Rover and I'll find that town, wherever it is."

"Why you?" Monaco countered. "Why not somebody else, someone who knows the area?"

The Games Room had become electric with each *duende*'s age-old desire to escape captivity within the earth. They all could feel it, and each probably had as good a reason as any for being the first one out, even the technician Stu Hagerty.

"This is a military maneuver, a reconnaissance, Kitteridge," Monaco said. "You heard Colonel Chaney."

Preston stood up. "That's all I've been hearing is Colonel Chaney."

"Preston—" started Dr. Wainwright, drained of some of his buoyance, his strength.

"No," Preston said firmly. "*You* think about it this time. The Soviets don't know it's a military situation, and *haven't* known for quite some time, especially the time it's taken them to establish an agrarian foothold in Kansas. Besides that, what's above us right now is what I've labored all my life in the Salina Ark to understand. I can evaluate the environment better than any 'spy' could, and I'm smart enough to recognize a military presence, despite what you think." He pointed a knowing finger at Monaco. "Add to that the fact that we don't even know if it's safe for *duendes* out there."

"What do you mean?" Monaco asked.

"Disease," Dr. Wainwright said from his quiet couch. "Mutations, the natural evolution of microbial species under the stress of so much radioactive debris. In six hundred years *anything* could evolve that might be harmful to us."

Monaco stood over the Appleseed. "But I only lived eighty miles from here. I grew up in this part of the country."

"We need somebody," Preston continued hastily, "who'd know if they were using human bodies for fertilizer."

Monaco's eyes widened, then he laughed. "What? Have you lost your mind?"

"Hardly," Preston said seriously. "What kinds of diseases would be in the air after two or three *billion* bodies, worldwide, began to thaw after a nuclear winter? What might the survivors do with them if they had to grow crops real fast?"

Clearly, Monaco hadn't thought of that. Indeed, it was too horrible a thought to think.

Preston continued, "We rig a Rover with a television camera hookup. I could even carry a portable for better views, better angles."

"We've got two serviceable Rovers," the Colonel quickly added. "We also send up someone from the Hive. Lieutenant Monaco *does* know this area and it'd be a shame to let that knowledge go to waste."

"Right," Monaco said. "It's still the twenty-first century to me." He crossed his arms on his chest, solid in his status as a lazarus.

"Now, hold on, men," Dr. Wainwright said, thinking things through. "We don't know if we're dealing with an occupying army, particularly this far inland, or just a lone farmer who just happens to own several hundred square miles of unfenced wild wheat."

Monaco indicated the screens. "You see those initials? CCCP. That harvester was probably dropped down from one of the Soviet sky-cities. Remember that the Soviet space program was entirely military in operation. In fact," he said emphatically, "that's probably where their Hive was located. Their space station was much larger than our own Asgard Station. It could have contained harvesters, tractors, earth-moving equipment—and soldiers."

"Then what's it going to be?" Preston demanded. "How are we going to decide this? I can't possibly believe that we're still at war. . . ."

"We have to decide here and now," the Colonel said. "I'm for sending up someone from the Hive and someone from the Mall."

"I'll vote for that," Monaco said, staring at Preston in an unmasked challenge to his authority as an Ark supervisor and an Appleseed.

They then turned to Dr. Wainwright. He slowly got to his feet, having recovered somewhat from his shock of the world above them. He said, "Duende Meadow was established to maintain life. Neither the Soviet Union nor the government of the United States exists any longer. At least as they were constituted hundreds of years ago. But only an Appleseed's going to know what it is he sees up there. One Rover will do. Preston should go up."

Kitteridge didn't have to vote. He simply shrugged in acknowledgment of the stand-off. It was up to the ranking Hive technician, Stu Hagerty.

Monaco and Colonel Chaney exchanged triumphant looks as they nodded to Mr. Hagerty.

"It's settled then," Monaco announced.

But Stu Hagerty had different ideas. He had a vote and he voiced it. "No, it's not. Preston is right. We've got to know for sure, and as long as the compound doesn't find out about it, we've got all the time in the world." He touched the Outcome Book as if it were alive. "We've lived far too long on mere speculations to rush out and start shooting the place up. I'm with Travis and Preston here."

Colonel Chaney went all dark and stormy. "I'm surprised at you, Hagerty. Turning on us like this."

The small technician held his own. "It's not a question of betrayal. It's just common sense."

"Then what about us?" Monaco said hotly. "We just sit around and twiddle our fingers?"

Preston jumped in. "You very slowly begin to go about preparing the lift engines, start unthawing the 'combs, and in general round up the more discreet personnel from the whole Meadow and let them know what's going on." He then added, more as a reconciliatory gesture, "And if we do need the military, then we'll be ready."

"I don't like it," Monaco insisted. "I know the land better than any of you."

"Land," Dr. Wainwright blurted out, "that has long since changed in character and climate. It's not the same at all, Sebastian."

They stood in the quiet of the Games Room as the implications of the vote settled in. There had been tyrannies and disputes in the Meadow in the centuries past, and some of them had been quiet costly. They also knew that many of those tragic conflicts arose from petty bickerings such as this.

But the tyrannies had been founded on simple unrest, dictatorial aggressions, and not an inconsiderable amount of utter boredom. This, however, was a completely different situation.

Colonel Chaney said, "We'll roll out a Rover at our end, here away from Saxifrage. We'll raise it to the surface on the east platform." He then stared at Preston. "But you're going to have to get your brother away from his observatory. By the time you're ready to go, the Bacchanalia will be about over. Everyone'll be conked out in their condos. But if Jay's in his observatory, though, he'll see the lift engines of the platform. I don't want that."

"Fair enough," Preston remarked. "I can handle him."

*I think*, he had to remind himself. With Wanderers all throughout the Kitteridge line, including their own mother, there was no genuine way to gauge what Jay might do if he saw a reconnaissance platform lift away from the Hive with a Rover sitting on it.

Then Monaco sought to add: "And don't tell Holly anything about this, either."

"What's she got to do with this?"

"Well, you tell her everything. And this is none of her business," Monaco said with all the vitriol he could summon.

"What I tell her is none of your business," Preston grated.

"It is this time," the Colonel said. "Just get back to your condo, clean up, and put a muzzle on your crazy brother. If you don't, we'll find him and lock him up ourselves. And the lieutenant here is right about Holly Ressler."

Preston was nearly livid at this point. If they didn't pick at him at one spot, they got him at another.

So he said, "Yes, but Holly's got the Rover I want to use."

"That's out of the question," Monaco then said.

Preston was firm. "Her Rover's long since been modified for something like this."

"You can use ours," Monaco insisted.

"I'm *going* to use mine!"

Colonel Chaney seemed to turn in circles, throwing his hands up in the air helplessly. "Nemesis! Don't you guys ever stop arguing?"

"You haven't given us a chance," Preston concluded.

With a quick motion, he abandoned the Games Room and ran for Saxifrage Mall.

# 5

Cast in the radiance of an occasional glow-globe set here and there among the leafy bushes and dancing fountains of the concourse, Preston carefully—and secretively—made his way back toward Saxifrage. The Busch brothers had long since returned to their stations in the Hive, and he did not encounter any more centurions.

He was presently worried about being seen by those *duendes* who knew that he was supposed to be still up on the ladder. However, no one was about, though much of the Bacchanalia's jubilance could be heard coming from the Mall.

The Mall recreation centers were between the Hive and the precious Arks. These Preston would have to avoid. Rapidly he stepped through a cluster of kudzu and mounted the stairs for the second level of the Mall. A few idle *duendes* were clumped together in some kudzu, but Preston easily avoided them as they dreamt their strange dreams.

His desire not to be seen just yet was coupled with his uneasiness at leaving Dr. Wainwright alone in the Hive. If the Colonel and Sebastian Monaco decided to initiate other procedures, the elderly botanist would easily be overruled. It was important that a balance be maintained until they all knew their best plan of action.

His other problem was Jay. It had been clear for a number of years that either one of the Kitteridges would inherit the chief Appleseed position, and that of co-ruler of the Meadow. But lately, Preston could feel it all coming down upon his shoulders. What made matters worse was his inability to control Jay. He would have trouble enough with the Hive, as the presence of Lieutenant Monaco suggested.

In the covered Mall, Preston skirted three boys chasing each other on their gyro-cycles. He slipped past two young mothers from the Denver Ark who were nursing newborn *duendes*, finally passing beneath the waterfall which plunged mistily from the floors overhead and flowed toward the center concourse of the Mall. He reached his condo above the Salina Ark without being seen at all.

All the other condos were darkened, including the one belonging to his brother. Even Holly Ressler was not at home. His apartment, however, had every light in the place burning.

"Those goddamn cats," he muttered to himself as he furtively stepped up to the kudzu-shrouded archway of the door.

He put his hand to the lock-plate, letting the computer register his identity. "Open up, you guys!" he spoke in a loud whisper to the voice receiver.

"*No!*" came a tiny but firm voice in kitty-trill.

He heard the computer dutifully unlock the door, but then the manual lock snapped into place from the inside.

"Ike!" Preston shouted, pounding. "Open up or I'll pull all your legs off! Tina, you listen to me!"

"Who is it?" trilled the voice.

"Who the hell do you think it is?" Preston said loudly. "Tell Ike to open the door, Tina, or I'll feed you to the Nemesis!"

The lock broke open instantly and the door wheezed aside.

Their tails in the air, his two mischievous cats, Ike and Tina, bounded in retreat across the living room of his condo.

Preston whipped inside and closed the door. "Ike, what's the big idea?"

Ike, older brother to Tina, turned and looked at him quizzically. He was not bio-engineered to speak, but he could—in a frighteningly human fashion—stand up on his hind feet and shrug, sort of. He held out his paws, paws which contained prehensile fingers instead of feline claws, and seemingly appeared to be innocent. *Sure*, Preston thought. *Right*.

Ike was the one, though, who had thrown the lock. Tina, the one who could speak, had no doubt told him. She had bio-engineered speech capacities—and the attendant intelligence faculties—but Ike was the tinkerer. And they both were *trouble*.

"Kudzu talks. Tina listens!" trilled Tina, a tubby calico whose eyes were bright with flirtations and pranks. Ike leapt across the floor and began strapping himself into the harness of a tiny cart he'd fashioned for himself while Preston had been climbing the ladder.

"What's that?" Preston stared as he began dimming some of the lights the cats had turned on.

Tina happily rushed over to the cart and watched as Ike prepared himself. She looked up at Preston. "We're leaving. Kudzu talks! Here we go!"

The condo was a shambles, as it usually was whenever Preston was away for any length of time. Tina's rudimentary ability to scheme continually got her and Ike into all sorts of trouble. Anything Ike could grasp, he could make into something else. Or just plain invent. It was scary.

What they had done this time was construct a cart. Loaded with all the items vital for their survival, they were indeed ready to go. The kitchen had been sacked and pillaged for cans of cat food, jars of fresh milk, and naturally they'd gotten Preston's hidden cache of catnip.

"Where are you going?" he asked them, but a glance at his couch where his cats usually slept told him the answer to that. A leafy curl of kudzu which had long ago pierced the upper corners of his condo lay fully exposed. Obviously, Tina had been sleeping in it and had overheard something, or perhaps had felt the disturbances the climbing robot camera had made. The two strange cats knew that something was up, but they didn't know what.

"We're not going anywhere," he told Tina, whose face, open and curious as it was, did not register any disappointment. Ike glanced around for other items he might attach to the little cart. They had become twice as animated now that their master was home. Some master, Preston thought.

"Okay, okay," he acquiesced. "We *might* be going somewhere, but I'll let you know when. Meantime, I want this mess cleared up."

Ike scrambled out of his harness as furry Tina leapt up onto the counter which separated the kitchen from the living room.

"Presents for Tina?" she trilled, snapping her tail from side to side.

"No presents," Preston said. "And put that catnip back where you got it!"

"We like presents," Tina purred. "Lots."

Preston headed for a quick shower. He knew when he was beaten.

When Preston came out of the shower he found a meal of lentil soup and freshly baked bread waiting for him. Ike had prepared it for him; at least he had instigated the programming for the food unit. Tina, meanwhile, was over on the couch, facedown in the kudzu, listening in.

Preston tabbed the intercondo, trying to locate Holly. There was no immediate answer, but that didn't mean anything. She was probably at the Bacchanalia.

He then tried his brother's number, in the hope that he might have returned. No dice. He was probably still at his observatory, but neither the kudzu nor the intercondo reached there. His desire for solitude was notorious.

As he spooned the hot, delicious soup, he spoke over to Tina. "Find Holly, best girl," he called out. "Try the Ark."

Tina perked her ears up, looking at him, then stuck her whole head down among the cool, leafy vines. She listened for half a minute, then surfaced. "In and out," she trilled. "Holly in and out of Ark." Her tail twitched.

"Good, Tina." He smiled.

This meant that he would be able to simply go downstairs to see her instead of walking back across the Mall. Jay was his next problem.

"Okay," he announced, rising from the kitchen counter, feeling recharged. "You guys behave yourselves. I've got work to do and when I get back, I want this place clean. You understand, cats?"

Tina declined to comment, licking her paw instead. Ike merely yawned.

"Right," Preston muttered.

He took his own personal dropshaft into the Salina, taking a shortcut to the Sonoran Ark. All seven of the Arks were much like the 'combs in the Hive in that most of the life they contained was in some form of storage. However, some of the animals and plants were always being used in research, and as Preston entered the lower level of the Salina Ark, he could hear a solitary cow lowing in its pen and some finches chattering away in their cages. The Ark was nearly always alive with animal sounds of one kind or another.

His own second-in-command in the Salina Ark, Betsy Morrissey, was the only *duende* in the building. She was one of twenty *duendes* who had chosen this week to catch her yearly cold, and as she sat with her feet propped up on the computer console with her dream-video headset on, she sneezed mightily into a handkerchief.

Betsy saw Preston and took off her headset, her red nose glowing with congestion, eyes tearful. She was otherwise an attractive twenty-five-year-old technician with long black hair and pale features and was married to one of his best friends. They were almost like brother and sister to him.

"Preston," she said. "You're back. How did it go up there?"

Her cold and her minor Ark duties apparently had kept her completely out of touch with the kudzu or the Bacchanalia.

"Everything went fine," he told her. "I broke all the records. How are you doing?"

She hauled out another handkerchief and blew her nose with gusto. "I feel like shit."

"You look like shit. Why don't you go back and let Mike take care of you?"

She pointed to the beast in its pen, wired to the computer for testing. "Cow needs watching."

Preston nodded. "Listen, have you seen Holly or Jay anywhere?"

She blew her nose. She then said, "Holly was in here about an hour ago. She needed some tools for her little sister. They're fooling with the trawler."

"What about Jay?"

"Mystery to me, Preston." She looked at him. "You better talk to him. He's a good biochemist, but there's something wrong with that guy. He's staying away longer and longer."

Preston nodded grimly. As supervisor of the Salina Ark, he knew that a good biochemist was indispensable. However, as much as the Ark needed a competent biochemist, he needed him as a *Kitteridge*. As a brother. Biochemists they could replace; they were running out of Kitteridges.

"I'll find him," he said.

He stepped toward the far exit of the Ark as Betsy watched him go. She sank back into her dream-video, coughing and sniffling as she plugged back in. The cow groaned mournfully behind her.

The Salina Ark was situated at the southwestern tip of the elongated Meadow. The Sonoran Ark was directly west. By stepping outside of the Meadow, onto the subsurface m-field itself, he knew he'd avoid being seen by any *duende* for sure.

Here, it was quiet. Few *duendes* spent their recreational time out on the m-field because of its horrible darkness. Those who did often never came back. As long as the individual m-field generators which each *duende* carried in his or her belt kept functioning, they could go anywhere outside the Meadow they wished. But as Preston stepped away from the comfort and security of Saxifrage and headed toward the Sonoran Ark, he could feel the emptiness, the loneliness, which often drew a Wanderer to his or her fate.

He looked up. Here, the southern "constellations" were quite apparent. Dimly, the ghost-lights sparkled. Only a year previously had Jay in his observatory discovered three new ones: the Trident, the Compass, and the Boomerang. They were quite distant and seemed to beckon Preston as he walked.

He hurried to the Sonoran Ark.

He found Holly. A giant spotlight from the rear of the Sonoran Ark cast down a crystalline cone of white light onto the trawler. At the base of its huge single center-aligned tread was the young supervisor of the desert biosphere.

The trawler, of which there were only two in the whole compound, was a machine thirty feet tall, full of tremendous pulling power, and was designed specifically to tow the individual Arks across the topside m-field to their respective places of seeding—when the time in the far future required it. Holly Ressler stood aglow in the Ark's beacon supervising its monthly maintenance.

The treads which ran underneath the behemoth seemed to dwarf her. Its foreplate was open and Preston could see the intricate spiderings of circuits and wires which, when activated, would allow each single tread to cling powerfully to the m-field floor. High above Holly, in the pilot's compartment, a solitary light blazoned and busybody noises came from within.

"Hi, kid," Preston hailed, coming at her from the ghostly darkness.

"Oh, Preston!" she said, startled. She then sneezed, and dropped the wrench she was holding. Her blond hair flapped wildly.

"Not you too," Preston began.

On her face were some smudges of grease, and she quickly brought up her own hanky.

"I didn't think it was your week," he said.

"It's not," she said, blowing her nose. "I'm not supposed to catch my cold for another month." She sniffed.

Their yearly bouts with induced colds and flu viruses was their way of keeping their immunological systems strong. Since they did not know what kinds of diseases awaited them if ever they should return to the surface, it had been their decision long ago to keep their lymphatic systems healthy. Apparently Holly had caught hers from Betsy in the Salina Ark.

She was very glad to see him. "It went okay?" she began. "I didn't think you'd be back so soon."

"Neither did I," he told her.

Tinny sounds came from the driver's compartment above them. Something dropped with a great deal of clatter.

Quickly he said, "Travis wants me to bring him your Rover. I've got to take it to the Hive."

"The Rover?" Despite her cold—or because of it—she seemed disappointed. "Oh, hoo. I thought we were going to the Bacchanalia when you got back."

"We will. I promise. But I have to do this first," he told her with a soothing smile. "You work too hard anyway."

Preston was having trouble hiding the excitement of his topside vision from her, and Holly, due to her incipient cold, misread him completely.

She then said, "No one's Wandered, have they? Is that why Travis wants my Rover?" Now she looked worried.

Preston laughed reassuringly. "No one's gone anywhere. Travis and the Colonel got into an argument and they want me to settle it."

He hoped that that explanation would suffice. Three weeks earlier a soil technician in the Sonoran Ark, and a very good friend of Holly's, had failed one of her important exams at their university. She disappeared. She had become their most recent Wanderer and Holly tried to find her in the Rover, circling the Meadow day and night in the Neptunian darkness. The girl was never located.

Yet, seeing Preston so unexpectedly had reassured her. "All right. But promise me you'll come back. I want to have some fun before the Bacchanalia's over." Her throaty voice seemed all that much deeper because of her cold.

"I promise," he said.

Suddenly the door to the pilot's compartment clanged open like a gong. A small blond-haired tyke came out, pushing ahead of her an indescribable piece of cockpit machinery.

Barrie Ressler, all of six years of age, bratty and cute as a button, appeared above them with a fussy look on her cherubic face.

"This doesn't work!" she pouted.

She shoved it out onto the metal ledge and left it there, presumably for someone else to fix. That meant Holly.

"Hi, pest!" Preston said up to the little person.

"Hi," Barrie muttered, and returned to the cockpit, slamming the door shut behind her.

Like so many children of recent vintage, Barrie, like her older sister, had received slight genetic alterings in her creative or mechanical capacities. It allowed for much precociousness.

Preston smiled at Holly. "She'll rework the whole trawler yet."

"She didn't want to play at the Gathering, so I'm letting her help me on the trawler." A sneeze came on as Holly spoke, then exploded when it arrived. She said, "Makes her think she's important." She blew her nose.

"Quit talking about me!" came a muffled little voice from overhead.

"Okay!" Holly shouted back. She smiled at Preston. "We won't even use the trawler in our lifetime, but she insists on making it better. I think it's like a dollhouse to her."

"Some dollhouse," Preston commented.

From Holly's belt he took out a remote unit and tapped out a command. A door slid open in the side of the Sonoran Ark and the Rover minibus, quite on its own, lumbered out, headlights on. Right next to the exterior garage door was the long, superalloyed hitch which connected the trawler to the Ark. The Rover dodged this and came to rest before Holly.

"I don't know how long I'll be," he told her. "But I'll be back around, pronto."

"You better," she sniffed.

He kissed her on the cheek. "Don't worry. You won't miss anything." He looked up at the pilot's cranny. "See you later, pest!" he shouted.

"I'm not a pest!" Barrie shouted down.

He smiled, surrendering to the strange Resslers. He often thought of what a couple more generations of altered Ressler women might be like, and shuddered.

He climbed inside the Rover and pulled out around the trawler. He had one other destination.

With human gene engineering, one never knew what to expect. Jay Kitteridge was one such example. Their long exile had often engendered eccentricity as a way to cope with the darkness, but there were times when Jay displayed signs of more disquieting unrest.

Ever since they had lost their parents years ago, one to an accident and the other to Wandering, Jay had not quite been the same. It had been the incident of their mother's disappearance which had done it. Like every family in the Meadow, theirs had been plagued with the Wandering mood. As the years of perpetual darkness wore at them, the instinct never seemed to go away. Only people did.

Jay, diligent all these years with his work in the Ark, had suddenly quit. He bore his mother's Wandering as best he could, but then one day began work on his observatory. He never returned to his biochemistry. He preferred solitude and the ghost-light phenomenon instead.

At first, Preston thought the observatory was a good thing. But then he realized that isolation was one of the first symptoms of Wandering. Next was despair, followed by alien- ation, then utter disinterest with life. Still, he let his brother build his fortress of solitude.

Several hundred feet away from the Mall, Jay had lo- cated his platform where he could best observe the ghost- lights in the darkness of the m-field. He managed to convince the Meadow leadership that his research in the "constella- tions" above them might contribute to a better understanding of morphogenetic field study. Since no one knew why the ghost-lights had begun appearing only recently, the Meadow authorities let him do it.

Preston had always had his doubts. Like any other *duende*, he had his inbred fear of the dark. But to watch Jay disengage himself from the other *duendes* was quite painful to him. He was the only family he had, except for Ike and Tina. He couldn't bear the thought of Jay vanishing. Jay had a bright, quick mind, and an inventive sense of humor. Everyone loved him. And love, these days, was the only thing which mattered.

Perhaps it was the only thing which *ever did* matter, but the forces which led to the Last War had apparently sprung from a different source. The Dark Nemesis, as they referred to it. Perhaps all of their Wanderers had been touched, in some way, by His dark whisperings. . . .

Preston drew the Rover up to the silvery dome. The large telescope, he could see, was aimed almost directly overhead, but no lights glowed dimly from within.

He got out and entered the dome. Jay was not home. Instead, his clothes were tossed helter-skelter and Preston noticed that many of his brother's most valued books were also missing. He knew what they were: the *Tao Te Ching*, the *Bhagavad Gita*, the *Gnostic Gospel of Thomas*, and the Buddhist holy book, the *Dhammapada*. All of which were duro-fiber paperbacks and could easily be tucked into the pouches of an Appleseed's tunic.

Especially if that Appleseed was going somewhere.

Preston stared up at the tubular scope which occupied most of the dome. Through the open partition of the roof, he could see that Jay had not been watching any of the ghostlight constellations.

The scope had been aimed precisely at the zenith of the ladder.

He then recalled their severed radio transmission. Had Jay overheard something the Hive had tried to prevent? Or had he done what many *duendes* in the past had done: assume that if the Soviets had survived World War Three—in whatever manner—then it meant that the Dark Nemesis, not God, had triumphed. Even Preston, in his worry, had felt a little bit of it.

So if ever Jay Kitteridge had a reason to Wander, this was it.

Preston rushed outside into the abrupt darkness of the eternal night.

"Jay!" he shouted to the emptiness in the distance. "*Jay!*"

# 6

The last time any *duende* got a topside look at the world was thirteen years before Preston's birth. The upper m-field was still—even after six hundred years—encrusted with black, glacial ice. It had been a routine reconnaissance, part of the Meadow's overall plan to check out the surface every fifty years or so.

No one had expected it to have changed, and to their dismay, it hadn't. But that was forty-six years ago, long before Preston was born and the ladder been devised for their amusement. No one dared think that the earth had healed. The Outcome Book was, to them, like the Bible. Fundamental in its truth; literal in its findings.

Their surface scoutings were conducted from an observation platform just adjacent to the Hive at the east end of the Meadow. As Preston sat nervously in the seat of his Rover, he felt the observation platform rise like a slow bubble in a viscous liquid, rising with a purplish underglow propelling him upward. The last time this had been done, there had been a mere robot camera on the platform; now, there was a modified Rover and a *duende* buoyed with an expectation of freedom.

Still, it was dark. The ethereal rock through which he rose betrayed only the distant shimmerings of the constellations of the Butterfly and the Spider's Lair. He briefly thought that the lift engines of the platform might be disturbing them, but that was an illusion. He was merely nervous, edgy. He had a lot on his mind.

Preston glanced out of the wide window of the Rover as the blackness of sedimentary rock sank past him. Numbers in soft blue shone from the computer dashboard of the Rover, indicating elevation.

"Two minutes," Stu Hagerty's firm voice crackled from his headset.

There was no steering wheel in the Rover. Hand controls at the ends of the armrests fed the driver's impulses into the Rover's autonomic nervous system. Preston felt his palms moisten on the controls and he could sense the Rover's readiness to respond.

"Thirty seconds," Stu Hagerty said. "Stand by for platform shutdown, Preston."

Kitteridge watched the dials. "I read you," he told them.

Then quite suddenly there was light.

From down below Hagerty braked the platform, locking it onto the surface m-field. The engines were then shut down, their gentle humming coming to a stop.

"Nemesis," Preston breathed as the late-afternoon light flooded in and around him as he sat completely enthralled in the seat of the Rover.

Because of his position in the Rover, he was now many feet above the field of shorn wheat, and he found the sensation rather disconcerting. There was so much space!

Quickly he switched the Rover's m-field to adjust to the surface m-field. The minibus lurched slightly as it touched down.

"We're getting excellent reception from the Rover's cameras," Dr. Wainwright's voice came at him. "We'll be able to follow you and watch wherever you go. But remember that you're going to need to come back down on the platform. So remember where it is. Find a landmark or something."

"Right," Preston said.

He was nearly speechless. He was struck with something he hadn't sensed when he was atop the ladder, and for which no one had prepared him: agoraphobia. He gasped and closed his eyes. He then opened them again and was struck this time with sudden, intense joy. The Rover's quiet electric engines hummed soothingly and he was suddenly ecstatic.

"I can see the ladder and the camera," he told them through his audio link. "I'm about three hundred yards east of it." Though thoroughly invisible to the rest of the world, his *duende* sight made it clearly visible to him. He turned to his right and saw a small hill several hundred yards off. The harvester had gone around it, so the wild wheat still grew there. He said, "There's a small rise to the east of the platform. I'll use it and the ladder for a parallax."

"We can see it," Hagerty informed him.

Nervously gripping the handholds, Preston eased the craft forward. "I'm moving out. Wish me luck."

"You've got it, Preston," Dr. Wainwright said. "But remember that the surface m-field is irregular. It will follow every contour of the ground where you're at."

Preston said nothing as the Rover drifted away from the lift platform. The Rover's sensors busily recorded what they could, and he could hear the idle talk of the *duendes* as they speculated to one another down below.

He was just trying to get used to such a bumpy, unexpected ride.

"Unbelievable," whispered a voice from the Games Room.

"Look at those trees in the distance. They don't seem like Kansas trees . . ." came another voice.

"There's a stream! I think there's a stream off to the left. There!" echoed another.

As Preston took the Rover to the north of the lift platform, out across the seemingly endless plain of harvested wheat, he felt intoxicated by the serenity of the land about him, his slight agoraphobia notwithstanding. Sunset was quickly approaching and as he reached a somewhat higher vantage point in the field, he was almost overwhelmed by its melancholy beauty.

This was a land long removed from the teeming presence of civilized humankind. The Salina, Kansas, region had been mostly farmland, with Salina itself being a medium-sized city of modest stature. However, the rills and ridges that funneled along the horizon were clear indications of not only recent glaciation and snowpack but also intense missile bombardment centuries ago. Craters now dotted the Plains, and that anything like wheat or birds or insects flourished here was a mystery to him.

He then looked at the leaves on the faraway trees and noticed something else.

It was autumn. *Real* autumn.

There were no seasons in the Meadow. They knew the time of year all right, but it rarely possessed any true meaning. Jay was forever quoting Chinese poetry to him, for the

ancient Chinese were perpetually enthralled with autumn
and the change of the seasons.

He recalled some special lines from Tu Fu:

> *An autumn wind rattles the stone scales of a sea*
> *    dragon.*
> *Among heaving waves sink the dark clouds of the*
> *    kumi seeds—*
> *In the cold dew pink petals fall from the lotus*
> *    pods . . .*

On a remote hillside, where the giant Russian harvester
had skirted it, stood a tall maple-tree grove which was already touched by the winds of autumn. It seemed to him as if
the cool autumn air was only a daring breath away. How he
wanted to opaque out and inhale that fragrance!

The stream which the Colonel had sighted through the
Rover's camera flowed off to his left. Preston swung the
Rover toward it.

"Fish!" someone said from down below.

The little dreamy creek seemed to pass through the
former field of wheat quite undisturbed or unfettered from
any intention the Russian farmer might have of maintaining
any symmetry to the wheat crop. Indeed, the harvester had
cleared up most of the wheat without so much as damaging
the creek or any of the isolated clusters of trees nearby.

Preston glanced down at the creek for a closer look as
Dr. Wainwright—who knew about such things—spoke up.
He said, "If fish have survived, then the biosphere is in much
better condition than we thought. There are even lilies. And
those things there are cat-o'-nine-tails."

Down in the Hive, they were almost like children.

Preston considered a wider perspective. Daylight was
waning quickly and he needed to find out where the harvester went. He knew it had forded this creek, so he took the
Rover up to a misshapen hill where he could properly scan the
whole field.

From his estimate, from what he knew about the amount
of grain which could be grown on an acre of land, he guessed
that this shallow valley—within which he placed Duende
Meadow at its epicenter—was capable of feeding perhaps
thirty thousand people. The vast field stretched for at least
twenty-five miles at its longest reach and appeared to be

about fifteen or so miles wide. There, a range of hills—impact craters?—boasted a family of deciduous trees of a kind he couldn't quite make out in the fading light. Only here and there in the field was an occasional undisturbed cottonwood or maple grove.

But nowhere could he see a human dwelling. There were no remnants of roads, or fences, not even a string of high-tension wires.

He stopped the Rover in the trees of a nearby hill at the edge of the flat valley.

"I'm going to step out of the Rover for a minute or two," he informed them, lest they become alarmed.

"Go ahead," Dr. Wainwright said, keeping the edge of excitement from his voice.

The door to the vehicle slid open and Preston stepped out onto the ghostly surface of the m-field, which exactly conformed to the shape of the hillside.

Standing there, just marginally away from his Rover, he almost felt like the first man on the moon. He now knew that it would take the *duendes* many, many years to explore and catalog everything this new world presented. More had changed than they thought.

The leaves of the maple trees nearby fluttered like tiny splayed hands in the wind that wafted up the hillside. But the leaves themselves seemed sturdier, slightly thicker than the maples they had down in the Arks. Protection against radiation? An adaptation for the colder weather brought on by an Ice Age?

A butterfly—what looked to be a black-and-white Weidemeyer's Admiral—danced in between the maple branches. It then sailed right through Preston and his Rover, disappearing into the trees.

"Did you see the size of that butterfly?" he heard Sebastian Monaco cry out for the first time. "It was huge!"

"Weidemeyers are normally two and a half inches long," Preston informed them. "That one was easily five inches. There have been a *lot* of changes up here." However, if the Outcome Book had encouraged them to think of the worst of all possible worlds waiting for them, the changes all about Preston were considerably more congenial.

The butterfly danced back into view and seemed to linger in Preston's vicinity, as if it knew—in its insectoid way—that something was there. But then it returned to its demesne among the autumn maples, not to be seen again.

Stepping further into the trees, Preston located another butterfly resting on a nearby branch, its wings easing slowly open and shut. Quickly he leapt back to the Rover and drew out a smaller video unit. He slung it to his shoulder and held it up to the colorful creature.

"I want you people to see this," he said.

What he sent down to them was an indication of the scale the world above had changed. *This* butterfly had feathers. Its antennae waved about searchingly.

"I'd swear the insect's intelligent," Preston reported into the pin-mike at his cheek.

Down below, they were silent as they watched their many screens.

Preston returned to the Rover and proceeded down the small hill. He drove north. "This is almost too much," he muttered under his breath. But they had heard.

"It just can't be Kansas," Sebastian Monaco told them all. The channel was wide open and Preston heard the lazarus' voice fill with an almost uncharacteristic poetic wonder. He said, "I used to live not far from here. I don't recognize a thing. Even the light is different."

Dr. Wainwright's voice sounded sympathetic. "After thirty or more ground impacts and a few hundred years of glaciation, I'm surprised it doesn't look like Mars."

The Rover registered an outside surface temperature a little cooler than Preston would have imagined for this time of the year. It was just marginally enough to suggest to him that if there had been an Ice Age, however brief, then it may barely have ended. He could discern clear signs of minor glaciation at the edges of the valley: small eskers, drumlins, and much of the topsoil down in the small gullies was permeated with a heavy peat growth, obviously laid down in the moraine of receding glaciers. How glaciers could get this far into the middle of the continent he did not know. But the evidence was indisputable. The War had changed the prevailing weather systems; that, in turn, changed the land.

It had also altered the river-flow patterns. Just to the north of Salina was the Saline River, and above that was the Solomon. Preston discovered that the Saline River was now a trickle in a mossy state of decline and the Solomon was nowhere to be found.

Monaco was right: The land was unrecognizable.

They had debated whether or not he should head south and find the ruins of Salina, but Preston had vetoed that idea. The harvester, the last they had seen of it, had moved toward the north. However, as he drifted invisibly over the sad, barren Saline River, he began to wonder if he had been mistaken. Wouldn't the ruins of Salina have provided a perfect foundation for a new Soviet settlement?

The Rover ghosted up a slight incline and quite suddenly Preston came across a brand-new road. Freshly graded in the black earth, it led away from the wide wheat fields toward the north. His heart began pounding as the Rover followed the tracks the harvester had left earlier that day.

"Something over there," Colonel Chaney's voice resounded. "See it, Kitteridge? Bearing up on your left to the northwest."

The Rover hadn't been traveling too fast, and it took him a second to make it out. Squinting through the vehicle's window, he said, "Right. I see them now."

The sun's light was weakening over the countryside, but a gently wooded rise just ahead of him revealed that behind it was a gathering of man-made structures.

His heart raced. The wheat plain was far behind him now, and mostly surrounding him were the swells of soft hills awash with a brownish sage studded occasionally with bushes of a sort he could not identify. The road, though unpaved, made a convenient pathway through the almost virginal terrain.

"The harvester went this way for sure," he said out loud as he turned one of the Rover's cameras down at the lizardlike tread the harvester had made. The tracks were quite fresh now. "I'll follow it as far as it goes," he told them.

In the approaching twilight he thought that he had seen the remains of a broken asphalt highway where the new dirt road crossed it. The highway came at an odd angle and Kitteridge privately wondered why the Russians would choose to make their own roads when simple repair of some of the remaining ones would have been more efficient. The road upon which the Rover was drifting seemed almost as if it had been plowed arbitrarily. Why this would be so was another mystery to him. He only knew that the Russians had done it, and that thought deeply upset him.

The objects, or structures, that the Colonel had sighted in the distance dipped behind another low hill as the Rover followed the winding road.

But then rather suddenly they appeared in full view.

"*Silos!*" someone shouted down in the Hive. It may have been Monaco.

The Rover rounded a bend, ghosted over another tiny creek, and pulled into sight of a row of sentinel-like grain silos.

"My God," Preston said, amazed. "Look at those things."

These new Russian-built silos were twice as tall as the old-time Kansas silos so common throughout rural America. These seemed to stand like towering rocket ships as their ventilation fans slowly turned, catching the orange autumn light of the sunset.

The clearing in which they stood had plainly been made specifically for them. Nothing else stirred around the four massive buildings except for a family gathering of grotesquely shaped pigeons on their conical roofs. Next to the grain silos was the mindless trailer bin which had followed behind the red harvester. There was no sign of the harvester itself or the farmer who drove it. There was some other machinery, no doubt necessary for the running of an automated farm, but Preston was unfamiliar with its design.

"Brand-new," Preston said as he eased the Rover nearer. "Look close. They are absolutely brand-new. The rust-proof paint, the wood of the shoring, the metal and fiber-rubber of the conveyor, even the pumps. If I could smell it, I'd know for sure."

"We can see it, Preston," Dr. Wainwright was quick to respond. "Don't opaque out just yet. We don't want you catching anything."

"I know, Travis," he said. "Just thinking out loud."

He couldn't take his eyes away from the four silos. They were taller than anything down in the Meadow, and they seemed to speak of so much abundance. They fairly bulged from the wheat contained within.

*American* wheat harvested by *Russian* farmers, he kept having to remind himself.

"I want to check on something," he then informed them.

He edged the Rover right at the nearest silo and passed in through its sturdy steel walls. Once inside, it was thoroughly dark and he knew that it was packed with wheat. He drove on out the other side and proceeded to check the other three.

All but the last silo was full of wheat, so far as he could tell at ground level. He told them, "There is still the east end of the river valley yet to harvest. I guess it will go in here."

"Preston," came Stu Hagerty's voice. "We're starting to pick up power readings nearby. Can you locate the source?"

Lights had twinkled on at the top of each silo in the sunset, some of which were sprinkled throughout the four buildings. Preston quickly found a small building which seemed to house a generator of some kind. He wouldn't know what kind until he could opaque out. It was completely dark within, indicating that the whole operation was as nearly self-contained and automatic as it could possibly be.

"Do you see any signs of life?" Dr. Wainwright then asked. "Are there any people around?"

"No," Preston said, scanning the terrain. "At least from where I'm at. I'll follow the road while there's still some light left."

"Do it," Dr. Wainwright encouraged. "We've got to know before the sun goes down entirely."

Preston drove the silent Rover out onto the small graded road which continued on north, away from the silos. Here, the landscape was a pleasure of greens and browns. The wind on the outside had died down and a hush seemed to embrace the land. Maples and oaks along the roadside had clearly been kissed by the cool autumn nights.

Preston noticed—but for now kept it to himself—that many of the larger trees seemed in intentional brakes along the road. They seemed too planned-out in their dispersal, as if the Soviets were trying to assist Mother Nature along in her healing process. He began to wonder if there were Russians everywhere on the continent, fishing off the coasts of New England or even farming the fertile San Joaquin Valley in central California. The harvesting there would be much more profitable and diverse. He shuddered to think of the Soviet conquest as being so complete. How they themselves survived their own pommeling by NATO and the United States was beyond him at the moment. Nonetheless, some of them had survived. That was the crucial issue at hand.

The harvester tracks were clearly getting fresher the further he went down the road. He was catching up to it although he had yet to see it.

"It should be appearing soon," he told them down in the Hive.

He had noticed that back in the silo yard there had been an unfenced maintenance area that contained several racks of harvester blades. Without the long, cumbersome blades, the harvester could probably do thirty miles an hour on a relatively flat surface. Here, however, it was going much slower.

The sun had just dropped past the horizon, fanning a soft fuchsine red light into the twilight sky. Preston could see no birds now, no insects. Nothing moved in the early-evening landscape that was slowly enfolding about the world. He felt a tingling rush of excitement dither up his spine as he anticipated the fall of night—true night. The darkness which surrounded the Meadow had a foggy, phantasmagorical quality to it which had something to do with the m-field process and the nature of the rock within which the Meadow had been situated. This, however, was vastly different.

This night would be natural, the way it was intended.

The temptation to opaque out was almost overwhelming. He had the capacity right there with him in his own m-field belt. He could even opaque out the Rover if he so chose. In that way, he could stay out forever. . . .

But he held his impulses in check. He had work to do and responsibilities to be met. He'd be out eventually.

And so would everyone else.

Thinking those idle thoughts, he came upon the harvester. A vague plume of dust had appeared at a bend in the road and the *duendes* down below saw it the same time he did.

"There!" came a voice. "There it is!"

"Right," Preston reported. "I'm on it."

The last fingers of sunlight trailed at the western rim of the world and the canopy lights of the machine were already on, guiding its way toward the small town which just then came into view.

"Nemesis," Colonel Chaney said. "The pot at the end of the rainbow."

The crimson harvester seemed ungainly as it bounced along the road on its large balloon wheels. Without its wide, crisp blades for balance, the harvester appeared to wobble somewhat, as if it were on the verge of toppling. But the farmer within obviously was a skilled hand at wrestling with the machine, despite its elephantine size. No sound came from it other than the squeak of its hydraulic shocks and the low humming of the engine within.

"John Deere never made a harvester like that," Sebastian Monaco told them. "Nor did International Harvester. It's too tall and too weird."

"And very functional," Preston added. "I imagine that it's totally electric." He scanned the console on the Rover, examining some of its data. "They've apparently got an economy that can afford to do without diesel."

"We don't know that yet," the Colonel said hastily.

"That's true," Preston admitted. It was much to soon to tell just what it was the Russians had created for themselves in their new homeland.

The crimson creature hogged the whole road, for as wide as the graded road was; but there was no other traffic coming opposite them from the village beyond.

In the town, Preston could see that small lights had been turned on in anticipation of night. Anxiously Preston gripped the armrest controls and pushed the Rover into the dust of the harvester's wake.

Then, within fifty yards, the dirt road ended and asphalt began. The harvester bounded up onto it easily. Preston coaxed his ghostly Rover along.

That was when they passed an Exxon station.

"Good heavens!" Monaco gasped, genuinely surprised. He recognized it as if he'd been there just the day before.

As Preston's Rover invisibly drifted by it, the *duendes* down below turned all available camera eyes upon the station, which was now all aglow in its neon blues and reds for whatever night business might come its way.

The station attendant, in clean-pressed overalls and a jaunty cap, was out hissing away dirt and grime from the pump area with a high-pressure water hose. The attendant waved at the farmer aloft in the crimson harvester as it passed, totally unaware of the spectral Rover following in its wake and the *duende* within from a defeated nation.

"That gas station's *exactly* like the ones in my time. I don't understand—" Sebastian Monaco said.

Dr. Wainwright was next on the horn. His voice now

seemed strained, as if the surprises were one too many. "Is it possible that there *wasn't* a war? That life went on?"

Preston looked around him in the near-darkness. "I'm not picking up any low-level radiation at all. Strontium 90 would've deteriorated within sixty years. So would cesium 137. Those are the most harmful isotopes."

"But the residual plutonium and uranium wastes—" Hagerty began.

Monaco cut him off. "There was a war, all right." He spoke with command and authority, suddenly coming to his senses. He was the only one among them who had a living memory of the bombs impacting upon McConnell Air Force Base that Christmas morning. The tone in his voice indicated that it wasn't likely—despite what they were seeing—that he was going to forget.

Preston pursued the harvester as it drove past the Exxon station. They entered the village proper. At the town's lazy entrance was a large wooden signpost which dangled various emblematic shields of the community's service organizations: Lion's Club, the Rotarians, Kiwanis Club, Knights of Columbus. . . .

The harvester lumbered gracefully down the center of town, passing as it went a J. C. Penney's hardware store, a dairy depot, a hometown grocery store, a feed-and-grain store. A real-estate office. A State Farm Insurance office. A flower shop. There was even a small pet store.

And the town had a name. It wasn't New Leningrad, Nuova Muskova, not even Kansasgrad.

*Anytown*. Population 318. "WELCOME," said the sign.

Alongside the main street were cars from all eras of the pre-War century. All seemed serviceable, some were even shiny and new. There were Fords, GM trucks, several Volkswagens—even Toyotas. Some seemed gasoline-powered, others electric.

Preston noticed how the wood of the buildings seemed newly cut and hewn. The paint and plaster lath seemed perhaps only a few years old. Trees freshly planted lined clean sidewalks.

It was a town built from scratch with an occasional addition of old-time relics fully restored and polished.

Preston discovered that he was shaking. This was not in their precious Outcome Book, their Anti-Bible.

This was not the way it was supposed to turn out. How

could it? After so many centuries of climatic upheaval and radioactive winds scouring the earth, how could so much color and vitality and freshness—and sheer mockery—exist in America?

None of the *duendes* spoke a word as the Rover's cameras panned about, absorbing every nuance before them. What they were feeling, Preston could only imagine. His view of things was considerably different. He was *here*.

And he was so confused, so perplexed, he was shaking.

The huge harvester rounded a corner on the main street, which led into the "suburbs." Preston ghosted after it, peering at the few dozen houses, each with their suppertime lights burning cozily within. These houses, he suddenly recognized, were *homes*. Not reconstructed from ruins or hastily nailed together from aberrant pine trees growing haphazardly outside of town. People lived here.

The Rover's computer screen indicated that the small farm community of Bennington, Kansas, was the nearest American town. It was some distance to the north, but from the looks of things, clearly no longer existed. This village, Anytown, had sprung up like a toadstool overnight, right in the middle of the great outdoors, as far from any leftover remnants of America as the Russians could manage. And they intended to live here. Permanently.

The harvester slowed and pulled up alongside one particular house, easing into an area built specifically for the machine. Another tractor of smaller dimensions sat nearby, as well as a Chevy pickup truck of late-twentieth-century design.

This could have been the farm household of an average Kansas farmer. Two-story home, screened porch, tire-swing hanging from the hefty arms of a box-elder tree—it couldn't have been more perfect. A happy mongrel dog bounded from the screen porch as the harvester's lights switched off. It barked and jumped excitedly.

Preston halted his ethereal Rover before this storybook scene just to take it all in. A tall, strong woman—not your standard potato-fed Ukrainian matron—came out on the porch upon hearing the fuss the dog had made. She seemed rather handsome, a wife and presumably a mother, in her late thirties. She wiped her hands on a dish towel and pushed a strand of brown hair back up away from her eyes.

"Irina!" she called. "Supper's almost cold!"

Preston glanced back at the harvester and was startled to

see the cockpit window open out to reveal the delicate form of a young girl.

Not a man, but a nine-year-old *girl*.

She took off the radio headset and shook her head, freeing the blond curls which framed her face. Down the rungs of the harvester she came, wearing overalls, hobnailed boots, and work gloves. The dog barked and wagged its tail, running up to her.

The mother held the screen door open for the daughter and spoke to her in very precise English. If there was a trace of an accent in her words, Preston couldn't tell; he was too dumbfounded to notice.

Irina, the blond-headed sprite, leapt across the driveway and clumped up onto the wooden porch. But as her mother moved to let the screen door slam shut, the beautiful little Russian glanced back out into the middle of the lawn.

She had apparently seen something, and so had the scroungy dog.

They both were staring at the shadowy box-elder tree and the very spot the Rover stood idling.

# 7

"The girl looked right at me," he whispered into the pin-mike at his cheek, as if he might be heard. "Is it possible she saw me?"

Dr. Wainwright, sitting at the Games Room console next to Stu Hagerty, had been watching closely. "There's no way. You're in another dimension to her."

"She saw something," Preston reiterated strongly. "And so did their dog."

"It's just your imagination, Kitteridge," Colonel Chaney stated harshly. "They probably heard a noise across the street."

The little girl, Irina, and her mother disappeared back into their farmhouse. The yellow porch light winked out and the screen door slammed shut.

"It wasn't my imagination," he told them firmly. "I'm going inside to see."

"Don't waste your time," came Monaco's admonition. "You've got to explore the whole town. That was the plan, dammit!" He heard the second lieutenant slap his palm angrily upon the console board of the Games Room. *These are Russians!* he could almost hear the patriotic lazarus shout.

But Preston chose to ignore Monaco's insistent demands.

He said, "We'll know just as much about the town and its people by examining one family. And besides, the sun's gone down now and there's no way I can effectively cover the whole settlement in one night. It's just too big. You saw for yourselves."

There was some protracted grumbling from down below in the darkness of the earth, but he let it pass unheeded.

He carefully pulled the Rover around in such a manner as to give its cameras the best view possible of the street in all directions. He then climbed out of the humming vehicle. Shouldering the portable video unit, he gingerly walked toward the house, his pulse increasing noticeably as he approached it.

Outside the Rover in the near-dark of the night, he turned around to notice that there seemed to be very little in the neighborhood that was clearly Soviet in manufacture. The farmhouse—and the other homes up and down the wide street—appeared to be rather a pastiche of Americana, as if drawn from ancient picture books by Norman Rockwell, a nostalgic vision of the Plain States circa the 1930s. Other than the orange initials of CCCP which rode high upon the bright red harvester's side, there were no other indications in the neighborhood, or the town, that *Russians* presently dwelled here.

Preston made a few brief adjustments at the thin belt around his waist which unified his own m-field with that of the house before him. The house had been built about a foot and a half above the yard and he needed to walk level with the floor of the structure rather than halfway down into the basement, assuming there was one.

So, hefting the portable video unit up on his shoulder, he mounted the wooden steps of the house and passed through the gossamer metal of the screen door, and drifted like a real ghost on into the house. He almost felt like saying, *Trick or treat!*

The *duendes* down below voiced no further complaint as Preston began scanning the living room of the domicile with the camera.

To their surprise—or perhaps disappointment—this part of the home seemed quite ordinary. This wasn't a military bivouac or temporary structure thrown together by a conquering army ready to move on. It was a home.

There was, however, a different kind of dog in the living room. It was the same size and color as the one which had happily met Irina outside, but this one seemed different. *Chubbier*. Then Preston looked closer as it hobbled into the kitchen area to the single dish of food the mother had laid out.

It was the same dog.

Inspecting the animal closer, Preston noticed that, as it ate, it was deflating itself; its outer coat seemed to be collapsing onto its skin in some hitherto unexplainable manner. The mother sang to herself as the dog snarfed up its food.

"Take a look at this dog," Preston—still whispering—said into his pin-mike. "I've never seen anything like it before."

"Forget the dog!" snapped Monaco.

Dr. Wainwright, though, was watching the screen intently. "It looks like one of your animals, Preston."

"Right," he said. The mother had placed a water dish down and the dog was busy absorbing it noisily. "A possible mutation or intentional altering of its genes to adapt it to extremes in climate variations. An all-weather dog."

"Kitteridge—" the Colonel started in.

"Okay, okay," he surrendered, and began surveying the rest of the scene.

The farmhouse was comfortable and tidy, and not the least bit ostentatious in decor. The furniture seemed functional, and while it could have easily been salvaged from the ruins of Bennington or Salina, he didn't think it likely. The upholstery was clean and lush and gave no signs of threadbare construction or poverty normally associated with farm living. Clearly, there were skilled craftsmen in the village who made their living building furniture. Even the varnish on the woodwork seemed new, shining in the wan lamplight. Macrame wall hangings decorated the walls, and there were several pictures and photographs as well.

Preston scanned the photographs closely.

These were definitely Russian—and quite peculiar. There was one shot of a fantastic underwater facility that clearly resembled a city. Another photo, apparently taken by a frogman, showed an ocean-going tug pulling something that appeared to be a geodesic dome. Another photograph—the centerpiece of the collection—showed an older man standing shoulder-to-shoulder with a younger man, perhaps in his late thirties. They were both wearing rather sophisticated underwater gear, not quite scuba equipment, more like space environment suits. This was taken on a dock somewhere and in the background blue, several seagulls lazed about in the sky, the tips of their feathered wings curling upward in the sunlight like shavings of balsa wood.

The eyes of the older man in the photograph seemed to awaken something in Preston. He was a man in his forties with a large nose and a friendly mustache. His eyes glittered warmly in the oceanside light. This was not the face of a conqueror, merely that of a man happy to be standing there by the sea with his younger companion.

*My God*, Preston thought. *Underwater cities? Fantastic watersuits?*

Who *are* these people?

The *duendes* far underneath the earth were strangely silent as they watched their screens and the pictures Preston sent down to them.

"Colonel," Preston spoke out, focusing upon the photographs on the mantelpiece. "I think you'd better run through the computer anything you can find concerning underwater cities built by the Russians in the years before the War. I think we've found something important."

He heard the Colonel growling beside Stu Hagerty and the lieutenant. "I don't like this at all," he said. Preston heard the Colonel's fingers tap commands into the computer keyboard.

Preston meanwhile walked through the living room into the narrow hallway that opened into the kitchen. Over the entrance to the hallway was the head of a deer—or what *looked* like a deer—stuffed and mounted on a large plaque. The glassy expression in its eyes bore both surprise and an alien desperation. Also along the wall was a gun rack, but it did not hold Kalishnikov machine guns or AK-47's. Instead, there were a shotgun and a Winchester, neither of which seemed to have seen recent use. They appeared to be decorative. And very much American.

The mother was in the kitchen stirring a bowl of steaming mashed potatoes. Preston ghosted up to her as close as he could without embarrassing himself. Not a voyeur by nature, he was beginning to feel guilty at his presence there.

The woman possessed facial features which radiated great internal strength and courage, the kind common at one time to America's own pioneers. Canning equipment—glass jars and metal tongs—were out upon one countertop and it was evident from the wide range of utensils that this woman was very competent.

She called out to her daughter, "Irina! Poppa will be

here soon. He will want to eat the minute he walks in the door. Please hurry yourself."

The dog waddled to a large basket where a blanket seemed to beckon it. It was almost like Preston's cats in its indifference to either the woman or the girl once it was fed.

Irina came down the hall from upstairs. She had changed into a pink jumper and her face was all scrubbed as well as her hands.

She stopped and glanced around.

Preston reflexively backed up, ghosting halfway into a wall hung with a rack of seasonings. He was only six feet or so from them and as Irina looked around the kitchen, his heart nearly leapt from his chest. But in the bright electric light of the kitchen, little Irina seemed not to notice anything peculiar by way of a goblinesque intrusion.

"So tell me, sweetest. Did you have a good day in the fields?" the mother asked above her welter of potatoes.

Irina jumped up on a stool at the counter. "Yes, Momma. We're way over our quota!"

"Poppa will be pleased," the mother commented idly as her daughter helped herself to a carrot stick in a condiment tray that had already been prepated. Seeing this, Preston assumed that there was a garden out back—a real one, not hydroponics. And why not? These people were farmers.

The mother said, "And there were no breakdowns? No problems at the silos?"

Irina shook her head. "No, Momma."

The little Russian was not a haughty child; she simply knew her job and knew that she could do it well. But a nine-year-old in a machine as big and complicated as that harvester meant that—perhaps like Barrie Ressler in the Meadow below—there had been some fine-tuning in the intelligence quotients of the children. Home-grown geniuses.

The mother proceeded to withdraw a roast pan from the oven which contained a golden-brown portion of roast beef surrounded with delicately cooked carrots and white onions. A salad had been prepared and was already upon the table. Preston flinched as he heard his stomach growl. The dinner looked so fresh, so natural, that he was nearly overtaken by the desire to opaque out his hand and reach for it.

"Abundance," he then heard Sebastian Monaco say after so much silence. "Look at the way they eat. There's a ton of food there."

Over the radio-link, Preston heard Dr. Wainwright counter with, "There's just as much food here, Sebastian. People have to eat wherever they are."

"But they don't have to feed off us," Monaco asserted.

Their arguing sounded so distant, pregnant with paranoia and scheming.

Preston then said, "You people quit bickering or I'll go off-channel. I can't concentrate. You don't know what it's like up here." Again he found himself whispering. He was an intruder, and he knew it.

The *duendes* quieted down, but evidently the tensions were very high. He had to admit that he followed their thinking. These Russians, *people* though they might be, were nonetheless living high off the hog. And the hog had definitely been raised on American land.

But Monaco wouldn't be deterred. He continued, "They're utter criminals. War criminals. Even in my time, the Russians did pretty well what they pleased, wherever they pleased. This is proof, gentlemen. Proof that they're still thinking that way. It's called self-advancement without labor."

Stu Hagerty chimed in. "What are you talking about? What do you mean, 'self-advancement'?"

"It's the normal mind-set of the criminal mentality. That's the way they think. You take the shortest possible route to getting what you want," Monaco said.

"It's also the American Dream," Preston said, not able to hold himself back. He wasn't about to let Monaco take control, especially when he was down there in the Hive where control was still important.

"What would *you* know about the American Dream?" Monaco argued.

Irina was before the pot roast upon the table; Kitteridge still remained in the wall.

Preston said in a throaty whisper, "Dammit, it's what caused America to decline. It's in all the histories. Most Americans felt that to work thirty years at some job was menial and degrading. Instead they took to waiting for the Big Kill. You had investments yourself. Isn't that self-advancement without labor?"

"It wasn't like that at all," Monaco countered loudly.

However, they all knew that it was exactly like that, and every American from the late twentieth century on into the twenty-first had become infected by it. Only fools worked.

Rich people were rich because they were either smart or God was on their side. Proof was in their success. And the poor were always wrong. That's why they were poor.

But apparently for all the self-aggrandizing myths the Americans had generated for themselves, they weren't smart enough to prevent the Soviet preemptive strike that permanently squelched America's right for a prosperous future.

These people, Russians though they were, plainly worked very hard for what they got, and no doubt worked hard to make the land livable again.

The truth was that they also weren't supposed to be here. But not in any ethical sense—at least as far as Preston could see. They weren't supposed to be here because the place was supposed to be uninhabitable. And unlike the *duendes* down below, he was face-to-face with a situation which totally defied six hundred years' worth of scientific and theological speculation on the fate of the earth.

The front door burst open and the dog jumped up from its basket in the corner of the kitchen.

Preston panned the camera around, as a handsome, tall man walked in. His angular features were those of the younger man in the photograph on the mantel.

Irina shouted out in perfect childlike English, "Poppa! Poppa! Hurry, I'm *starving* to death!"

The dog clattered over the polished wooden floor, seemingly encumbered by the thickness of its special, adaptive pelt. It ran up to the tall brown-haired, brown-eyed man and leapt at him happily.

"Our daughter is starving!" he said with playful sarcasm. He petted the dog and roughed its ear. "We shall have to feed her Ura, don't you think, Yelena?" he said to his wife.

Ura wagged his stubby tail as Irina's father took off his light jacket and hung it on a coat hook next to the gun rack in the hall.

"Ura!" said Irina down at the dog. "*Ick!*"

Preston found himself smiling at this little domestic scene. He could imagine six-year-old Barrie Ressler intoning the same words in the same manner.

But Irina never left the table and took her father's entrance to be a signal to dive into the food. Which she did. Yelena, her beautiful but sturdy mother, gave the man a welcoming kiss as he came directly to the table. Ura, the mutant dog, was now full of energy and was everywhere underfoot.

"And what did the Mayor have to say, Lev?" Yelena asked as she began cutting the roast for her husband. "Will there be another train shipment soon?"

Here, Lev seemed almost exasperated. He drew a white linen napkin across his lap. "The Mayor says that the metals coming down from the north must be shipped out first. The grains can wait, since we've surpassed our quota expectations."

Irina, wolfing down her potatoes—and avoiding the spinach salad—looked up. "I filled one whole silo today, Poppa! One's left. When I'm done, I can then go with Uncle Yuri!"

Lev slowly began chipping away at his plate of beef, potatoes, and vegetables. Yelena gracefully seated herself opposite her daughter. She said to the rambunctious child, "We'll see if Yuri has room for you. Remember, he has a dangerous cargo."

"You promised!"

Yelena smiled and pointed to Irina's plate. "Eat your dinner, Irina. And mind your father."

Irina brooded. She began eating, but then managed to comment, "I don't like the Mayor. He smells funny."

The two parents smiled and shrugged at each other. Their offspring was apparently full of non sequiturs.

The *duendes* far below were now arguing heatedly amongst each other.

"Mayor!" Monaco sneered. "Listen to them talk. It's a mockery of Middle America. Jesus!"

"Be quiet!" Hagerty snapped. "I want to hear what they're saying."

"Don't tell me to be quiet!" Monaco rasped.

With a touch at his belt, Preston did what he should have done sometime back. He turned down the audio link in his earphones by a few dozen decibels.

"Yes," Lev said to his wife conversationally. "The Mayor says that we are in a better position to deliver the metals needed for the Great War. The grains can wait since they won't spoil and can be shipped out during the winter."

At the mention of the Great War, little Irina glanced up excitedly. "I wish Mikhail could come home soon," she sang. She reached for a tall glass of milk her mother had poured.

"Africa is a long way around the world, child," her mother remonstrated.

"And Indonesia, too," Irina added. "Isn't that right, Poppa?"

"Yes, it is," Lev said evenly. "But I wouldn't worry about Mikhail. He is a big boy and can handle himself well in the service of the Awakener."

With that there was a pall of silence, respectful silence, as they continued eating.

"Great War?" wondered Colonel Chaney. "You mean it's still going on? After six hundred years?"

"Who's this Awakener they're talking about?" Monaco asked.

Stu Hagerty then said, "And they're fighting in Indonesia, of all places." Preston could barely hear their gabbling.

"It looks like they're in the process of conquering the whole world," Monaco said.

"Well," said the Colonel unhappily, "they've certainly conquered America."

The dinner-table conversation prattled on. Irina's day on the wheat plain was discussed; Yelena spoke of her canning and her expectations of an early frost. Ura begged for table scraps, which Lev staunchly refused and Irina surreptitiously doled out underneath the table. A grandfather clock somewhere in the house chimed out the hour.

"Preston," came Dr. Wainwright's call after a prolonged silence from the *duendes* in the Hive.

Preston had been busy setting up a remote-controlled stand for the video unit so that he would not have to be there continually to hold it up and pan it around when it was needed.

"I'm here," he told the chief Appleseed. "What have you got?"

"The Rover's picking up some very minor radiation readings out in the street," Dr. Wainwright said. "It's too dark for us to see where it's coming from. But it's definitely out there."

His voice sounded heavy; Preston wondered just how the Appleseed was taking all this. He said, "I'll look into it right now."

He aimed the camera at the dinner table and left it going.

Ura, the bulging dog, jumped up and wandered from the

kitchen as Preston moved for the front door. It was as if he were following him. Ura passed straight through his legs on the way to the living room.

Preston ghosted down onto the lawn and stepped on out to the quiet street. Darkness had fully cloaked Anytown. A single streetlamp down the block cast out a circle of feeble yellow light.

A long flatbed truck, apparently electrically powered, was pulling up in front of the home of the Russian farmers.

"That's it," Preston heard Monaco say. "We're getting the emission readings from that truck."

"Plutonium," gasped Stu Hagerty. "There's a trace of residual plutonium on that thing!"

Preston could nearly feel the horror in the Hive technician's voice.

The truck, which resembled the diesel eighteen-wheelers from the videos of ancient America, halted in front of the house, just opposite the Rover. The driver within honked its loud horn like the voice of a stegosaur.

The front door opened and Lev, still chewing his dinner, stepped out. He was followed closely by Irina and Yelena. Ura thundered out in their midst, yapping wildly.

"Uncle Yuri!" little Irina shouted with surprise.

The man in the cab, Yuri, stuck his head out, and in the light from the house, Preston could make out his features. Long nose, bright blue eyes, drooping mustache like a hairbrush, and a fire-engine-red cap gave Preston a perfect picture of another hardworking Russian. Yuri appeared to be Lev's age.

Yuri waved at the approaching family. "Ladies and gentlemen," he announced himself. "The man who has done more for the color red than Lenin or Trotsky! Yuri Kreutin has arrived!"

Kreutin stepped out of the cab. From top to bottom he was entirely dressed in red. It was some kind of protective work tunic, with red boots as well. He smiled hugely.

On the back of the flatbed were several metal ingots, appearently reconstituted steel. Although from what Preston could ascertain, there might be some aluminum and copper ingots among them as well.

In the fore of the trailing flatbed was a large crimson barrel. It was the source of the radiation, albeit small doses of it.

*Surplus for the Great War*, Preston suddenly realized. *Metal gleaned from the ruins surrounding the community, no doubt.* It was all that was left of American labor.

Yelena approached Uncle Yuri and she gave him a great big kiss as Lev looked on. He, too, was glad to see him.

"Ah, Mrs. Magin. How well you look," Yuri said to her. Then to Lev Magin he said, "You treat my sister well. If I could find a woman as good as you, then I'd be a happily married man!"

"She'd probably shoot you!" Yelena said with a sisterly smile.

Irina was climbing onto the flatbed without any protests from the grown-ups. She made for the large metal barrel which seemed designed to harbor radioactive materials.

Yuri Kreutin said, "Be careful, child. The monazite shells are still fresh, some of them."

"That's right, Irina," Lev called out.

Irina glared at the red barrel. Carefully she opened its metal lid. With a pair of steel tongs she reached inside, pulling out an obsidian stone of almost circular proportions. It was the size of a peach.

"Don't touch it with your fingers," Yuri said.

The nine-year-old gingerly returned the monazite stone to its berth. She replaced the lid and tightened down its locking screws.

"How much of it did you find?" Lev asked of his brother-in-law.

"Fifty grams," he reported as Irina scampered from the flatbed trailer. "An old warhead, unshielded and a hundred feet deep in a battered silo. The last in the region, if our maps are correct." With a thumb he indicated the other contents of the trailer. "We almost have the region clean of metals, too. What we can salvage."

"They'll be sending you to Topeka next," Lev Magin said. "You better watch out. No funny business." He wagged his finger at his in-law.

Yuri shuddered visibly—and comically. This made Irina laugh. He mussed her hair as she held onto him affectionately.

Preston stood close to the gathering and listened as the *duendes* watched from the Rover's cameras.

"There are fifty grams of residual plutonium in that barrel? That's impossible!" claimed the Colonel down in the Meadow. "Those people would be dead by now."

"That's what the Rover is indicating," Hagerty said. "But that other Russian mentioned monazite. It's just possible that they've rendered the plutonium bits harmless in monazite shells made from phosphate. It's hard to say what the mineral derivatives are, though, unless we can get a sample of it ourselves."

"Not on your life," Preston said quickly. "I'm not going to rummage through that barrel unshielded!"

No one said anything, though. Too much data was filtering down to them.

"I am on my way to the depot to store my bounty," Yuri Kreutin informed them.

Irina turned to her mother. "Can we go? Can we, Momma?"

Yelena seemed to vacillate for a moment or two, but Lev nodded ever so slightly in that invisible manner known only to parents, and Irina bounded around to the front, climbing inside the truck.

"I guess it's all right," Yelena said. "But don't be gone long. We still have dessert waiting."

Lev Magin followed his daughter. The two men climbed inside the truck as Irina called out of her side of the cab, "Ura, *up!*"

With a bark of joy, the strange canine leapt with more agility than Preston thought possible. It landed on the flatbed and barked once more. The truck pulled away as Yelena returned to the porch.

"Follow them in the Rover, Kitteridge," Colonel Chaney commanded from down below. "I want to see where all that plutonium's going!"

Preston wanted to see, too. He swung the Rover into the street, keeping what cameras he could focused on the plutonium truck. Lights all across the Rover's computers and sensors were twinkling like the ghost-lights above the Meadow as they took in all the data around the Rover. Preston shook his head. It was like a chess gambit where every move changed the whole character of the board. These people, despite their apparent simplicity, ranged from highly advanced wheat and grain farmers to radiation engineers and metal harvesters.

Whatever they were, they had nothing in common with the Soviets of any century, past or present.

The flatbed went down the block of sleepy farm homes,

then rounded the corner which took it back to Anytown's main street. The train station and storage depot was its destination and it was not too far away. Preston hadn't come this way originally and was nearly crushed with nostalgic melancholy seeing the station for the first time. It was lifted right out of America's past, with its open wood platform, single lonely light dangling above it, and an illuminated sign announcing "Anytown" for all to see.

The flatbed truck drifted toward a smaller building beside the depot.

Preston drove as near as he could, but even in the light from the flatbed's headlights it was still hard to make anything out. This clear Kansas night was going to be a pitch-black one.

A door facing the flatbed gasped open from some hidden command from Yuri Kreutin in the truck. The Russian drove the whole vehicle deep inside the building as Ura barked all the way.

Preston watched from the doorway as mechanical lifting arms removed the ingots and single ominous drum from the trailer bed. Other, smaller ingots were piled neatly against the opposite side of the building, the one closest to the rails outside.

The Russians then got back into their vehicle and drove out, the doors of the storage facility closing silently behind them.

Preston wasn't staring at the red lights on the console before him.

It took a question from Dr. Wainwright to enlighten him of the danger indicators.

"Preston," came Travis Wainwright's call. "Are you getting the same readings as we are?"

Preston glanced at the console of the idling Rover. The radiation meter had risen measurably.

"Yes," he said. "But I don't understand. Where's it coming from?"

Sebastian Monaco said, "It's coming from the storage depot. There's enough plutonium and uranium in that little building to construct several tactical nuclear bombs." He paused for a few seconds, then said, "If you ask me, friends, I'd say we have a *serious* problem on our hands."

# 8

It had been a long day and an even longer night, and Kitteridge had been very reluctant to return to the Meadow. However, upon reaching the lift platform in the dark, night-cloaked wheat field, he discovered that he was indeed bushed and that for all that there was left to examine and explore in the Russian colony of Anytown, he was practically asleep when around midnight they lowered him back beneath the earth.

His exhaustion, both physical and mental, had been so complete that he hardly recalled being led to one of the Hive dormitories wherein he could find some peace and quiet, away from the revelries of the Saxifrage Bacchanalia. Dr. Wainwright and Colonel Chaney had decided while he had been topside to spend some time going over the Rover's data—and what the camera left in the kitchen of the Magins recorded—before extending the expedition further. But it had also been decided, and Monaco had contributed to this decision, to keep Preston away from the other half of the Meadow for the time being, since it was evident that they were going to need another scouting sortie.

So Preston made himself at home in a comfortable room above the Hive 'combs and tried to ignore what had occurred over the previous twenty-four hours. Moreover, he had also to forget his promises to Holly and he had to put from his mind the disappearance of his brother, Jay. That would have to wait until the morrow. Everything would have to wait. . . .

\*     \*     \*

When Preston finally roused himself, took his nourishing brunch in the dormitory's automated kitchen, he then made his solitary way back to the Games Room. Upon arriving, he discovered just how quickly things could change in the Hive: The Games Room was now a War Room. It had been converted overnight back to its original form and a number of military *duendes* had been enlisted to help with the analysis of the Rover's data. All of its tapes and readings were presently sifting through the Hive's mainframe computer. Even the air-conditioning had been turned up to accommodate the increased computer activity.

However, as Preston suddenly noticed, the only other Appleseed represented in the War Room was Dr. Wainwright. That seemed foreboding to him. But Dr. Wainwright apparently noticed the expression of unease on Preston's face, and called him over with a reassuring tone in his voice.

"Preston," he called out. "Come on in, son. We thought you might want to sleep longer, so we started without you."

"You could've woken me, Travis," he said. He indicated the gathering of military personnel. "Why aren't there any of us here? At least Lee Williams should be here—"

Sebastian Monaco, wide-awake and primed for action, came up to them holding a computer printout. He said, "We've got the situation in control, Kitteridge. We don't need anyone else."

Preston glared at him. "Why don't you let us be the judge of that? Our vote counts just as much as yours does."

Monaco seemed uninterested. He said, "In case you've forgotten, Kitteridge. This isn't a democratic society. We do things by the Outcome Book."

Travis Wainwright, though inwardly drained by yesterday's discoveries, surged between the two younger men like an ice-breaker. "Boys, we can do without a fight about this."

"We should have all the Ark supervisors down here," Preston insisted, "if only to examine the data on the biosphere up above."

Colonel Chaney, sitting at the glowing console beside an alert Stu Hagerty, spoke out, clearly taken with a newer sense of mission. He said, "The whole situation's changed, Kitteridge. They'll be called when it's time. Right now, we've got some matters to discuss."

"Military matters, I suppose."

"Perhaps," the Colonel said. Dr. Wainwright did not

seek to contradict him. It appeared that, upon closer inspection, the chief Appleseed had been up most of the previous night and had lost some battle between them for authority. He should have been the one to spend ten hours sleeping, Preston realized.

He glanced around at the other Hive personnel assembled in the War Room. Abe Koch, the 'combs supervisor, seemed somewhat hung-over from last night's festivities. Dark-eyed and dark-haired, he was the opposite of Tom Winehall, the blond-haired, crisp Armory supervisor. Winehall was completely awake, sober, and anxious to be of use. But Sid Rankin, portly and bovine, was not. Rankin was the Hive logistics officer, which in peacetime meant that he was a glorified secretary. However, that could change if they now had to move soldiers and pilots and chemical-warfare specialists around instead of typewriters, word processors, and paper clips. He was brooding because he was currently having troubles with his wife, a woman whose flagrancies were turning him into a laughable, Meadow-wide cuckold. And that Sergeant Rankin did not like.

"Let's start with the dog," Sebastian Monaco began, waiting for Kitteridge to take a seat.

Preston, though, was already well ahead of them in their thinking. "Forget the dog, Monaco. Let's talk about the goddamn *town*."

"We'll get to the town in a second," the Colonel breathed heavily. "Let him begin. You've missed a lot and we have to make sure that we all understand the parameters of the situation up above."

"I was there. Remember?"

Monaco ignored their banter and started in. He said, "The dog clearly shows that there has been a vast number of changes."

"Very good," Preston said sardonically, arms crossed and waiting.

The second lieutenant continued without breaking his stride. He went on. "Obviously they have mastered not only the art of suspended animation, as we have, but they have made the same kinds of advancements our Appleseeds have made in the field of genetic engineering."

"Don't forget what the ecosphere can do on its own," Preston said, scowling. "Recall that butterfly I saw. The thing had the insectoid equivalent of feathers. The Russians didn't do that."

Abe Koch, at the coffeepot to one side, spoke up. "We have to assume the worst. They've had at least six hundred and some years of freedom, evidently underwater most of it. They've had enough time to do their experiments."

"Yes," Monaco told them. "That means that they had planned all along to survive the nuclear winter in the same fashion we did."

Preston, now sitting next to Travis, who seemed to labor in his slow breathing, said, "You're looking at the trees, Monaco. You can't see the forest. Whatever those people are, up there, they are *not* soldiers. Russian soldiers don't speak English in their spare time, and they don't fill their idle moments with chatter about grain silos and canning tomatoes."

"You forget the nuclear material contained in the barrel," Tom Winehall, the Armory manager, said. He rechecked the data sheet. "Yuri Kreutin had found and stored enough residual material to make a number of bombs." Winehall spoke with authority; he came from a military family who'd spent generations maintaining their nuclear-weapons cache. Preston feared Captain Winehall's knowledge the most.

"Monazite," Preston said quickly, "is permanent. Each hot atom of plutonium, neptunium, or uranium 235 is encased in a phosphate molecule bond to contain it. What kind of substance they derived the phosphate from would determine how easily they could retrieve the fissionable material. But monazite stones are permanent bonding structures."

Monaco glared at him. "As far as we know, they are. But they've had six hundred years to improve waste-storage technology and we haven't. The Meadow has never had any fissionable waste material to get rid of, so the problem's never existed for us. Those Russians"—and here he pointed angrily at the computer television screens—"have inherited a whole continent with radioactive debris strewn all over it, and evidently they've found an efficient way to collect it and contain it."

Preston was silent; he had no argument for this. However, he could conclude one thing: "But we don't know that they're using it to manufacture warheads."

Instantly he knew just how stupid that sounded. All of the Hive *duendes* stared at him.

Dr. Wainwright, visibly older now, ran a tired hand

through his thinning white hair. "Preston, that's exactly what we have to presume. The Magins have a son fighting another major war in Africa somewhere, led by a person they call the Awakener. We know that they're shipping out the scrap metals, grains, and the stored wastes from the ground-burst nuclear reactors in the vicinity."

"Just whose side are you on, Travis?" Preston asked. "This is all conjecture."

"I'm on our side, Preston," the older man said, but he seemed rather sad in saying it. "You have to remember why we put ourselves down here in the first place."

Sid Rankin, previously silent, spoke out when the lull had appeared between the two Appleseeds. "But notice, men, what we actually have here. This is not quite a Russian society six hundred years in advance of the Soviet Union of the twenty-first century." He had been doing his homework, perusing the Rover's tapes and data while Preston was asleep. He went on. "All the evidence shows that these people are first- or even second-generation Russians *from the time of the War*."

"They have 'combs," Abe Koch said darkly as he sipped his coffee.

"Right," Monaco concurred. "From the photographs in the living room it seems that most of the people have been asleep for hundreds of years, and then were aroused, somehow fully prepared to take over America."

"The Awakener." Stu Haggerty nodded. "Their leader."

"Exactly," Monaco continued. "But the residual radioactive debris isn't the real problem at the moment. The real problem is in the dog."

"That's where you started," Kitteridge gibed.

"The dog and the girl," Colonel Chaney hastily pointed out to his second-in-command. Preston noticed how Dr. Wainwright seemed to turn away, as if revulsed by something which had passed between them all earlier that morning.

"What does the girl have to do with this?" Preston countered.

"This is really your field of expertise, Kitteridge," Monaco said grudgingly. "But the dog has been genetically altered and so has the little girl. We don't know enough about the adults yet."

"We've done the same down here," Preston asserted. "Barrie Ressler, the Brancatto twins in the Gulf Ark, Ed

Steinhoff in the Appalachia Ark, are all products of careful engineering. One way or another they're geniuses. So are my cats. What are you suggesting?"

"I'm suggesting that their alterations may be more severe than we imagine," Monaco responded.

"In what way?"

Sid Rankin sat in his chair and folded his arms over his thick chevron-laced chest. He did not smile. He said, "They might have had to make adjustments in their genetic makeup in order to withstand the radiation that's still out there. Then they'd have to endure any kind of bacteriological or chemical-weapons residue which might have lingered—"

"Or was left undamaged in the original attack," the Colonel interrupted.

"The Rover didn't pick up anything like that," Preston pointed out.

"The Rover wasn't equipped to probe for any bacteria which may have been floating in the wind. Chemical agents would endure for no telling how long," Monaco said.

"So where's this all leading?"

Monaco stood before him holding his authoritative print-outs. He said, "The Russians might have altered their immunological systems to such a degree that they might very well be different kinds of humans."

Kitteridge laughed so suddenly he almost fell out of his chair.

"*What?* Are you insane?" He gestured toward the screens with their many playbacks of his first trip topside. "Look at them! They're just like you and me and the rest of us. These aren't *Homo sapiens moscovus* we're seeing. My guess is that they are, as Sergeant Rankin has pointed out, second-generation Russian survivors of whatever agency prolonged their lives after the War. No more than that. And *that*, friend, is just too short a period to alter or adjust any kind of chromosomal structure. The genetic changes wouldn't manifest themselves for generations."

"*But we don't know that, Preston,*" Tom Winehall said, his pale blue eyes stern in their urgency and military paranoia. "That's the whole point."

Kitteridge threw up his hands. "Nemesis! Give you clowns a few hours overnight and you come up with the wildest ideas."

"We believe"—Monaco spoke for the militarists—"that

the Soviets intentionally planned for this, and they have also prepared their people to endure any kind of remaining dangers on the continent."

Abe Koch brooded over his coffee. He said, "And that means that when we opaque out, we're going to have problems other than just explaining to the Russians what a shopping mall and a former administration building from McConnell Air Force Base are doing in the middle of a wheat field."

Sid Rankin then said, "I don't think we'll have any difficulty taking care of the villagers. Our rocket-mortars can lob a tactical warhead over—"

"*Whoa!*" Preston stammered. "Just what the hell are you people talking about? You're not thinking of killing those people, are you? You just can't opaque out and flatten a whole town! Those are real live human beings out there. And besides that, I'm not sure we have all the facts of the situation."

"This is war, Kitteridge," the Colonel said solemnly. "Whatever else you might think, those people are dangerous to us. We have to deal with what we know, and we *know* that they're in the middle of a Great War and they're using American wheat fields and metals to help in the Soviet conquests. And they are also proof that nothing remained of America's military force after the War. These people are too far inland. If any of our people have survived, they'd have rebuilt some kind of nation and would have fought back in some manner. The Russians have beaten us. *They've beaten us!*"

Right there in that room a thousand feet inside solid rock, Preston felt the age-old human dialectic at work. Peace versus War. Love versus Hate. There rarely seemed to be any middle ground. The Tao or the Way, as Jay would call it. No one in that humming War Room remembered the Santayana dictum: Those who do not recall the lessons of the past are doomed to repeat them.

"You're a bunch of idiots," Kitteridge said, angry at himself. "You don't know what you're talking about and you haven't a shred of evidence."

"These are facts!" Sebastian Monaco thundered, throwing the printout down before him. "You forget, I *lived* through it! I did, not you! The Soviets were like a disease in my time, an evil cancer. NORAD barely had time to respond when their submarine-launched cruise missiles came in from the Atlantic. They knew what they were doing. All this"—he pointed at the screens—"merely proves to me what I've known all along."

At that juncture, the centurions—the Busch brothers again—had come into the War Room upon hearing the heated debate. Colonel Chaney waved them off, but neither Clark nor Brian took his eyes off Preston, the implication being that whatever was going on, it was *his* fault.

"It's okay, boys," the Colonel told the centurions. "Just a minor disagreement."

"Disagreement, my ass!" Kitteridge said. "We're talking about eradicating several hundred Russians before we know anything at all about them!"

The centurions reluctantly withdrew from the room, though they itched for some sign or provocation from Preston. He could see that they were going to be a big problem when the Meadow got out. *If it got out* . . .

Abe Koch, master of the 'combs, turned to Preston. "We're not talking about killing them off yet. That's about at Stage Three of any possible operation. We've got a couple of stages to get to before that."

Preston was livid. His fists were nervous balls of hard knuckle ready to dance a few times on Monaco's face.

However, it was Dr. Wainwright's lack of interest in defending what was in effect an Appleseed creed that bothered Preston the most. They believed in the preservation of life. And that presumably included Soviet life. What had these last six hundred years been all about, if not the preservation of life?

Clearly, to the Hive personnel, it had meant something vastly different.

Monaco, though, retained his self-control and narrow-minded outlook. He stepped to the computers. There he took up a rather large but shallow black box which had been sitting on top of the console. He placed it on the small table before Preston.

"So what's this?" Kitteridge asked.

Monaco stood up. "Abe is correct when he says we are a stage or two from taking any kind of retaliatory action, and you're right in pointing out that there's so much we don't know."

Seething, Preston locked his eyes upon Monaco's.

Monaco opened the shallow box. Inside were two large,

if peculiar-looking, guns. He said, "You're a qualified geneticist. No one disputes that." *What's going on here?* Preston suddenly wondered. One minute Monaco is antagonistic, the next he's conciliatory. *Watch out, son. . . .*

Monaco held up one of the strange weapons. He said, "What we need to know is if any of our speculations about their genetic makeup is accurate."

"The Soviets?" Preston said. "You mean if they have wings and fly around at night?"

"That's not what I mean and you know it," Monaco said as he unlimbered the gun. A spring-coiled cord with a jack came with it and plugged into the pistol grip. The lazarus continued. "It's possible that each Russian might be carrying diseases deadly to us but harmless to them. Like the yellow-fever virus of the nineteenth century. People in equatorial climates had been living with it for ages, but it was only the white man who caught it and died from it."

Tom Winehall, of the Armory, knew what bacteriological weapons could do. He said, "It's possible that the Russians could be carrying Typhoid Mary-type diseases, to which they'd be immune. But should they be captured by any surviving Americans—such as ourselves—they could inflict them with sicknesses no one could prevent."

"That's pretty farfetched," Preston said.

"Not really," Dr. Wainwright conceded. "I think you'd better hear them out."

The strange gun had a rather large barrel, and it was apparent to him that it didn't shoot any kind of projectile, nor was it a laser gun.

Monaco said, "This is an assessor gun. We had them designed and built in my time and it's been in storage in the Armory ever since the War."

Preston took the gun and examined it. "Okay," he said glibly. "Give me a clue. What's it supposed to do to people?"

"Nothing," Sebastian Monaco said. "If you aim it at a person, whether you're opaqued or not, it will transmit data back to our computers down here that will enable us to determine not only their genetic makeup but also whether or not they're carrying any time-bomb bacteria or viruses."

Preston looked questioningly over at the chief Appleseed. He held up the gun. "Have you ever heard of these things, Travis?"

Wainwright indicated Captain Winehall. "I'd heard about

them a long time ago, when I was much younger. Tom's father told me about them. But since there was never any need for them, I'd forgotten they existed. Tom pulled it out of storage last night."

Winehall shrugged. "I didn't know where it was, really, until the lieutenant here told us where he thought it might be in the Armory."

Kitteridge held the gun and considered it before them. "So I'm supposed to go topside and 'assess' all the Typhoid Marys and mutant Russians. Is that the idea?"

"That's the idea," Dr. Wainwright said. "It'll give us a lot more to go on, Preston. We don't want to rush this thing if we can help it. Resurrection Day can wait until you make a full assessment of the population."

"Well, I can't canvas the whole countryside by myself," he told them. "Are these the only two you've got?"

He looked over at Captain Winehall, preferring not to acknowledge Monaco's authority any more than he had to. He knew he was caught up in some kind of intricate chess game and he had to make all of his moves with precision.

But Monaco was in charge. He said, "These are the only ones. They were experimental and no more were made at the time."

Dr. Wainwright slowly rose to his feet. To Preston he said, "If that little girl named Irina was out by herself in the fields all day, then there is no doubt that there are other farmers and workers throughout the vicinity. The gun only has a ten-mile range from the Meadow's apex. But we think you can assess all of the Russians in Anytown with it."

Preston considered him, "And I can do this in either state? Either as a *duende* or opaqued out?"

Travis said, "We'll inoculate you as best we can. We have decided that there might be some situations where it might be best if you opaqued out. But that's up to you."

For the first time during the conference, Preston felt a surge of genuine excitement. But he swiftly suppressed it. He suddenly felt as if they were dangling candy before him in order to get him to participate in something devious. Monaco was smiling ever so slightly, as if he had won a battle. And in a real way, he had. Preston, by taking the gun, had tacitly approved of his plan. Another chess piece slid across the board. . . .

"I still don't believe we have to do this," he told Dr.

Wainwright. "And I'd like to add that I don't approve of the way you're letting Monaco here take control of things."

Colonel Chaney came over and faced him. "Listen to me, Kitteridge. I'll make this plain. I don't care what you believe or just who you happen to disagree with in this affair, but the fact is that we're at war. Those *are* Russians topside, and in deference to Wainwright here we're postponing any military action until we know what the situation is. You don't have to do it. We can send up someone else. Either you go or you don't." He prodded Kitteridge in the chest. "You decide."

Dr. Wainwright nodded in a fatherly fashion and seemed to indicate that not *all* the power had slipped over to the waiting hands of the militarists. Even though theirs was a rigidly structured society, they did have to trade off responsibilities or the Meadow would just not run.

An assessor gun did make sense, after he thought about it—although he couldn't possibly see how such a thing worked. But then, he was only an Appleseed. And it was true that the *duendes* might have lost their immunological edge over the centuries, even though their required bouts with horrible colds and crippling flu bugs were an attempt to keep their systems up. Perhaps the Russians *had* come up with something new.

"So who goes up with me?" he asked. "There are two guns."

Monaco was all smiles and about to open his mouth to volunteer his services when another voice sounded out from the opposite, unguarded end of the War Room—the side which connected to the Hive proper.

"Let's make this a family affair!"

And Jay Kitteridge walked in as if he had a free rein of the place. Everyone jerked around, astonished.

Jay was all dressed up and ready to go. He said, "After all, two Appleseeds are better than one."

# 9

The two Rovers rose upward into the eternally black night as the ghost-like constellations shimmered in the incalculable distance.

For the second time in two days, *duendes* were about to breach the topside world, but for Preston Kitteridge, this particular expedition was made more exciting, for his brother Jay was now with him.

As they stood beside their Rovers, not *in* them this time, the lift engines of the platform hummed and glowed. A fawn afterlight illuminated Jay's features as he walked to the edge of the platform. Like all of the Kitteridges, he was tall and lanky. Wisps of gray graced his temples and sprinkled the trim mustache he continually wore. His eyes were nearly always hooded in wrinkles of impish delight, and because of this Preston never really knew what his strange brother was thinking.

Neither, however, could the members of the military Hive contingent.

Jay Kitteridge was well-liked and got along easily with the technicians of Saxifrage, but like a great many of his American forebears, he did not like being told what to do. As a consequence, he did not relate very well to the Hive personnel whose charter it was to take control in times of obvious crisis. And clearly, this was such a time.

Jay, though, seemed to circumvent any kind of authority, and to do this he even had to baffle his own younger brother.

As Jay stared at where they were going and where they were coming from, Preston tried to talk some sense into his errant brother as the darkness of solid rock passed around them.

"You shouldn't push them, Jay," he said above the groan of the lift engines beneath them.

Jay's eyes had a puckish gleam. "There is a time for even the most gentle persuasion, my son," he said theatrically.

"That wasn't very gentle," Preston responded. "It was blackmail. Those people down there are ready to engage another Tyranny."

Jay's temporary "disappearance" was due to the fact that he had known all along that Preston had encountered the topside world upon the ladder. However, Jay took a more meditative approach to the possibility of Resurrection Day by hiding in the kudzu and "feeling" the Meadow, perhaps for the last time in their history. In the same way as Ike and Tina discovered, Jay knew that something was going on.

His "blackmail" consisted of a message he had left in a sequestered section of the Meadow, where a computer "tapeworm" would appear and override the military programs, announcing what the Hive was doing unbeknownst to the other *duendes*. Jay was a master at computer overrides, much to the chagrin of those in power at the moment.

Sebastian Monaco had been all set to go topside with Preston, but this had changed his plans. There was nothing he could do about it. There followed something of an argument, but Jay was invincible.

But as Dr. Wainwright pointed out, two Ark specialists topside were much more appropriate to the task of assessing any kind of mutagenic drift in the human population. The militarists didn't like it, but the chief Appleseed was right.

"Jay," Preston said as they rose, "I don't want you to do anything stupid, that's all." His brother wandered about the lift platform, watching the ghost-lights in the distance, as if he wasn't listening. "Travis is having a very difficult time with the Colonel right now. Those people are trigger-happy."

Jay smiled magnanimously. "They should be just plain *happy*, like us!"

"Well," Preston acceded, "just watch it. Let's do our job and see what happens after that."

All this time, Preston had been gripping the assessor gun

he had been given, almost as if it were a kind of talisman he didn't know what to do with. Jay, however, merely kept his odd gun in his holster; his mind was on other matters of more cosmic importance. Indeed, Monaco had to repeat a portion of his whole lecture to Jay in order to convince him that the assessor gun wasn't actually a weapon.

"But now the truth shall be known," Jay said as the platform magically pierced the upper m-field.

Bright sunlight crashed down upon them in an ocean crest of impenetrable glory. Preston blinked rapidly as the lift engines shut down and the platform once again locked itself into place.

"Stay close to the Rover, Jay," he told his brother in the harsh noon light, recalling his own initial agoraphobic reaction to so much wide-open space. "It'll take a few minutes to get used to it."

Jay staggered as if struck with a beatific vision. His smile, however, remained in place.

"Now, this is what I call a beautiful day," Jay said, looking around him at the wide meadow of wheat stubbles. He turned to his younger brother. "I should say 'day' with a capital D. You shall go down into the annals of the Meadow. He who saw the light. Look at all you have given us!"

"I don't think I had anything to do with it, Jay," Preston said cautiously, watching his brother's reactions.

"Thou art far too modest for one who's taken upon himself so much responsibility," Jay said with a flourish of his hand. "Far too modest indeed."

Dr. Wainwright's voice came in over the radio channel in their earphones.

"We see that you've made it," he said, relieved. "Good. Now, remember the plan. Each gun has an effective range of about ten miles. But you must assess everyone you come across. No exceptions. Understand?"

"We got it, Travis," Preston affirmed, speaking into his pin-mike at his cheek.

"Jay?" Dr. Wainwright hailed. "Jay, do *you* understand?"

But standing in the center of the shorn wheat field was a fully fleshed human. A *duende* Appleseed.

Jay Kitteridge had opaqued out.

"Jay, wait!" Preston switched frequencies so that his brother could receive his ghostly transmissions.

"Boys," came Dr. Wainwright's plaintive call. "What's going on? What's happening up there?"

"Jay's opaqued out," Preston informed him.

"*What?*"

Preston watched as Jay seemed to wobble as he breathed in his first lungful of *real* air. His body shuddered as it reacted to being fully opaque with color, mass, and density.

Preston was stunned that his brother would do this.

A tiny whirlwind had gusted about Jay's body as his own m-field belt adjusted for the interpenetration of molecules. Wheat husks danced about his feet as they were thrust aside for the space his boots came to occupy. He was *out*.

"Intoxicating!" he said alone in the wheat field. "Absolutely intoxicating!" He looked around him for his brother. "Hey, Preston! Give this a whirl! It's a kick!" He laughed; he danced. "It's even better than sex!"

The *duendes* down below had switched on the cameras mounted in both of the Rovers, and they could easily see for themselves what Jay had done.

"Get him back in," ordered Sebastian Monaco. "I don't want the Russians to see what we're up to, dammit! This is important!" He then apparently turned aside and addressed the other *duendes* in the War Room. "I told you we shouldn't have let Jay go up. Why didn't you listen to me? The man's irresponsible."

Monaco then returned to the channel and spoke directly to Preston. "You get your brother back into his *duende* state, Kitteridge. That's a direct order. He's going to jeopardize the whole mission."

Jay twirled in ecstasy, his feet brushing the brown bristles of wheat stalks in the field. Looking in the direction in which he knew his younger brother to be standing, he shouted, "This is heaven! Come on out and play, Pres! We've made it to the fields of heaven! It's Resurrection at last!"

"He's going off the deep end," Sebastian Monaco said into Preston's earphones. "Stop him, Kitteridge."

Preston himself was fighting the urge to opaque out and join his brother. After all, the *duendes* in the War Room were a thousand feet underneath them, lodged away in solid earth where they would be unable to prevent the two brothers from cavorting the day away in the Kansas sunlight.

But Preston, already used to many years of responsibilities in the Salina Ark, couldn't just simply opaque out and roll in the dirt. His hand sweated over the pistol-grip of the assessor gun. They had work to do and it had to follow a plan, if they were all to survive. Not only had they their own Resurrection to deal with, they had the Soviets as well. Jay had yet to see any of those.

"There's nothing I can do," Preston finally said into his pin-mike.

Jay whirled around, arms out and head thrown back in the sun. He spun like a dervish, laughing and tripping about. Like Christ taking upon himself the burdens of mankind, so did Jay Kitteridge take on all the joys of the *duendes* below as he frolicked through the barren wheat field.

"This is great!" Jay shouted to no one. "The earth lives and breathes!"

He took off running for all he was worth, his grasshopper-like legs bounding out, carrying him across the stubble of the field.

"Hey, Jay!" Preston hailed into his pin-mike, holding onto his brother's frequency. "Come back here!"

Jay the Older was now acting like Jay the Younger. He ran right for the little stream Preston had come across the previous day.

"Follow him," Preston quickly ordered Jay's semi-intelligent Rover. Both of the Rovers were programmed to respond to either brother in case one broke down.

Jay's Rover obediently trundled out in silence, ghosting through the shorn wheat field.

"Nemesis," Preston muttered. At least his brother would be in viewing range of the *duendes* down below. If he could stay in sight of the second Rover's camera eyes.

Preston climbed inside his own machine and sat briefly debating with himself. Jay was now knee-deep in the lilies and cattails of the creek, splattered with mud—mud which Preston knew could contain an incredible range of bacteria, parasitic nematodes, and no telling what other kind of life that might be radiation-altered.

He decided then not to opaque out. His body said *yes*, but his mind said *no*. Not now. There would be plenty of time later.

But it was too late for Jay.

Dr. Wainwright came back on channel. "We can't reach him, Preston. He's switched off the Hive frequencies."

"I know," he said. "I think he can hear me, though. I'll try to reason with him if I can."

Dr. Wainwright then said, "Preston, we're going to have to bring him down. We'll send Sebastian up in his place. We think his threat to release the information to Saxifrage might have been a bluff."

"No," Preston immediately said. "Jay will come out of it. Give him a chance. He's only doing what I wanted to do originally. You don't know what it's really like up here. And I can't blame him. Besides, this'll give us a good chance to see if there's anything inimical in the environment. Jay's up to his knees in it." He found himself cringing as he said those words; but it was true. Jay was now effectively their first guinea pig.

He also cringed for another reason: He was playing politics. He didn't want to share this particular mission with Sebastian Monaco, and he knew that his line of reasoning would placate the authorities down below. Jay wasn't *that* crazy, and once his adrenaline level stabilized, he would get back to his *duende* form and proceed to explore the terrain.

Or so Preston hoped.

Eighty yards away Jay's whoops of joy could be heard amid explosions of creek water as he crashed in and out of the stream.

Preston decided to leave him be, at least for the moment. There really wasn't much he could do. However, as he got inside his own Rover, he called out to his brother.

"Jay," he spoke. "I'm heading for the village. Your Rover will get you there if you don't want to drive yourself. It's already programmed. But that's where I'll be. Use the train depot as a rendezvous point."

In the distance Jay's soaking head jutted up above the creek bank. He waved, but he was waving in the wrong direction. Preston was still invisible to him, but that fact hadn't impressed itself upon his brother.

Jay disappeared back into the creek, like an old frog: the sound of water . . .

The first people Preston "assessed" were a man and a woman driving along in a hay-filled pickup truck just north of the Magin grain silos. Little Irina was not to be seen anywhere and Preston reasoned that she must have been off in another part of the landscape working to gather grain for the remaining silo. The wheat fields in the area seemed to stretch for miles and miles.

But the two farmers in the pickup had been slowly driving close to the outer fringes of Anytown. Preston had his doubts as to the feasibility of the assessor gun, but when he passed the couple in the dust-spewing pickup truck, aimed, and fired, he was informed from down below that the Hive computers were recording the impulses that the gun generated.

The elderly couple apparently hadn't felt any sensation whatsoever. They merely continued their bouncy journey toward town in the silence common to lonely drives along deserted country roads. Preston made a mental note to himself to locate their farm. It might be useful to know just which Russians lived in Anytown and which Russians lived far out on the prairie.

The gun, however, seemed to function best at a range of twenty to thirty feet. It plugged into the m-field generator circuits at his waist and nestled comfortably in his lap as he drove along. The gun itself, when fired, only registered a faint vibration. He distantly wondered if his brother would ever "assess" anyone at all.

In fact, he himself was feeling an urgency to get within Anytown as quickly as possible before word of a madman in the fields to the south of Anytown reached the small settlement. He began to regret his decision to leave Jay alone. He felt as if he had the world on his shoulders and that there was no one interested in helping with the load.

"Are there any readings coming from Jay's gun?" he sought to ask.

Dr. Wainwright's voice appeared over the channel. "No, I'm afraid not. We can't even locate his Rover now."

"What?"

There was a pause, an almost embarrassing silence which seemed to throw most of the blame back upon his shoulders. But Dr. Wainwright came back on the radio frequency. He said, "He got out of the creek and ran back to his Rover. Apparently to change his clothes. We don't know for sure since there aren't any cameras inside the Rovers. But we registered a lot of commotion, then he unplugged the assessor gun from his belt and turned off the outer Rover cameras and sensors." His voice sounded leaden and so far away.

Preston said nothing, but he was surprised—though he did not openly express this—that none of the military *duendes* were insisting that he somehow locate his brother and bring him downside. True, there were no spare Rovers and it would take the 'comb and Armory personnel some time to de-mothball one of the armored personnel carriers, lift it up, then search out the errant Appleseed. But if Jay wanted to stay gone, then there was almost nothing the militarists could do about it.

Still, he had enough faith in Jay to suspect that all his brother was doing was enjoying his own personal Resurrection. He would return to earth shortly, and hopefully in his *duende* state, before the Soviet settlement suspected that anything peculiar was transpiring.

Anytown, USA, was quite busy that day.

In the full light of the noonday sun, Preston was rather astonished by the completeness of the colony. The previous evening he wasn't able to observe the exact nature of the buildings or the very land upon which the Soviets had founded their town. His natural curiosity had embraced a number of reasonable deductions, but the utter newness of the township truly startled him. Anytown was no temporary settlement.

The train depot, of which he had only gotten an incomplete vision last night, was a very modest and almost storybooklike structure. Its gabled roof and open freight platform seemed to beckon characters out of *Anna Karenina*. Preston could easily imagine Count Vronsky waiting for a train to the Crimea or Constantine Levin off to his Petrovsky estate. Even the oak of the benches on the platform glistened as a Russian farmer or two idled about, waiting for whatever train was due at the station soon.

He also noticed the nature of the railway tracks themselves. He glided in his goblinesque fashion through the sleepy depot over to the wide-gauge rails on their asphalt cinder mound which snaked off toward the flat horizon. Here, he could see no sign of ruins from the holocaust of the past. These locomotive rails had not been laid upon the same railway route which had existed here in the past. The Rover's computer memory showed that no rail line had passed this way before. Indeed, Anytown itself had been founded where no previous Kansas city had been located.

It was as if the conquering Russians were purposefully avoiding all of the sites of atomic destruction. But then,

Preston recalled Yuri Kreutin's cargo on his flatbed truck: "harvested" metals and radioactive waste in monazite shells. He was going to have to follow the extroverted Kreutin someday to see where he harvested his steel, iron, copper, and aluminum ingots. He was equally certain that there were also other *duendes* interested in the process by which such harvesting was done.

There was so much to see!

However, he didn't want to make a motor race of it and decided to park the Rover at the train depot, beside the storage facility where Yuri Kreutin had driven his flatbed. With a tiny homing signal left beeping silently for Jay to loacate, he knew that his brother would be able to find him. *If* he chose to do so. Otherwise, he himself would not be seen by his brother unless he was about twenty-five feet from him. *Duendes* could be just as invisible from one another as from normal corporeal incarnates on the surface. Out here, they would need a reliable way to find one another, and the homing device in the Rover was the only way he could think of at the moment.

He started assessing at the train depot, adjusting himself to the elevated station platform. There, in the cool shade of the station, he assessed several arriving individuals who had business at the depot, noticing as he went their manner of speech and dress.

What bothered him greatly was their constant, and efficient, use of standard American English. To be sure, each had his or her own particular accent, but at no time did anyone fall back upon the use of his native tongue. For all he could tell, these people could have been simple immigrants to the Midwest who happened to settle upon this vacant spot on the prairie, much as the Swedes had done in Wisconsin or the Dutch in Pennsylvania.

Across the fresh asphalt of the main street from the train depot was a large country store. The paint seemed so new on the sign above that it shone in the sun's light as if recently daubed. A water tower which he hadn't noticed before perched above the settlement at the far end of town. The word "ANYTOWN" was freshly emblazoned upon its massive steel hulk.

Preston ghosted over to the country store, passing right through its very walls. The *duendes* down below were silent in his earphones and he chose not to give them a blow-by-blow account of his every footstep. He felt bad enough about being an eavesdropper and voyeur, but he also knew that the *duendes* would be going over the data he was sending down by way of the assessor gun. That was enough for them.

The country store was . . . a country store. Canned goods (labels in English), hunting and fishing equipment, gardening tools, feed bags, fertilizers in sacks and metal canisters, pesticides, even a pickle barrel could be found within. Every item seemed of recent manufacture; nothing was gleaned from the ruins themselves of the larger nearby Kansas cities. And absolutely nothing seemed *Russian* in character.

*These aren't Soviets*, Kitteridge realized as his assessor gun hummed throughout the store. *These are Americans*.

He counted twelve adult Russian farmers in the store, including the aged, yet active, storekeeper. Several small children, perhaps three to four years of age, were also present, getting in the way of things as all children their age seemed to do.

The store appeared to be something of a focal point for the village, and in the space of an hour Preston had assessed over forty people. Citizens came and went, each with a particular complaint or need from the storekeeper, and through it all Preston drifted invisibly, removed from their world.

However, there was nothing about their behavior this close up which might have suggested that they were walking genetic time bombs or Typhoid Marys. Still, there was no way he could know for sure, since appearances could be deceiving.

Preston ghosted through a side wall of the store which was hung with rakes and shovels and shiny hoes, and found himself inside an old-fashioned ice cream parlor. Here, several parents with about a dozen children were facedown in confections of a sort he hadn't known down in the subterranean confines of the Meadow. There were even different kinds of yogurts available, which meant that somewhere was an efficient dairy in full operation. He felt envious of them somehow: This was a scene right out of old-time America. And the Russians were clearly enjoying themselves.

Jay had yet to make an appearance.

Preston roamed about Anytown, staying relatively close

to the main street where the bulk of commerce and traffic was. He drifted back time and again to his Rover, hoping that the elder Kitteridge would have shown up.

Midafternoon came around and Preston had already assessed the folks in the town's only bank, the people who ran the small hospital at the north end of the village, and most of the children in the town's only schoolyard. But Jay could not be found anywhere. He could not even be raised on the radio, and Preston had no idea where he could possibly be. He was beginning to get worried.

So in the meantime, he took to ghosting in through the homes of the "suburb" behind the main street of Anytown. He'd saved them for last.

There was nothing new here.

The wives were busy at work, doing what farm wives and farm mothers have done down through the ages. He assessed young wives with squalling babies; he assessed grandmothers and grandfathers poring over tissue-thin newspapers; he assessed the sick and infirm, the lonely or heartbroken. In all these centuries, human nature had not changed. He took in the town block by block, corner by corner, until he felt sure that he had canvassed the whole village.

And through it all, he felt a little bit angered by Jay's absence from the assessing process. He needed Jay's own authority and knowledge to help maintain the balance of power in the Meadow, and his not being present did not help matters much. However, the *duendes* had made no move to send Monaco up to the village, and that seemed to be a positive sign.

He decided on making a final circuit of the northern edge of Anytown, and this swing took him by the little Russian's home. Irina's mother, Yelena, had been home alone all day, singing to herself, doing some occasional sewing and mending. The kitchen apparently had seen some active canning earlier that morning, and Preston did manage a visual survey of their sumptuous back garden. Autumn was in the air along with the wordless tune of Irina's attractive mother, and the land was being prepared for its fallow sojourn through the harsh winter months. That meant canning for the women of the town, and harvesting for the men. *And*, he had to remind himself, *for those precocious nine-year-olds among them*.

He was in the midst of being hypnotized by Yelena's wifely duties when Stu Hagerty's voice suddenly blossomed over his earphones.

"Jay's in town," he called out quickly.

Preston hastily withdrew from Yelena's presence, ghosting out onto the front lawn before he spoke.

"What? Where is he?"

"He's just passed your Rover at the train depot," the Hive technician reported. "He's still riding silent, but he just ghosted right on by and your Rover's cameras picked him up. He's out of range now, but wasn't going too fast. We're sure he's nearby. You'd better find him, Preston."

There was a sense of urgency in Hagerty's voice that seemed to say *Monaco, Monaco*. . . .

"Right. I'm on it," he acknowledged.

This was the first he'd heard from the War Room in several hours, and both the silence and the tone in Hagerty's voice told him that he was to make a beeline back through the suburbs to the main street. Pronto.

Jogging through houses, trees, and white picket fences, he called out on his own *duende* frequency, "Jay! Are you there? Do you read me? Come on back."

There was no response. He was going to have to find his own Rover and backtrack from the depot.

He found Jay's Rover. It was parked at the other end of the train depot, just far enough out of range of the first Rover's cameras not to be seen too well. He had found it only because he had been coming in that direction. Jay, though, was at least obeying orders. He *had*, after all, rendezvoused at the train station. But somehow he had missed Preston's Rover and driven on by.

Jay, though, wasn't anywhere near the depot.

In fact, by the time Preston had reached the station, he discovered that a great many Russians had assembled at the depot. He wondered what all the fuss was about. Jay, he knew, was in there somewhere, but it was impossible to make another *duende* out, especially with all the bright colors and the bright afternoon sunlight overhead.

"Jay!" he shouted, but the m-field process was such that while their ghostly *duende* voices could not be heard on the outside, they also had to mingle with all the sounds coming in to m-field on the inside. There was just cacophony surrounding the station.

"Nemesis," he swore to himself, looking around, passing in and about the milling farmers.

Into the crowd appeared Lev Magin, home from the wheat fields, and Yuri Kreutin, still dressed in his red tunic, with goggles on his forehead and red gloves tucked in an epaulet upon his left shoulder. Preston drifted close to them.

Everyone seemed to be in an expectant mood, but only a few people upon the platform actually seemed to be waiting for the train for the sole purpose of traveling upon it. Obviously the train which was due to arrive was bringing someone or something of great importance to the villagers. Or perhaps they were just there to *see* the train. Like true farmers, any diversion in their humdrum lives was something to look forward to.

Lev Magin, perhaps the most level-headed of the two relations, turned to Yuri Kreutin, who boisterously laughed with the other farmers nearby.

Lev said, "There are rumors that the Great War goes well. But how rumors of any kind reach us here is beyond me."

"It must be the women." Yuri smiled roguishly. "I am convinced it is the women. They communicate mysteriously at night with each other, perhaps on moonbeams. Gossiping in their sleep."

Lev grinned at his brother-in-law. "You should know. You are the expert on women."

Yuri held up his hands. His mustache curled upward with a playful smile. "Any man who claims absolute knowledge of women is either a fool or a madman."

One farmer, a sturdy man with very shaggy eyebrows, turned to Yuri Kreutin and laughed. "I hear you've found a device that reads moonbeams, Yuri Kreutin. It is not the ruins you haunt by day, but bedrooms by night."

"Moonbeams will do it to you every time," Kreutin said.

Everyone at the station laughed, some of whom slapped Kreutin on the back. The metal harvester relished the attention as if there might be some truth to the matter.

As Preston drifted invisibly among them, he noticed that most of the idle talk centered around the faraway Great War and the rumors that it was nearing the end of its present phase. What phase this might be, Preston could not determine. But evidently many of the townships scattered throughout the Plains had sent their sons and daughters off to engage the enemy in the service of the Awakener. Many of the Russian farmers expressed considerable pride in this fact.

There was also much talk concerning the farmers themselves. Mostly they discussed their trials with the harvesting of wheat and corn, and its basic processing for shipment. This included the metals which Yuri Kreutin had harvested.

"Rover?" Preston called out on the minibus' frequency.

He glanced over into the parking lot beyond the station platform. The Rover's rounded form ghosted up to him as close as it could without having to rise to the platform's own m-field level.

"I'm here," it said in its computer voice.

"Turn your cameras on the station and magnify the audio. Catch as much as you can and relay it down to the Meadow," he ordered.

"I understand," it said.

The excited conversations among the people of Anytown, USA, seemed to build until a cry broke out among the townfolk sheltered on the platform and a very distant air horn could be heard coming up from the south.

Preston hastily ghosted through the crowd with no problem until he reached the lip of the platform, which was only inches from the asphalt trail of the silvery tracks.

From the southeast, cutting across a wide glacier-changed prairie, came a train of a kind he'd never seen in any of the old videos of the twentieth and twenty-first centuries. The single engine appeared to be run by massive electric batteries, or by a process of electrical conversion which might have been fusion in nature. In fact, he noticed just then that the rail tracks themselves were a bit wider, perhaps by two whole feet, than tracks laid down before the War.

A cheer ran through the crowd as the unusual locomotive drew its bounty across the horizon. However, the train did not stop at the Anytown station. What few passengers there were waiting at the depot were apparently due for another train yet to pass through.

But that wasn't what got his attention. The single engine, with its waving engineers inside, bore behind it rail cars linked in such numbers that it stretched back down the tracks for a mile and a half.

Over his own earphones he thought he heard someone far down in the Meadow War Room gasp at the train's cargo. Nearly every car was a mountain of harvested crops. Sugar beets. Corn piled high, husk-hairs whispering in the wind. Wheat. Barley. Potatoes in car after car after car.

About a third of the long passage of freight cars was devoted to flatbeds which boasted the squatting figures of metal ingots similar to those Yuri Kreutin had harvested in the ruins near Anytown. Iron and steel. Copper shining orange in the sun. Aluminum, a dull silver. Ingots of lead and what might have been zinc. Car after car rumbling by.

All of it was bound for the Great War; all headed for barges that were no doubt waiting on a profoundly altered Missouri River. Preston staggered to see such wealth, the *true* wealth of any nation.

The crowd of Russians waved and shouted at the long, long train, whose whistle-stop hoots stampeded out across the fields to the east of Anytown, which had themselves yet to be harvested.

Once the caboose roared past the station, the crowd began to disperse, everyone chatting excitedly among themselves. Preston's heart crashed in his chest and he did not know if it was from the sight of so much defeat, or if it was partly related to the infectious nature of the crowd's natural exuberance over the harvest. As an Appleseed, he was thrilled that so much of the ecosphere had survived. It meant that insects and bees abounded far and wide and that pollination was still going on in the fields and forests.

He felt humbled now. And defeated. After all, their long ghostly exile deep within the earth had been undertaken to eventually accomplish what these Russian men and women had apparently been doing now for a number of years.

He stood alone with his shame, assessor gun held impotently at his side.

The Russians returned into town, crossing the main street to the stores, to the single tavern, to their electric farm trucks. Some had further chores to which to attend; others had finished for the day. All that seemed to remain at the station were the original passengers who still awaited the arrival of their particular train.

However, he discovered that he now had a problem. A *big* problem.

His brother, Jay, dressed as a Russian farmer in workshirt, rugged pants, and leather boots, was fully opaqued out and conversing with one of the townspeople. And the cameras of his Rover were watching.

# 10

Jay's hair was still slick with pond water, but the farmer's cap which he wore concealed that fact from the man with whom Preston found him speaking.

Just where Jay had gotten the clothing was anyone's guess.

Jay said to the older individual, "I am up from the south," and he put into his speech a Georgian inflection gleaned from years of videos watched deep within the Meadow. "I would have taken one of the trains, but the countryside seemed to beckon me all of its own."

The farmer, a capable man, luxuriating somewhere in his mid-forties, seemed taken aback by the stranger's words. "Up from the south on foot? Centerville is such a long way from here and there is much unpleasantness in between. You are a very brave man."

Jay tossed it off with a friendly wave of his hand, letting the natural curve of his mustache and the playful glint in his eyes disarm the man's suspicions. It seemed to work.

The farmer, reddened from long hours in the sun, held out a strong hand and greeted Jay officially. "But let me welcome you on behalf of Anytown. I am Foma Zhvakunin, dairy farmer. One of many here."

Jay's eyes danced delightfully. He smiled. "Call me Jay. Jay Kitteridge, formerly of—" He paused slightly. "Centerville. I am a biochemist by trade."

The two new acquaintances stepped away from the train station, seemingly with no particular destination in mind.

Foma Zhvakunin appeared to be in Anytown after a day of chores, and was in need of a respite from the tedious life he lived somewhere beyond the outskirts of town. Jay companionably fell into stride beside the dairyman.

"Kitteridge?" Foma Zhvakunin said, eyebrows arching up provocatively. "That is an American name I am not familiar with. Have they begun the name changes already in the South? I was told that we would not be taking on our new names for another year or so."

Jay walked like a man with one foot in one world and the other foot somewhere else. And always did a smile adorn his face. He laughed. "We are who we are, is that not so?"

Foma Zhvakunin, a simple dairy farmer and technician, liked the philosophical ring to Jay's words. "You are a strange one, Jay Kitteridge. Yes, I suppose we are. I have often wondered myself why we must wait for the Great War to end before the name-changing occurs." Foma Zhvakunin shrugged casually. "But that is the desire of the Awakener. However, Jay Kitteridge is a nice name for a biochemist from the South. I do not suppose that either the Awakener or his *mandali* would mind."

They headed for the tavern next to the general store. Preston, in his apparitional form, leapt from the station platform and followed them. Jay was totally unaware—and uninterested—that his younger brother was close by.

Foma Zhvakunin, hands in his pockets, turned to the visitor from Centerville. "And how goes the Centerville harvest? Well, may I presume?"

"It goes very well," Jay said happily, eyes forward, giving nothing away. "Indeed, it is better than any of us ever expected," he commented.

"As a chemist, I would guess your talents are more useful than most," Zhvakunin said conversationally as they crossed the street.

Jay grinned. "I can make fertilizers and pesticides from nothing!" he said, holding up his sensitive, long-fingered hands as if he were a magician. "And do not forget the metals and plastics."

"Ah!" exclaimed Foma Zhvakunin. "Yes, there is much of those in between our towns, or so I am told. That is a region I do not . . . haunt."

Zhvakunin said this with some trepidation, but then quickly changed the subject as if that were an area of discussion forbidden by some kind of social convention or unspoken taboo.

The dairyman said, "We have no chemist in our town, but Yuri Kreutin does some metal harvesting. He's the only one who knows how to use a Khoury converter properly. I myself"—he turned to his new friend—"know nothing of these matters. I stick to my Holsteins and my farm."

"Kreutin," Jay said musingly. "The name may be familiar to me."

Foma Zhvakunin laughed slightly. "It is a name, I suppose, more familiar to the women of Centerville, if the rumors are true!"

"I shall have to inquire when I return." Jay smiled.

They came to the tavern and Jay's eyes widened. "Intoxicants! Just the thing to finish the day with." He turned to the older gentleman beside him. "I have but little money to squander, but enough, as they say, to wet our whistles."

Coins of uncertain denomination jingled in Jay's pants pocket.

But Foma Zhvakunin, always the polite host, slapped Jay upon his shoulder. "After such an interesting journey from Centerville, across so much dangerous territory, let me be the one to 'wet our whistles,' as you say."

Jay bowed to the man's invitation.

The tavern was simple, filled with pipe smoke and the sound of many conversations going all at once. Several of the citizens who had gathered to see the bounteous train rumble through town were there, most of them crowded around tables or leaning back in their chairs against a far wall in the dark ambience of the place.

Proston carefully ghosted in through the walls before Jay and Foma Zhvakunin reached the ebony bar which was just to the left of the tavern's entrance. He found several Russians within who had not originally been assessed upon the station platform or on his previous tour of the town.

At least with Jay present, he didn't have to worry as he went about his spectral duties. The assessor gun hummed.

Mostly off-duty workers and farmers inhabited the tavern's dark spaces. But several of the younger men appeared to be genuine cowboys. They wore fringed riding chaps around their long, muscular legs, their heels spun with spurs whenever they shifted positions in their chairs. On the hat racks inside the door clustered hats of all descriptions, hanging like grapes on a vine. Several cultures came together here in an odd mix.

Preston watched his brother closely, wondering what he himself might have to do should Jay get into trouble. That he *would* get into trouble was only a matter of time. Nervously Preston holstered the assessor gun and watched.

Jay seemed to stagger from the inrush of all the conflicting odors and fragrances hovering about the bar. If there were any airborne diseases or organisms which could affect a *duende*, such a closed area as the tavern would definitely make an impression on Jay.

But Foma Zhvakunin, true to his own convivial nature, escorted his new friend to the long bartop. Zhvakunin pulled off his cap and laid it upon the bar as the bartender came over to serve them.

"It is Foma Zhvakunin," said the bartender, a man of much girth and several chins. "Fleeing from his many cows and his wife. Or is it his many wives and his cow?"

A couple of barflies next to them laughed in their beer.

Foma Zhvakunin smiled sheepishly at Jay and indicated the jovial bartender. "His sister, whom I somehow married long ago, has come to look like him over time. I think I prefer my cows."

The barflies laughed even harder. The bartender's face seemed to flush with embarrassment, but he did not lose his smile. Foma introduced them all to his new companion.

"Comrades, we have a visitor from distant Centerville. Jay Kitteridge is the name he has already chosen, and he tells me he is an expert chemist by trade."

Jay beamed.

The bartender's eyes widened, partly with surprise and partly with a friendly welcome. His hands were nearly crimson from rough dishwater scrubbings, but he reached out and shook Jay's lean hand eagerly.

"A new face in town is always a pleasure," the bartender said.

Foma whispered to Jay, "Watch out. He has several sisters left."

The barflies, huddled over their foamy beer, laughed again.

"Chemist, you say?" the bartender queried, ignoring his brother-in-law.

Jay nodded. "Yes, sir. I work with the bioengineers of the Salina—"

He caught himself and laughed. He seemed thoroughly intoxicated simply by being where he was, taking in all the raucous sights and smells. Preston clenched his fists and inhaled sharply through gritted teeth. *Careful, man. Careful . . .*

Jay went on with a smile. "Anyway, I deal in fertilizers, pesticides, and other miracles of the technician's craft."

Drinks were poured. The noise level increased. A few more Russian men entered the bar. Foma Zhvakunin and Jay leaned together at the bartop as clear vodka appeared in ounce shot glasses, accompanied with steins of beer chaser. Down they went.

Preston gently ghosted over to his brother and made a slight adjustment at the controls of his m-field belt.

*"Just what the holy hell do you think you're doing?"* he whispered into his brother's ear harshly.

Jay merely grinned foolishly, though clearly he had heard the admonition.

"Nemesis!" Preston said, inaudible now, standing away in total frustration.

The liquor went down easily, although it was evident to Preston that Jay was having to fall back on his drinking skills engendered during his apprenticeship days when he was a younger man at the university in the Meadow. Preston wanted to reach out and slap the shot glasses away, but he knew that while he could do it and remain a *duende*, it would no doubt cause too many problems

And he had more than enough to deal with at the moment. He halfway expected to see a few *duende* centurions come crashing into the tavern to arrest his insane brother.

But Jay wasn't out of control yet.

"I am curious about news of . . . the Awakener," Jay said to Foma Zhvakunin, who'd already had twice as much liquor as he. "And news of the *mandali*. You mentioned them earlier." He sipped his beer slowly, methodically.

The easygoing soul which comprised Foma Zhvakunin was given to great respect for the Awakener. He said, "Ah, the Awakener! Now, where would we be without the Awakener?"

Several of the nearby Russian barflies nodded in complete and solemn agreement—though their solemnity was more reverential than grim.

But Jay continued to pump his friend for information. "That is why I am up from the South," he reported. "I have a great curiosity for many, many things upon the earth. The Awakener is one such."

Foma Zhvakunin, forgetting about his cows and wife, became lost in thoughts of the Awakener. He smiled at Jay. "They say that when he is done with the War in Africa, he will come here. There is to be a meeting of the *mandali* in a year's time. That will be a great day indeed. My father, were he still alive, would relish meeting with his old friend again."

Foma Zhvakunin's eyes went bleary with the memory of his long-departed father, and in those eyes radiated something that spoke of his relationship with the distant Awakener.

"Africa," Jay muttered. The vodka was being sipped slower now.

Preston stood by in his frustration. All he could do was watch. He hadn't the slightest idea what Jay was up to.

"Perhaps when the Great War is done, even in Indonesia and India," farmer Zhvakunin said almost tearfully, "he will be able to see what we have accomplished in his name."

Jay glanced sideways at him. "In his name?" he said.

Foma signaled the bartender for another round. "A manner of speaking." He then looked squarely at Jay, not as drunk as he appeared to be, merely high and happy that a new person had come to town. He said, "You are a funny one, Jay Kitteridge. You speak like one who's spent too much time with test tubes and beakers and not enough time in the world."

Jay lifted his shot glass and studied it. "You don't know how much of the truth you speak. That is why I seek the Awakener and his company."

"*Careful, buster,*" Preston whispered as he briefly cast his voice into the real world just an inch from Jay's ear.

Jay ignored his little brother.

"I live in a closed world," Jay confessed somberly. "We think of the Nemesis only and how much God has punished the world. The Great War is too far away. And the Awakener—"

Foma Zhvakunin struggled with Jay's words. "Nemesis? What is this Nemesis of which you speak?"

Evidently Foma Zhvakunin was used to the ingestion of

massive quantities of vodka and beer and was equally able to maintain his senses about him. Jay, however, was not.

"The dark force of history," Jay told him. "After what we've been through, someone had to be blamed. The Devil. Nemesis. Not that it could be *our* fault, of course. When things go right in a man's life, he says that God is on his side and has blessed him. But when things go wrong, well, it's the Devil to blame."

The other men at the bar, though quite drunk on their own, stared at Jay. They were not hostile, merely attentive.

"*Jay!*" Preston switched in. "*You'd better watch it!*"

Jay continued with his reverie. "My friend, Foma Zhvakunin, I feel as if I've truly lived my life among ghosts—"

The men nearby began speaking among themselves. One of them, a young cowboy or ranch hand, said, "*Prevedenir, prizrak!*"

Then the man next to him said thickly, "Use the new tongue, even when you speak of ghosts, Oleg." He indicated Jay. "Our friend is only a visitor. He does not speak of these things in a literal way."

Jay, though tipsy, saw that he had transgressed. He said, "Forgive me, friends. We all have our own specters. I did not mean to suggest anything by it."

Foma Zhvakunin took a larger pull upon his vodka glass. He set it down slowly. "So few of us travel that visitors from the other communities remind us that there is a big world beyond our fences and fields."

"It is a big world, indeed," Jay confirmed, and smiled disarmingly. "Let us just say that I find my life filled with emptiness and aimlessness. These are my ghosts."

Foma Zhvakunin nodded, understanding the import of his words. "Were it not for the ruins we would have more places to harvest. We do as well as we can, but at least there is land here to cultivate. It is not the same . . . elsewhere." He looked disapprovingly down into his empty shot glass as if it reflected the emptiness in his soul.

Preston, listening and watching closely, thought that Zhvakunin had almost said *in Russia*, and by the way the others in the tavern turned away at the dairyman's words, he knew that Jay had struck a sensitive, if melancholy, chord.

Preston watched as Jay continued to gamble with the Soviet farmers. He said, "But at least we have something toward which to work. We have the guidance of the Awakener."

At this, everyone seemed to be cheered. Their moods were many and their lives afforded them rare opportunities to explore their innermost feelings. Jay, despite his drunkenness, was playing his hand very carefully. Preston couldn't tell if this was because he had told him to do so, or if Jay had other reasons in mind.

He knew his brother. Jay *always* had other reasons.

Jay continued, "I, for one, would like to meet the Awakener. He seems to be behind everything we do."

The vodka glasses were refilled. Foma Zhvakunin assembled more coins on the bartop for payment to his portly brother-in-law.

"We would all like to meet him," said the barkeep with a proud smile.

Through a red veil of bloodshot eyes, Foma Zhvakunin pondered the biochemist. He said, "Perhaps you should reconsider your travel itinerary."

"What do you mean?"

"Perhaps a glimpse of the Awakener might do you some good, since Centerville seems to hold little for you at the moment," he told him. "The Awakener is a man of great power, but the *mandali* say his spirit is large."

Jay leaned back on his barstool, gripping the edge of the bar. "I would not know how to find him. There is, after all, the Great War."

The man next to Foma on the other side was much less drunk than his friends. He said, "There are many wars, but they say that the Awakener spends his time in eastern Africa where there is much work yet to be done."

Everyone nodded in agreement. The bartender silently polished a shot glass.

Another man then said, "But it changes all of the time. Next he is supposed to go to Indonesia."

"Indonesia?" Jay said.

The same man returned with, "My wife tells me that our next harvest of corn will go directly to Indonesia. And most of the metals."

Foma Zhvakunin turned to him and grinned. "Perhaps we should send your wife instead of the corn. She'd put an end to the Great War. *All* of the Great Wars."

The man blubbered in his embarrassment as thighs were slapped and howls fell about them all.

\* \* \*

Preston watched his brother closely as Jay and the Russians continued to drink. He noticed how Jay's dangerous eyes glittered in the same way as their mother's had after they had lost their father years ago. And his brother, now three sheets to the wind, was beginning to appear remote, mulling over his dark, mysterious thoughts.

So far Preston hadn't heard a peep from the Meadow. Since he had been channeling Jay's conversation with the Russians down to the Hive, he was hoping that Dr. Wainwright would offer some suggestions as to how he might go about retrieving Jay from the outer world without alarming the farmers and the ranch hands.

However, the Meadow was silent and still.

The door to the tavern burst open just then, letting in a bright shaft of orange afternoon light. A boy in his late teens, a store merchant's son, came inside.

"A plutonium car's coming!" he shouted to the men within the dark barroom.

Nearly all of the Russian farmers, with the exception of the bartender and one profoundly drunk individual over in a far corner, got up and exited the tavern. The boy led them out.

Only then did Preston hear from the Hive.

Colonel Chaney came in over the earphones. "Kitteridge, you'd better look into that. The Rovers aren't situated well enough for us to see. We think this might be important."

Vacillating between his duties and his loyalty to his brother, who was brooding over his vodka just then, Preston finally gave in. A plutonium car *did* sound important.

Foma Zhvakunin was also one of the Russians to remain inside the tavern when it was evident that Jay was not going out to see the spectacle of the plutonium car arriving. Foma had seen such things before.

Reluctantly Preston turned and walked through the tables and chairs of the dark tavern and passed on out through the wooden walls of the bar. More vodka had been poured for Jay and farmer Zhvakunin, and Preston knew that Jay wasn't likely to go anywhere. He was just concerned that he might start blabbing.

The plutonium car came up from the south on the railroad tracks. However, the engine which drew it was somewhat different from a regular train engine, and there was only a single car in between the huge engine and the caboose. Even the caboose was unusual, being studded with a vast array of communications equipment on the outside. *This* train had a special mission.

Preston signaled his Rover to turn in a more advantageous position so that its many camera eyes might better scan the train's approach.

This train was their first real indication that there was a war going on somewhere in the world. Its colors were a military green and a khaki brown, with leafy patterns on the roofs. This train, clearly, had little or nothing to do with the harvest season.

Still, the train bore no signs of weaponry—no missile racks, no machine-gun turrets, nothing.

The train approached Anytown slowly, but it did not stop at the depot platform. Instead, it eased on past it, pulling to a slow stop at the warehouse-like structure into which Yuri Kreutin had driven his flatbed truck the night previous.

Several Russians had returned to the depot to see the arrival of this unusual train, but there weren't nearly as many people assembled here as before. It may have had something to do with what the train carried: *plutonium*.

Yuri Kreutin and his brother-in-law, Lev Magin, were there waiting. The doors to the warehouse storage facility were open, and Preston could see the two Russians inside. Other citizens had gathered, at a cautious distance, outside.

From the communications caboose, a voice boomed from a recessed loudspeaker. "Is Yuri Kreutin there? Will Yuri Kreutin please come forward?"

Yuri, in his bright crimson tunic with his goggles on and his gloves on his hands, stepped out onto the cement loading dock nearest the train. Lev Magin was right behind him. He, too, wore leather gloves.

The crowd watched as Yuri Kreutin and Lev Magin exchanged some low words with the men in the communications caboose at the rear of the train. Up front at the engine, the engineers and the lone conductor waited patiently.

"Wow!" someone down in the Meadow commented. "That center car is *loaded* with radioactive waste! I'm even picking up isotopes of neptunium." Preston recognized Sid Rankin's strained voice. "Where the hell are they finding neptunium?"

Stu Hagerty was conversing aside with Sebastian Monaco. The data from the Rover must have been overwhelming.

Preston walked out onto the cement loading dock and stood beside the assembly of Russian technicians.

One of the men in the caboose stood at a side door. He wore a headset and pin-mike and gestured to Kreutin and Lev Magin.

"This load comes from Vance," he said to them in inflected English. "We'll have the area cleared out by next spring, if all goes well."

Kitteridge heard Monaco's voice suddenly. "That's Vance Air Force Base they're talking about. It's got to be. They must have come up from Oklahoma."

"Quiet," Preston said into his pin-mike. "I can't hear."

Yuri Kreutin, uncharacteristically grim, pointed back over his shoulder into the concrete storage bunker. He said, "I need more monazite foam. There's more to be harvested where I found all this."

As he spoke, an automated forklift, controlled by Lev Magin, came up out of the bunker on rubberized wheels, rising up the cement incline.

The operator in the caboose, surrounded by his own subordinates, threw several switches. A door in the side of the center car opened slowly. Preston noticed that the center car was windowless and thoroughly shielded. The forklift rattled past them with the crimson barrel of monazite shells on into the center car. Also within the plutonium car were other barrels of various sizes and shapes. A technician was there to assist the awkward robot with its burden.

It took them another ten minutes to empty out the Anytown bunker of the other radioactive-waste barrels.

Yuri said, "I would appreciate more foam, if you have it. It would spare me an extra trip."

The head technician said, "I'm sorry, Yuri. We've run out ourselves. We're on our way to Missouri Landing to get this"—and with a jerk of a thumb sideways he indicated the booty in the center car—"transferred."

"Well, then," Kreutin continued, "can you bring down more canisters of monazite foam? It sure would help."

The technician shook his head. "Not unless you can wait a week, my friend. We are not scheduled to pass back this way until then."

"That is not convenient," Yuri mumbled to himself, looking aside to his brother-in-law.

Lev tapped him on the shoulder. "There is another train due soon. We can reach the Landing by morning."

Yuri gave this some thought while the forklift backed out of the plutonium rail car for the last time. The doors rumbled shut.

"I do need to get a few parts for our thresher," Lev Magin then said to his brother-in-law. "And Irina has been asking for a short trip like this."

The operator in the caboose smiled down at Kreutin. "You should think about these things, Yuri. You should get twice as many canisters as you're going to need. You never know when or where you're going to come across debris in the ruins."

Then the sun shone through Kreutin's character. He grinned wolfishly. "But then I'd have no excuse to visit the women of Missouri Landing, now, would I?"

The operator and his subordinates laughed. One of the younger men behind the chief operator leaned over. He apparently knew of Kreutin's prowess. He said, "And when they've swept the country clean, what will you do with your time, Yuri Kreutin?"

Yuri leered, fishing in his tunic pocket for a mythical piece of paper. "I seem to have your sister's address somewhere. I'll think of something."

Everyone laughed at both Kreutin and the younger technician. The operator in the caboose then signaled the engineers up front and the giant engine began to grumble as its massive pistons began to move its wheels lugubriously on the track. The crowd of Russians around the bunker waved. Lev and Yuri backed off.

Preston listened as the *duendes* down below argued among themselves.

"There were several hundred pounds of plutonium and uranium in that train car," Monaco's voice sounded.

Stu Hagerty followed with: "Those people don't know what they're sitting on."

Colonel Chaney: "Sure they do. They know exactly what they're doing. They've figured a way to make the ruins pay off for them. Those bastards."

Then the conversation turned to Preston suddenly.

"Kitteridge," came the Colonel's voice. "You didn't assess the Russians on board the train!"

"So?"

"So you're supposed to assess everyone, dammit!" This last bit came from Sebastian Monaco.

"I don't think our data base is going to be hurt by the few Russians I forget to assess," he said.

"When I said everybody, Kitteridge, I meant *everybody*!" Monaco stated.

Preston stood alone on the bunker as the Russians walked away. He touched his pin-mike. "Just who the hell do you think you're talking to, Monaco? I'm not one of your lackeys. I'll do what I goddamn well please up here. I don't even think this is a good idea."

"You're not qualified to think, Kitteridge," Monaco told him with full authority blossoming in his voice. "This is a military operation, and you're going to respond accordingly."

"Fuck you," he said angrily. He switched off all communications to the Meadow.

But even in his anger, he knew that Monaco was right. All he had to do was ponder the receding form of the plutonium car on the far horizon.

It was a converted troop train. It had all the colors of war, and it was full of fissionable—and recyclable—material.

"Damn!" he swore to himself.

Suddenly several Russians bolted out of the tavern with frightened expressions on their faces.

"What now?" Preston grated.

He ghosted down into the street and passed through various individual farmers and ranchers. He swept through a cowboy who was in the midst of throwing up all he had consumed in the saloon. The boy was frightened to death—and sick because of it.

Preston leapt through the wall of the barroom.

Jay was nowhere to be seen.

A small group had gathered inside the bar and were, to a man, greatly agitated. Everyone was talking all at once, waving their arms about, shouting. Foma Zhvakunin looked palpably green with terror. The bartender had lost all of his humor.

"I knew there was something strange about that young man!" the chubby barkeep swore. "I just knew it!"

One man said, "He said he was from Centerville, didn't he? Didn't he say that he was one of us?"

Another interrupted. "But who travels the roads at night? Centerville cannot be reached but by train, and he did say he came to us on foot."

The bartender then said, "He came by train. There *are* no roads between here and Centerville. That is the Awakener's original plan."

Foma Zhvakunin, older than most of the Russians present, said with a heavy voice, "No, he did not come by train. I only met him at the depot. No train had stopped there for him to disembark from. No. He told me specifically that he had traveled on foot."

"*Prevedenir!*" someone cursed.

And they were suddenly quiet.

The bartender held up his hands. "Please, my friends. Do not use the old tongue. There is no call for obscenities. We must remember the Awakener's wishes in these matters. There must be some other explanation."

They all turned and faced the single restroom which was at the rear of the darkened tavern. The very dust in the air seemed alive and electric.

The barkeep concluded, "He must have slipped out some other way."

"No!" shouted another Russian. "He disappeared. I swear to you, friends, that he just disappeared. I was right behind him as we headed into the restroom."

Then one of the remaining cowhands said, "He is one of the ghosts." He had fevered blue eyes that took in all of them. "You heard what he said. He came from the countryside. And it is true, no one travels the old roads. No one."

His words were almost toneless, funereal.

Preston dashed for the restroom, passing through the long smooth bar with its overturned glasses and silver amoebas of spilled vodka.

The restroom held a toilet and a tissue-clogged urinal. Above the toilet was a six-inch-square ventilation grid. A tiny fan was churning away, gently rattling the grille, and some bulbous mutant flies with large yellow wings were buzzing up in a corner where a spiderless web hung in gossamer threads.

But there was no Jay.

His brother had deopaqued and had apparently been seen doing it.

Since his brother was now back within the m-field as a *duende*, he called out, "Jay! *Jay!*"

Jay would still be wearing his filched farmer's clothing and probably wouldn't have yet put on his communications gear. And with so many voices and sounds, both within the ghostly m-field and out in the real world, there would be no real way his brother would hear his shouts.

Preston sped from the tavern and ran for the two idle Rovers across the street. If he could reach Jay's Rover in time, then he might be able to cut his brother off.

When he reached the depot, though, Jay's Rover had already vanished.

Suddenly he felt sick.

His spirits sagged and he thought that his very heart would break.

Almost automatically he switched on the com-link with the Meadow a thousand feet underneath him.

Dr. Wainwright—and not Sebastian Monaco—was instantly on the horn. "Preston, we've been trying to reach you. What's going on with you two?"

For a moment Preston was silent as he stared off into the distant wheat fields beyond the Anytown train depot. He felt the cancers of responsibility gnawing away at him—and it hurt.

"Jay's gone," he finally said. "He's Wandered, Travis."

"*What?*"

"He took his Rover with him. He's probably on his way to Africa by now, if I read him right."

He switched off the com-link and stood alone in the silence which six hundred years of Meadow history threw about him.

# 11

Preston should have known that his elder brother would have tried something like this.

Even as they had prepared that morning for their journey topside from the north end of the Hive, Jay had brought to his Rover all sorts of mysterious items which he had claimed were necessary for his job as an assessor. Each Rover had a plentiful supply of food and water, and Preston knew only too well how capable the minibuses were of traveling almost indefinitely along the upper m-field of the earth's surface. Unless Jay's Rover met with some kind of mechanical failure—which was unlikely since his Rover belonged to the militarists and was constantly serviced—it would be able to draw from the incomprehensible energies from the m-field itself. Jay was on his way.

Preston, though, could not understand Jay's apparent fascination for the figure of the Awakener. That the man was in control of those parts of the world which survived was indisputable. But the *duendes* had long held, almost superstitiously so, that the force which had brought mankind to its knees—the Nemesis—was bigger than any one man, or nation, could deal with. Preston had also believed it was their duty, as *duendes*, to learn the lessons of history, rather than go against them. What Jay thought he could do in Africa or Indonesia completely baffled his younger brother.

It was probably also baffling the *duendes* far down below, whose plans had now been significantly altered by Jay's wandering off.

"Dammit," he muttered to himself. "I just knew he'd do something like this. I should've seen it coming."

Expecting all sorts of vituperative remarks and recriminations from the Meadow, Preston switched the com-link back on.

However, none were in the offing.

Dr. Wainwright's tired voice seemed strained but sympathetic. "There's nothing we can do now. The boy's gone from us. At least you have sense enough to stay."

"I can go after him," Preston quickly told the older Appleseed. "I've done all the assessing I'm going to be able to do today, unless more people come to town. The terrain to the east seems to be fairly flat. I might be able to raise him on the radio if he left it on."

Dr. Wainwright came back. "But we don't know which direction he took. He might be heading for Topeka, or he could have gone directly to the southeast. That would be the quickest way to the equator and Africa."

They all knew his brother too well. As such, Preston could almost hear the political authority as it eroded in Dr. Wainwright's weighted voice. The Appleseeds needed that parity. With Jay gone, it would be harder to keep Colonel Chaney and Sebastian Monaco in check.

"Damn," Preston said.

"And at his greatest rate of speed," Dr. Wainwright continued, "it would take him days to get to the Atlantic."

"And we don't have days," Kitteridge said in a low voice.

That meant that they would lose Jay for certain.

Jay's fate—insofar as he maintained his *duende* form—no matter where he was, would be linked to the Meadow computers. They controlled the Resurrection Day machinery which, when activated, would opaque all *duendes* everywhere, topside or bottomside, regardless of their condition or where they were. Jay and his runaway Rover would instantly come to occupy whatever space they might be ghosting through. And if Preston knew his brother, Jay would deduce that the fastest way of reaching Africa would be by taking the sea-level m-field where there would be no time-consuming hills or valleys to slow him down.

But if he had reached the Gulf or the Atlantic region when the Resurrection Day machinery went into effect, then Jay and his Rover would immediately sink beneath the gray-green waves. Rovers did not float, and neither did *duendes*.

Long, long ago they had done away with their only swimming pool in the Mall. They needed the space instead for further plant cultivation. As such, no *duende* could swim.

Jay was now officially a Wanderer and would have to be written off as a casualty of the Resurrection. Preston's only hope now was that Jay would opaque out on his own and learn to survive, somehow, off the land—a land of undoubted dangers.

It was with that meager thread of hope that Preston was able to return to his scouting duties. His only comfort lay in the fact that he was, after all, out upon the earth's surface and that Resurrection Day would soon be upon them.

Transmissions from the Meadow were at a minimum. He knew that the Hive mainframe computer was working overtime, but he did not press them for results. They were not requiring that he return to the Meadow, and that meant he was still considered to be useful by the powers that be.

The sun was lingering near the western horizon and Anytown was awash in the final colors of the autumn day when Preston decided that he wanted to return to the Magin household. Despite himself, he found that he liked the hardworking family. Already they were familiar to him, and he knew that there was some security in this. He felt grounded being near them, but he kept this sentiment to himself. It was difficult, however. He could feel his deep need for a family, and he began to suspect that Jay had felt it too, being in the company of the hard-drinking Russians in the tavern. It was their closeness which aided in their survival in the changed world.

Preston drew his Rover up to the Magin home to find that the father, Lev, was underneath the giant harvester, banging around in the glare of a utility light, whose long black cord snaked all the way back to the side of the house. Irina, with grease-blackened hands of her own, stood beside him. Ura, their peculiar dog, panted next to her, his long hairs puffed out in the cool fall air.

Lev backed out from beneath the mammoth machine and in his hands he held a differential gear about the size of a dinner plate. He pointed to a serrated edge that apparently wasn't supposed to be there. "This," he said to his diligent daughter, "is what broke."

Irina looked at him with adult concern. She said, "We can't find anything like that here, can we, Poppa?"

Lev, smudged and dirty, wiped his hands on a bandanna as Irina contemplated the damaged gear. "Not here," he confirmed. "But we're going to have to find another one soon if the west fields are to be harvested in time. And our thresher needs a new ignition switch as well."

Yelena, this time wearing sturdy coveralls with her hair tied back beneath a colorful scarf, came out on the porch. Ura barked and waddled over, wagging its frilly tail.

Lev held up the wounded gear to his wife. "This is our problem right now."

Little Irina jumped happily. "We have to go get another one. We're going to take the train!"

Ura barked as she bolted up onto the porch and on into the house to get cleaned up. The decision had evidently been made.

Preston kept his Rover about thirty feet from them and watched.

Yelena frowned at her greasy husband. "She has other duties she can attend to, Lev. And you can have Yuri bring you back the right part. Just give him that," she said, pointing to the broken gear. "He'll know what to get."

Lev walked up to the porch steps. "I think I already promised her. She's worked hard all week and we both could use a short trip to Missouri Landing."

Yelena clouded with concern. "They will be unloading the silos tomorrow. They could use our help, and Irina's little friends will be there."

Lev gave his wife a tiny peck on the cheek. He said, "An overnight trip won't hurt. And besides, our Yuri Kreutin is easily distracted by the fairer sex wherever he goes. He should not go unescorted in these matters."

"And what about Lev Magin?" Yelena asked, but now she was being coquettish. "Isn't that where I met you—or have you forgotten so soon?"

Ura barked playfully around them as they stepped within their home arm in arm.

Preston jumped out of the invisible Rover and ghosted up into the house. Missouri Landing had been mentioned before, but he had no inkling where it might be located. Unless they were going directly to Kansas City, the trip would be a little over a hundred miles. Had the conquering

Russians renamed the ruins of Kansas City? Whatever the case, there was a port facility nearby on the Missouri River.

And that, he realized suddenly, would take him due east. Where Jay had gone.

"Is anybody listening in?" Preston hailed out through the pin-mike.

"Stu, here," Hagerty said from his console underneath the earth. "We've been following you."

"Let me speak with Travis," he said.

A few seconds later, the chief botanist was back on the line. "What have you got, Preston?"

"Have you been monitoring any of this closely?"

"We're taking all that the Rover's sending us, trying to make sense of it. Why?"

"The Magin family is planning to take an overnight trip to a place not far from here called Missouri Landing. I think it's where the railway system ends. A train's coming to town tonight and I'd like your permission to board it. See where it goes."

"That's out of the question," returned Dr. Wainwright.

"Why? Give me one good reason why?" Preston demanded. "I've assessed almost everyone in town and there's really nothing for me to do up here."

"You can come down until we figure out what we're going to do next." Dr. Wainwright was firm. "We've got an awful lot of data to go through and I don't want anything to happen to you."

They were still thinking about Jay.

Preston gritted his teeth. He could almost imagine the Colonel and Sebastian Monaco leaning on Travis, watching the chief Appleseed's every move.

Kitteridge said, "You know me better than that, Travis. I'm not at all like Jay. But I've been hearing so much about Missouri Landing and the *mandali*—"

"The what?"

"*Mandali.* I think it's the plural for a kind of regional governor. They relate in some way to the Awakener, apparently seeing that his orders are understood and carried out. I believe that a couple of them are in Missouri Landing. At least from what I've been able to overhear."

There was a terse pause as a few words were exchanged down in the Hive War Room. Preston could hear Colonel

Chaney's deep voice in the background, but Monaco did not seem to contribute to the discussion.

Dr. Wainwright returned. "You've got to let us track you."

"All right," Preston acknowledged. "I don't see any problem with that."

"And you've got to take your assessor gun with you," came the Colonel's voice over his earphones.

"Colonel," Preston began, assuming some authority of his own. "The population of Anytown is a large enough sample to give your computers enough data on any kind of mutagenic drift. I can't imagine that the population in Missouri Landing is any different."

"We'll be the judges of that, Kitteridge," the Colonel reported. "The more we know, the better we'll be at handling the situation when we opaque out."

"But—"

"Just do it, Preston," came Dr. Wainwright. "We still need to know more than we've got, especially now that we no longer have Jay to help us."

That hurt. He didn't want to confess to them that a trip eastward might assist him in finding his Wandering brother.

"What am I going to do about the gun itself?" he then asked.

"You'll figure out something, Kitteridge," the Colonel stated. "Just make sure that you *do* use it."

It was a trade-off he could live with. With Jay roaming about the surface of the earth somewhere, he just couldn't bear to return to the darkness of the Meadow all over again. Even if Holly Ressler and her family were down there waiting for him, he'd wait for them on Resurrection Day here on the surface. Holly, he knew, would understand.

"I'll do it," he told them. "It'll be risky. Guns don't seem to be part of their lives, and if they find it, they'll be very suspicious. Especially after what Jay did to them in the tavern."

"You can handle it," the Colonel said almost disinterestedly. "Just make sure you get the layout of the town and the countryside. Look for military buildup, troop strengths, communications—"

"All right. I get the picture," Preston interrupted him.

He switched off his com-link with the Meadow. He was

beginning to wonder just how much more of their authority he was going to be able to withstand.

The Magins were seated at dinner when Preston made one last survey of the family. Lev had packed an overnight bag, and little Irina, who downed her dinner excitedly, had a bag being prepared by her mother.

There was plenty of time to prepare himself for the journey.

The first thing Preston had to do was find the right kind of clothing. Where Jay had gotten his duds would probably always be a mystery. But Preston had to be doubly careful now that the townspeople had already had some experience with "unusual" visitors. His disguise had to be authentic, and it had to accommodate his assessor gun.

So he left the Magins to finish their brief meal and drove his Rover back to the train station as quickly as he could.

There, the locomotive had already arrived and was being on-loaded. Some passengers had disembarked; others were in the process of getting on. The train, though, had some time before it was due to leave. The Magins no doubt were aware of this.

The train was designed for passenger traffic only. The massive single engine rumbled like the purr of a dinosaur as it waited to pull away with its few cars. Including the caboose at the rear, there were only five cars altogether. And even within the three passenger cars there appeared to be few people traveling that night.

A porter shuffled various bags into the baggage car, and it was there that Preston formed his plan. Among the assorted luggage were several coat-carriers suspended from long rods which were eventually stored in the baggage car. When the porter withdrew and closed the door behind him, Preston ghosted through the walls of the train and placed himself within its own m-field.

Light from the depot filtered in weakly from the doors at either end of the baggage car, and Preston was able to find his way. This was critical because when he opaqued out he had to make sure that he wasn't located directly within a valise or a crate or a suitcase. The resulting explosion of interphasing m-fields would probably level the depot and toss the cars of the train all over the place as if they were plastic toys.

He looked around to make sure.

Then he opaqued out.

He took a deep breath—and nearly fell over with a laugh of delight. He quickly clamped his hand over his mouth, hoping that no one had heard him.

Jay had gotten to opaque out in a field of freshly mown wheat with a creek nearby and birdsongs filling the air. Preston had only to laugh at the irony of his situation. His first appearance in the real world had instead been in the closeted spaces of a musty baggage compartment of a Russian passenger train, not a fresh wheat field.

The richness of it all nearly knocked him over. He staggered in the heady air of the dozens of lives packed away in the murky compartment. There were perfumes . . . powder smells . . . stale tobacco odors . . . and the leather of the luggage pieces seemed to fill with the life of the animals from which they were taken.

He could smell farms and fields and the dust of small-town streets. There were oil fumes here, and the sweat of ranch hands. He could even smell the slight frizzling of a weak electric current trying to make it past a bad connection somewhere.

These were not the sterile aromas of the Mall down below. This was *life*.

No wonder Jay had gone crazy in his little creek. The urge to Wander was there. Preston had to lean against a tall crate just to keep himself from falling over. Six hundred and nineteen years is a long time to be away from the world.

He stood up in the dim light of the baggage car. Night had fallen outside and there was a chorus of motion on the train platform, with heavy boots thumping and people wishing one another off on their journey.

He heard Yuri Kreutin's cheerful voice as it teased away at little Irina, who was laughing excitedly. A conductor shouted for everyone to climb aboard and the whole train lurched as its couplings tugged at each other with a great deal of complaint.

Preston wobbled slightly in the baggage car, his head still swirling with the input of so many sensory impressions. He regained his equilibrium and quickly found what he needed for his disguise. He drew out a pair of pants, large enough to fit comfortably over his tight-fitting tunic, and a workshirt and jacket. He made sure to remove these items from different suitcases and boxes, lest their original owners recognize them all at once on a complete stranger.

He then found a tote bag for his assessor gun. He kept his m-field belt around his waist where he could replug it whenever he needed it. The belt would also allow him to deopaque back if necessary. However, he did not plan on returning to his *duende* manifestation if he could manage it. The utter richness of the world around him was too compelling.

With a little further digging, he unearthed coins and bills which he felt he might have some use for. He shoved them into his worn pockets. The money was ancient American. Touching it, he felt as if he was poring over the bones of his ancestors. There was an old expression that Americans were made out of money. In a vague, almost pagan way, he felt somewhat ghoulish standing there with so much money and the clothes of other people upon his back.

But then, he had to remind himself that he was an American and that this was his country.

He stepped out into the corridor between the cars as the train slowly pulled away from the lights of Anytown. The wind in his hair sent a thrill up his spine and the rattling of the powerful engine shook him down to his bones. He walked into the next car.

There were very few passengers, as he had originally surmised. In this car only a farm couple and an elderly matron were to be found. There was room for another thirty people, though.

Nervously he made for a seat at some remove from the other passengers, not being brave enough to explore the train any further. He found a seat close to a shaded window. He noticed that all of the windows had shades made of a durable plastic, and all of them were tightly drawn shut.

Cradling his tote bag in his lap, he tried not to glance at the other traveling Russians in the compartment. He was nearly dizzy from the circulating smells. The farmer next to his wife resonated with days of toil in hot summer fields and Preston thought he was going to swoon from the downwind draft of the older matron's perfumed hairdo.

But soon the rocking motion of the train quieted everyone and Preston found it easier to relax.

That was when Lev Magin, his daughter, Irina, and Yuri Kreutin came into their compartment. Weaving slightly back and forth, they searched for the most congenial seat they could find.

Little Irina, dressed warmly for the trip and carrying her

own overnight bag, came bounding down the aisle ahead of the grown-ups.

Suddenly she stopped before Preston. Her small, intelligent eyes locked onto his.

"Ghost!" she gasped, pointing right at him.

# 12

Preston had barely adjusted his mind to this new sensory world, when suddenly he was thrown into direct conflict with it. Time seemed to freeze in the passenger compartment as he sat there trapped before the three Russians. His heart almost exploded.

"Irina!" admonished her father as he and Yuri Kreutin came up to the long seat which faced the one in which Preston languished.

The passenger car had seats which resembled those of ancient European rail travel in that they faced each other, seemingly to allow for more companionable journeys—definitely a Russian affectation. But Preston had not counted on someone sitting opposite him, which was why he chose to sit so far from the other passengers. He hadn't expected anyone else to wander back this far in the compartment.

It was just his luck that the three Russians were of the sort who liked traveling companions across from them. They sat down across from him even though there were a good many other seats they could have selected.

"Irina, do not be so rude to strangers," Lev Magin said, removing his cap. He sat directly across from the American Appleseed.

Preston grasped tightly the tote bag with its high-tech gun within. He smiled thinly.

Irina, though, sat right next to Preston and bounced playfully on the seat which was already rocking to the train's accelerated motion. She kept her bright blue eyes fixated upon him even though he was supposed to be a "ghost" to her in some way. He began to feel considerably uneasy.

Yuri Kreutin removed his coat, still wearing his red tunic underneath, and stashed it along with his small traveling bag above them in the overhead rack.

Kreutin laughed, speaking to Preston. "Never mind my niece, friend. She is like all the young ones these days. She sees ghosts we are all trying to forget."

"No problem," Kitteridge muttered.

Lev Magin reached over and thumped his daughter on the head with a finger.

Irina tried to duck, but it didn't work.

"Behave yourself," Lev said. "Or we shall leave you out in the middle of nowhere and let real ghosts eat you."

Irina was in a playful mood and ignored her father. She rested her knee upon the tote bag and glared continuously at Preston.

Lev Magin made himself comfortable, letting his daughter unravel more of her mischief.

Her lack of propriety and seemingly uncontrollable innocence appeared to overflow in her. The little Russian said, "You look like a ghost to me. Are you?"

There was no fear in her eyes, just the simple conviction of her perceptions.

"I don't think so," Preston said, thinking faster than he thought he was capable of. "I guess it's the light in here."

He rolled his eyes upward, indicating the dim ceiling lamps, hoping that that would do.

When he saw that it wouldn't, he poked her gently in the stomach, forcing a smile from the blond-headed girl. "Do ghosts poke nosy little girls in the tummy? I don't think they do. Not where I come from."

The elderly matron, overdressed for the trip in an ornate black shawl and too much makeup, glanced disapprovingly at them. She returned to her crocheting.

But Irina did not take her eyes from him.

Yuri Kreutin turned up his sleeves, exposing sun-bronzed forearms and a scar or two. He said, "There was a sighting in our town today. Our Irina is busy thinking about ghosts now."

Preston, playing his part of the ignorant sojourner, quizzed the metal harvester before him. "A sighting?" he queried in a conversational tone.

Irina ignored her uncle's remark. "I saw a ghost last night in our kitchen!" she blurted out. She turned to her father for confirmation. "Ura saw him too, didn't he, Poppa!"

Lev Magin smiled, leaning his head back upon the upholstered rail couch. "Ura sees many things. I would not favor the intelligence of a dog. Particularly someone as stupid as Ura."

Yuri Kreutin laughed.

Breathing easier, Preston relaxed somewhat.

Sitting so close to the little girl, he could suddenly smell the soap Yelena Magin had used to scrub down her daughter. Irina's hair was a fine platinum color in the faint light of the compartment and seemed to Preston like the glow of moonlight from behind a cloud at night. It was an image he'd only read somewhere in the past, but it seemed to fit: she was a beautiful, healthy child.

Affably, Preston laughed. "I wish I had been in your kitchen last night," he told her. "At least my dinner would have been better there." He leaned close to the little Russian. "Choose your restaurants well the next time your father takes you to Centerville."

Yuri Kreutin, crow's-feet wrinkling happily at the corners of his eyes, laughed and pointed at Preston suddenly. "Carmen's Café, am I right? Third and Elm. It must be the one!"

"Right." Preston nodded. Sounded good to him.

But Lev Magin was a bit more sober-minded than his mildly quixotic brother-in-law. He turned to face Preston. "No, our ghost today was seen by one of our dairy farmers, Foma Zhvakunin. Several others reportedly saw it as well."

Probing them further, Preston said, "I hear that sightings are rare in the towns."

Yuri Kreutin shrugged. "It is the price we must pay in the fields. Soviet guilt."

Lev Magin looked serious, grim. Irina fiddled with the loose strap to Preston's tote bag.

Kreutin went on. He said, "The more of us come to harvest for the Great War, the more we see of them. They are truly everywhere. I am afraid that they do not like us here."

Lev turned to his in-law. "I, for one, do not believe in them. I have enough to worry about," and he bent over to pull Irina's busy hands away from Kitteridge's stolen bag. "Such as keeping a bratty daughter in line."

"Poppa!" Irina cried, but then she turned to Preston. "Mikhail is helping the Awakener fight the war!" She was very proud to say this.

"Mikhail—" Preston started.

Lev Magin smiled. "He is our son."

"Ah," Preston acknowledged.

Magin continued. "He turned sixteen last year and we decided to let him go assist the Awakener and his *mandali*."

Yuri Kreutin winked. "But only because he couldn't be tied to a wheat harvester. That boy's no idiot."

Irina, thinking her nine-year-old's thoughts, shifted gears in the conversation. She jumped in with, "I was born here in America. I am an American!"

Neither Lev nor Yuri Kreutin sought to contradict the blond-haired imp. Lev Magin considered Preston with an expression of abject fatherly helplessness. He shrugged.

Then Irina burst out with: "Where were *you* born?"

Preston's heart fell somewhere down around his feet. He paled visibly.

"Irina!" her father retorted, gently nudging her with his booted foot. "We do not implore strangers with such questions."

However, Preston had managed to come up with a response of a kind. He said, "I was born far away from here. But I, too, am an American."

The two adults across from him accepted the cryptic nature of his remarks and did not push the issue any further.

The friendly Kreutin asked, "What is your trade, may I ask?"

Preston felt a trifle more confident. He said, "I am a . . . farm supervisor. I am on my way to Missouri Landing to purchase some new equipment for the harvest." Knowing what he did about Yuri Kreutin, he said with a slight conspiratorial wink, "And I have some personal business to attend to."

Kreutin laughed. Irina looked at them both, quite puzzled.

Kreutin said, "I've often thought that the women of Centerville looked like potatoes."

Irina scrunched her face up at her foolish uncle. "Potatoes!" she said. "Uncle Yuri!"

Then Kreutin said, "No offense, mind you."

Preston held up a hand and laughed. "The truth should be told more often."

The adult men laughed heartily.

But Irina kept staring at him.

Preston, in one swift motion, looked at her quickly and leaned down, saying, "*Boo!*"

The little blond Russian jerked back in her seat to the laughter of the men in her family. She managed an embarrassed, if penitent, smile.

But Preston recognized that he was going to have to be much more careful. Evidently the little Russian was capable of seeing something having to do with the m-field's interaction with the real, corporeal world. Apparently the adult Russians did not possess this ability.

Was there something currently happening to the m-field process itself? Morphogenetic fields were simply not visible in the material world, and as far as he could tell, the Russians did not have the slightest technological means to sense morphogenetic fields anywhere.

He suddenly began to regret temporarily switching off communications with the Meadow. This was information which might be of value to them, for its implications were many. If the adult Russians didn't have mechanical means of detecting m-fields, what was it that allowed perky little Irina to do so? Was there some slight alteration in the child's genes which allowed her perceptions to transcend the ordinary? Recalling Jay's easy acceptance in the tavern by the Russian farmers and ranch hands, Preston suddenly realized that it was possible that the adults were unable to see what their children could. The ghosts of the American dead would be both real to the children and imagined to the adults, thus affecting their whole culture down to the deepest levels.

Though he found the little Russian cute and likable, Preston knew that he was going to have to treat her with care. She possessed the same talents as six-year-old Barrie Ressler, and that could only mean trouble.

Lev and Yuri spoke idly to each other, but in voices loud enough to include Preston in the conversation. The rocking motion of the train added a sleepy backdrop to their gossip.

"The Mayor told me only last month," Kreutin began, "that should more ghosts appear we will have to move Anytown itself. We cannot harvest where the ghosts do not let us."

"I can," Irina chirped. "I am not afraid of ghosts!"

Were these a superstitious people talking metaphorically, or were they speaking literally? Preston couldn't tell, even though he knew Yuri Kreutin was a practical man and would not speak lightly of such things. Unless it had to do with women . . .

Lev Magin took on an air of a crafty old man as he looked at his impetuous young daughter. "It is true that ghosts cannot harm anyone. But I hear that a hundred—"

"Or a million!" Yuri Kreutin interjected.

Irina's eyes widened.

"Well . . ." The father waved it off. "There's no way of telling what a *million* ghosts can do."

Irina teetered on the edge of her seat.

"Then we would have to return to our cubbies in Barents City," Lev said with a theatrical sigh meant only for his gullible daughter. "Unfortunately, though, it is impossible to harvest wheat under the sea."

"That is correct," Yuri Kreutin teased. "You would have to harvest green yucky kelp. And smelly tuna fishes!"

Little Irina brooded, crossing her arms defiantly. She sat back with profound resolve. "I'm not afraid of any ghosts!" she said, scowling. The men laughed.

Preston, like a sponge, took it all in, recalling the photographs on the Magins' mantelpiece of a vast undersea complex. *Barents City? Cubbies?* Could cubbies be something like the 'combs down in the Hive? Cubbyholes full of sleeping Soviet technicians?

There must have been—*or must be*—dozens of such cities around the globe, he realized. For no single city in a thirty- or fifty-year span of time could yield up so many Russians as there were in Anytown. Centerville sounded as if it were about the same size. And Missouri Landing sounded even larger than that.

But clearly Barents City was the largest of the havens. It was barely possible that one such underwater city could reseed the world, perhaps doing so through automatics as the rest of the survivors of the War slept on elsewhere. But where?

He mentally kicked himself. He should have been funneling this information down to the Meadow, but it was too late to manipulate the controls at his m-field belt. He didn't want to give his traveling companions the slightest indication that he was another ghost. At least not yet.

Suddenly the interior coach lights went out and little Irina jumped up with alarm.

The elderly matron across the aisle gasped, dropping her crocheting needles. The farm couple behind them were also just as startled.

Preston glanced around. "What happened?" he asked.

Irina sat rigidly as the compartment went entirely dark as night closed in from the outside. The train, however, did not slacken speed.

"Poppa?" the little girl cried out.

"It is nothing, child," Lev Magin said. But little Irina—as brave and as smart as she was for a nine-year-old—rose and crawled into her father's lap.

"It is the ghosts," Yuri Kreutin volunteered.

He reached to undo the lock which Preston had noticed shuttered each window.

The lock easily snapped loose and Kreutin lifted the shade, as did the farming couple down the aisle. Even the elderly woman had the courage to lift her own shade.

Privately, Preston had speculated what the rest of the Kansas landscape might have looked like beyond Anytown, and now was his chance to see. The night sky, however, had enshrouded it with a musky blackness. There was no moon yet and high thin clouds washed the stars, casting down little illumination.

But much to his surprise, off in the immeasurable distance, there were a few lights.

"*Prevedenir*—" cried little Irina, huddling on her father's lap.

"Shh!" Lev Magin hushed. "Do not speak of them that way," he admonished, but there was no bite to his words. He was just as enthralled as his daughter.

But Yuri Kreutin, a man of great courage and curiosity about the world, pointed out the window. "There. You can see them."

Preston leaned close to the glass. If there were ruins left over from the War, he could not see them at all. It was just too dark. He knew that for the most part this would be nothing more than Kansas farmland. However, he also knew that there would be a scattering of small towns and principalities, and in the daytime their ruins would be clearly visible.

"Ghosts," Irina whispered.

Out in the countryside, beyond the train, Preston could make out greenish pinpricks of light decorating the horizon. None of them appeared too close to the iron trail which bore the Soviet engine; however, some of the lights did appear to be brighter than the others.

"Incredible," Preston breathed, wishing for one of the Rover's video units and a telephoto lens.

At least he now knew that the adults—as well as the children—were seeing *something* out in the countryside.

They were not the kind of lights, though, that one might have witnessed while crossing the Kansas plains at night in old America. Their geenish luminescence was the color of dreams, and they winked in and out of sight as the train made its cautious way through groves of trees themselves made invisible by the night.

When the train did make a turn in the tracks, Preston could see that all of the lights of the locomotive had been extinguished, from the engine's cyclopean headlight to the lights of the cars between it and the dark caboose. A funeral train burrowing through the night.

It was as if the engineers up ahead did not want to disturb the greenish vapors hovering in the spectral distance.

Soon the engine rounded a particular corner in the countryside and the eerie lights danced from view. The ceiling bulbs in the passenger compartment, however, did not come back on. The train continued to forge through the quiet Kansas fields in complete darkness.

What those lights were, Kitteridge had no idea. They certainly were not ghosts in any sense he had known of. What literature of the twentieth and twenty-first centuries survived on the subject suggested that the sighting of a real ghost—in a haunted house or mansion—was of a different order from what they had just witnessed.

Those lights beyond the train were indescribable, beyond anything in his experience. They were too large, as seen from their distance, to be individual spectres.

But what *were* they?"

Whatever they were, they were real enough to startle the Russian passengers. They were also sufficiently alarming to compel the engineers up front to shut down all illumination on board the locomotive. Preston noticed how the shutters in the windows seemed to be made of a reinforced plastic, perhaps with a metal alloy of some kind molded within it. And the very train itself, he suddenly realized, moved with the sluggishness more commonly associated with heavy radiation shielding.

Could the ghosts in the distance be related to radioactive ruins? If so, then the Russians might have some real-world grounding for their superstitions.

As he observed little Irina fade away into the corridor of sleep in her father's lap, Preston realized that for conquerors these people had not quite inherited the fields of heaven.

Theirs was a world full of real terrors and nightmares. And only the train's thick shielding seemed to protect them as they rattled through the wraithful night toward the faraway security of Missouri Landing.

# 13

The long day and even longer night had nearly been too much for Dr. Wainwright. Somewhere high above the Meadow, and quite far away, Preston was being swept along with the Russians off toward Missouri Landing. The further the boy got from the epicenter of the Meadow in the wheat field, the lonelier Travis got, feeling as he did the anguish most parents felt for their children when it was time for them to go away and make on their own in the world.

This was a little different; but he felt the same about the two Kitteridge boys as he did about his own children.

It was with that sense of grief that greeted him when he awoke from a night of fitful sleep. For he too had seen some Wandering in his family. Though his wife had died of natural causes several years ago, his two sons had long since vanished out onto the preternatural m-field which sustained their world. There was just too much darkness in their lives.

And now, as the bioluminescent pods of a glow-plant filled his Ark apartment with a dim morning light, he felt as if he could no longer stand the leave-taking. Wandering was one thing, leave-taking another.

Wandering was where the body actually left the secure confines of Duende Meadow; leave-taking was when the mind and soul began to leave. Its signs were harder to discern—on the outside—but they definitely could be felt by those whom it affected.

He felt it now. During the night, as the Hive personnel continued to monitor Preston's journey eastward, Dr. Wainwright was forced to leave the War Room because he'd begun to feel his own ghostly spirit dissolve in his chest. It was just too much of a burden to bear. Without Preston, he could not fight as he should.

He managed a disconsolate shower from the waterspouts of the gene-altered mist plant, and while he normally would have savored its accompanying perfumes and fragrances, this morning he could not. Even a mist plant was foreign to him now, an artificial creation of their artificial lives.

*Was this old age?* he wondered. Toweling his thick shock of white hair, he stepped from the bathroom out into the living-room area. Was old age the slow leave-taking of the soul? The abandonment of hope? The loss of interest in life?

Perhaps that was why Jay always seemed so young, so childlike. He refused to grow old. Preston, on the other hand, was already beginning to show signs of physical aging: bags of responsibility could sometimes be seen beneath his eyes in times of stress, and there were even a few wisps of gray already appearing in his hair.

Sometimes even the *duende* children of the Meadow seemed older than their years would belie. Perhaps that was their curse as surviving *duendes*, their burden. Many great religions of mankind's past had been based solely on the guilt that man was supposed to feel for merely being his limited self—as if he was somehow supposed to aspire to more and was now to be punished forever because he had failed. All of the *duendes* had felt it in one way or another, and their six-hundred-year history spoke of the revolts, tyrannies, and harsh adjustments they had to impose upon themselves because of the weight of so much guilt. They did not need a Nemesis; they had themselves.

Travis heard noises coming from the kitchen. At first he thought that the Hive personnel were already in the process of "bugging" the Ark Appleseeds and that some military technician or centurion was presently bungling his job. It was rather early yet. Most of the Appleseeds in Saxifrage were still asleep.

However, upon stepping into the kitchen he saw two cats up on the countertop helping themselves to plastic containers of ersatz fish meat which they had removed from his bachelor's refrigerator.

"Cats," Dr. Wainwright called out.

Ike and Tina looked up at the portly Appleseed and their tails wagged with excitement.

"Hi!" Tina trilled. "We're hungry!"

Ike, a gray tabby, looked up with something of a devilish smile, then went back to his deft manipulation of the plastic box's lid.

"Our true innocents," Travis said as Tina rubbed up against his belly as he moved up to the counter. "Here. Let me help."

He fed the cats and looked around the kitchen area to see how they had gotten in.

A ventilator grille had been delicately removed from a bustle of leafy kudzu just above the hallway entrance. Ike was wearing a small sling-pouch, and Dr. Wainwright could see four narrow screws contained within.

Distantly he wondered just how Preston's strange cats would do on the outside. Would they survive well? Would they breed true? In fact, would *any* of them survive? The Hive personnel were acting as if six hundred years—and so much planetary devastation—had not changed a thing. Was mankind going to have to change physically—as had the cats—in order to adjust to a new world? Jay had often insisted that the military lobotomize themselves, but that was taking their solution too far.

He didn't know what the solution was. All he knew at the moment was that he needed coffee—and more time to think.

The com-link from the Ark computer center chimed and Dr. Wainwright rose from his breakfast. Instantly he thought of Preston.

"Yes?" he answered, feeling quite nervous now.

"It's Lee, Dr. Wainwright. Sorry to bother you so soon," the man at the other end said. Lee Williams was their head integrator. He oversaw all of the computer interfaces between the Arks and the Hive. So many experiments were continually being done that someone was needed to make sure that all the data did not become lost or scrambled in the process.

"What is it, Lee?"

"Have you authorized any blackouts between the Hive and the Ark?" The silence which passed over the com-link was ominous.

"No," he told the integrator. "Not at all. Why?"

"Well," Williams began, "I came in this morning and found a total shutdown. I called Stu Hagerty and instead got one of Colonel Chaney's adjuncts. He said that I wasn't authorized even to ask, let alone get any kind of answer. Do you know about this?"

Travis was silent for several seconds. Preston's cats were already climbing back up the kudzu braids toward the ventilator shaft.

"This is news to me," Dr. Wainwright told him.

"In fact," Lee continued, "they seem to be doing everything they can to separate themselves from the Mall. All of the power leads are being switched over to their own generator."

"They've done that before," Travis found himself saying, and hating himself for covering up for the Hive's clandestine activities. "Perhaps they're just running a systems check while everyone's asleep."

For a moment that seemed to placate the Ark integrator. Then Williams said, "I don't know, Travis. Not right after the Bacchanalia. It just seems funny to me, that's all. I thought you'd want to know."

"Thanks, Lee," Travis said. "I'll look into it and get back to you."

He switched off as the ventilator above the hallway rattled with activity as Ike replaced the grille, tightening the screws.

Dr. Wainwright didn't like what was happening. Even without plugging into the ubiquitous kudzu he could feel that something was wrong.

He dressed quickly and stepped out into the Mall. The day-globes had already come up to their full luminescence. Night, for the *duendes*, was a standard eleven-hour period of a vast dimming of the Meadow's light sources. However, at this particular hour, no one was normally about. It was just too early, even for the day after the Bacchanalia, which was a holiday for them anyway.

A small creek flowed down the lower Mall of Saxifrage, and it was the only sound Travis could hear as he took the elevator down from the Ark condominiums. Waterfalls and fountains were plentiful throughout the long former shopping center, and it was perhaps the only natural phenomenon they had to remind them of what life was like topside. He began the hike to the Hive.

That was when he found the centurions. These were not the Busch brothers, but other individuals enlisted from 'combs supervisory personnel.

They were struggling with Holly Ressler's father, Hugh, a man in his forties, still quite athletic and strong.

"What's going on here?" Dr. Wainwright demanded of the uniformed centurions. They bore their stingers and their badges—and considerable authority.

The first centurion said, "We've orders to keep the concourse clear." His blue eyes seemed harsh in their sternness.

"Travis!" shouted Hugh Ressler. "I want to see Sebastian Monaco and they're not letting me through."

"The concourse is to be cleared," the other centurion maintained firmly. "Those are the Colonel's orders. No one passes."

Dr. Wainwright separated the angry Hugh Ressler from the two centurions. Hugh, a former wrestler in his youth, could easily topple the young Hive officers. However, Dr. Ressler was also one of the Ark system's more respected scientists and was clearly indignant that he would have to resort to physically scuffling with anyone, let alone two centurions.

"First things first," Travis said. "Maybe I can help." He held Hugh's thick arm, calming him.

"Holly's upset because of what Monaco did last night!" Hugh said loudly.

"What did he do?"

"He tried to rape her!"

The centurions were indifferent, holding their positions. Lights in the Hive were burning brightly across the concourse behind the police officers.

"What?" Travis said, surprised. "Are you sure?"

"You're goddamn right, I'm sure!" Hugh said blackly. "Barrie called us from Holly's apartment when Monaco locked her in her room. Holly spoke with him for a while, but then things started happening."

"When did this—" Dr. Wainwright started.

"It went on all night," Ressler stated. "He only left a half-hour ago and Holly called Peggy and me just now."

Dr. Wainwright turned to the centurions. "This is a pretty serious charge, gentlemen."

"No one passes," the first centurion said. They both had their stingers out and were clearly ready to use them.

"I'm tired of Monaco coming around. I don't like him and he scares Barrie," Hugh Ressler insisted. "Holly hasn't the slightest interest in him at all."

"He *is* one of us, Hugh," Dr. Wainwright said, trying to be diplomatic. "But perhaps I can talk to the Colonel. He'll listen."

"Sebastian Monaco," Hugh began, "doesn't listen to anybody, not even the Colonel."

"I'll see what I can do," he said. "Go on back and take care of your girls. If they're all alone in their apartment they might be scared."

Hugh had simmered down somewhat, staring defiantly at the two somber centurions. "We have laws, you know. Monaco might not be used to them, but he's got to obey whether or not he wants to!"

"Okay, Hugh," Travis said. "I'll look into it."

"You two are next!" Hugh Ressler shouted at the centurions as a parting shot. He stalked back into the Mall proper, kicking angrily through the kudzu that dipped into the creek.

The centurions let him by on authority from the Colonel, who was already up and about deep within the Hive.

Striding across the concourse, out where the creek ended in a pebbled depression which recirculated the water back underneath the Mall, he came across several technicians— more Hive personnel—who were fussing about the kudzu.

They were examining the Meadow locks beneath the leafy fronds.

The locks, which had been placed in position six centuries ago, linked the Hive administration buildings and Saxifrage Mall into a stable unit. Indeed, over the years, so many plumbing and electrical conduits had been laid underneath the Meadow that the Hive and the Mall with its Arks had seemed to be an organic whole.

Only now, as the technicians pored over the kudzu, locating the locks, did Dr. Wainwright realize how wrong they all had been: Military paranoia simply did not jibe with Appleseed thinking.

"What are you doing here?" he demanded of the technicians.

One man looked up. He had a headset around his ears

which led to a peculiar metal detector. The flat circular plate
of the device hovered over a spot in the thick kudzu where
they believed one of the many Meadow locks to lie.

"Orders, Dr. Wainwright," the man said.

"*Whose* orders?"

"The Colonel's," he returned. "And Lieutenant Monaco's."

They went back to their hunting. They weren't centurions, but even so, he didn't have the authority to make them
stop. Why they were probing for the Meadow locks he didn't
know. There were several centuries of decay and dirt around
this part of the concourse, and there was no real need to
disturb anything.

Dr. Wainwright approached the administration building
and was met by more centurions. This time, the Busch brothers were among them, wide-awake and prepared to follow the
Colonel's orders.

The glare of activity from the east end of the Hive
indicated that something was going on within the Armory and
quite possibly down in the 'combs.

Dr. Wainwright noticed this, and began to head in that
direction, avoiding the main entrance to the Hive altogether.

Centurion Brian Busch prevented him, rushing over.
"Sorry, Dr. Wainwright. Off limits."

Dr. Wainwright pointed toward the Armory windows.
"Don't be absurd," he said. "I can go anywhere I want. I've
got the clearance."

He shouldn't have had to say it. He was a co-ruler of the
Meadow, and he could go anywhere his duties required.

"The Colonel says to send you up to the War Room,"
Clark Busch said from beneath his shiny helmet. "Everywhere else is off limits to all Appleseeds. No exceptions."

"Well, I'll see about this," he said to the centurions,
stepping around them.

The Hive was crawling with military personnel, and had
apparently been churning with activity all night long. Furniture had been moved, walls had been taken down, even
newer uniforms had been put on by many of the militarists.

Travis bolted into the War Room and clearly the same
kind of frenetic preparation had made its effect here as well.

"What's going on?" he demanded of Colonel Chaney,
who now wore his full fighting fatigues, which included a
military pistol on his hip.

The Colonel, though, was surprised to see him—as was

Second Lieutenant Sebastian Monaco. Monaco had the look of a man who'd been up all night baying at the moon. Especially the moon over Holly Ressler's house.

The Colonel quickly stood up from the computer printout which was coiling from the word-processor unit.

"Travis," he began. "We decided to make some changes while you were asleep."

"I don't understand," he started. "We were to wait until Preston's made his final report."

Monaco, suppressing his frustration, snapped, "We're done with Kitteridge. We've got all the information we need."

Dr. Wainwright stared around him as personnel came and went. Many of the men were now sporting rifles about their shoulders.

One technician came in from the Armory wearing protective clothing and goggles. He carried with him a sheaf of papers. He ignored Dr. Wainwright's presence there, or had perhaps simply not seen him.

The technician said to the Colonel, "We've prepared the troops with wolfsbane, as you ordered sir. It'll certainly save on bullets."

"What?" Dr. Wainwright stammered.

Sebastian Monaco held him back with a strong, forceful arm. "We're taking matters in our own hands. We've begun arming the troops with aconitine-nitrate shells. We're going to have to sneak up on the Russians since we don't know about their communications yet."

Dr. Wainwright staggered against the console. "You can't do this. It goes against the original Resurrection charter!"

The Colonel recovered from his shame at being caught with blood on his hands at engineering a military coup. He said, "Look, Wainwright. It's got to be done. Those people are shipping out nuclear material for making bombs. They've got wars in Africa and Indonesia. We know this for a fact. And we're the only ones who can stop them."

"We've gone over this before," Dr. Wainwright claimed. He indicated the technician who'd just come from the Armory. "And the use of the toxins is entirely prohibited except in times of extreme emergency. Wolfsbane is very, very powerful."

"This *is* an emergency," Monaco asserted. "And we're going to use everything we have. That includes wolfsbane and BZ."

Dr. Wainwright looked around. He reached for the com-link which would connect him to Lee Williams in the Ark computer room. "We should notify all of the Ark supervisors immediately. You can't do this without their approval."

But Monaco was quick to stop him. "All lines are severed, Wainwright. We don't need anyone's approval for this. Not even yours."

Dr. Wainwright stared at Colonel Chaney—a man he thought he knew. "Colonel, how can you let him talk you into this?" he beseeched. "It's *all* wrong! Wolfsbane and BZ are the two most potent chemical agents we've got. We need skilled personnel to deliver them, and your men aren't capable of doing that."

Monaco jumped on him just then. "*Our* men? What about your men? Jay Kitteridge's *gone*. And Preston is off on some joyride to the Missouri River. Those knuckleheads can't do anything right! We've got a crisis on our hands, in case you haven't noticed yet."

"But this is crazy!" he found himself shouting. "We don't know how many of them there are!"

"They've got cities scattered all throughout this part of Kansas and Oklahoma," the Colonel said, his dark eyes glowing indignantly. "It's time someone put a stop to them once and for all."

Travis stammered. He was shaking violently now even though no one had physically assaulted him. He said, "Colonel, that's not what I meant. We don't know how many Russians there are because we don't know how many survived. We can't eliminate them as if they were vermin. We might need them someday."

"Bullshit," Sebastian Monaco said, standing before him. "The Russians always were paranoid. They couldn't stand the notion that there was someone as powerful as them in the world."

Wainwright's head began to swirl. *How to argue with these people?* Everything was falling around him. . . .

Slowly he tried to convince them. "The ancient Russians lived on a continent that was almost totally flat. They saw wave after wave of invaders, including Napoleon and Hitler."

"So?" Monaco asked.

"So, those were the ancient Soviets. These people might be different."

"*Might be, might be,*" interrupted the Colonel. "We

know what might be and what already is, Wainwright. Every last Russian dies."

"No," Dr. Wainwright said, trying to keep his voice steady. "We might *need* them. You don't understand. We might need their gene-pool. They're a hearty people—"

"And they eat hearty, too," Monaco said. "Remember that family chowing down on food from our country up there."

Dr. Wainwright found a chair and fell into it. He could feel his pulse quicken and already he was going crimson in his cheeks and neck. His arm had begun hurting. He clutched it to him.

"Can't you see? That was six hundred and nineteen years ago. A long time in human history—"

"We're goddamn lucky to even *have* a history anymore, Wainwright!" Sebastian Monaco said, standing above him, virtually throwing the words at him. "I consider myself damn fortunate to be alive with the hope of seeing daylight once again. I'm not going to let anyone take that from me!"

"This is the only chance God's given us to start over again," the chief Appleseed said finally. "Our only chance."

"God has nothing to do with this," Monaco said.

"He never did," the Colonel said as he stood up against one of the computers. "God is just an excuse. Only men are responsible for their actions in the end."

"And God isn't going to help us with the Russians," Monaco told the botanist.

The Colonel could see the effect of their words on the Appleseed. He came over to Travis Wainwright. He said, "Only this time, we take care of the Russians piecemeal. One town at a time. We'll need your Appleseeds to help us establish our cities and towns, but eventually we'll get America back. Then we'll tackle Africa and the rest of the world."

Travis breathed heavily. "Man never changes. Only his circumstances."

Suddenly, from somewhere far underneath them in a dim recess of the Armory, they heard a dull roar.

Wainwright looked up at the Colonel. "What's that? What are you doing now? You aren't engaging the lift engines yet, are you?"

The horror was evident on his face: Had they blown the Meadow locks on the concourse already?

The Colonel smiled triumphantly. "No," he said. "Don't be stupid. It's just a test firing of one of our rocket engines."

"The missiles?"

"Just the engines," Monaco told him. "We're going to place a few spy satellites into orbit and track down this Awakener. That's what the toxins are for."

Dr. Wainwright felt a heavy weight place itself on his chest, and he closed his eyes.

But the weight didn't go away. The last thing he knew, he had slumped to the merciless tile of the War Room floor. Darkness pervaded everywhere. . . .

Jay Kitteridge had stopped when the moon got too dim to see and the sun looked so bright as to set his eyeballs on fire. Dawn had washed the world in a soft pink, but it had been the crystal horseshoe of the last quarter-moon which had drawn him further and further eastward.

"Now look at that!" Jay said enthusiastically to the Rover, which had not been programmed to respond. "What a *real* sunrise! A *real* sunrise! Preston ought to be here to see this."

The Rover ghosted invisibly to a halt in a broad, undefined meadow that was carpeted with a bristly sage. Birdsongs spirited into the morning air from hidden crannies on the prairie grass as the world filled with sunlight.

"But he's always too serious," he mumbled to himself. "Wouldn't appreciate it." He sighed heavily. "Still, it would do the boy a world of good." He patted the dashboard of the Rover. "Isn't that right, Rover?"

Jay had rerouted the Rover's computer capacities so that the Hive wouldn't be able to track him. In the process, he had brain-damaged some of its circuits. He would've enjoyed having the Rover talk back with him, but it was a necessary sacrifice.

Mist from a nearby river channel had drifted in over the low fields, though the river itself was miles away still. Assuming that the Rover's maps were accurate . . .

However, as he had learned during the night, the Rover's maps hardly described the terrain he'd been encountering. Hills and rises appeared where none were indicated; small rivers and creeks twined about the countryside where none had done so before. It didn't bother him one whit. He took everything in like a child turned loose in a toy shop.

Still, he remained in his *duende* form. It made travel easier in the Rover that way, and while he maintained the vehicle on the upper m-field of the earth's surface, he was able to take the best routes across the countryside.

The moon in its final stages had intrigued him. But what he was really waiting for was dawn. He wanted to see the country across which he was driving.

Now was his chance.

The low-lying mists weren't so thick that he couldn't discern what lay beneath them, and carefully he drew his Rover further to the east.

That was when he could clearly make out his first-ever ruins.

Kansas had been pulverized in the Last War. And following that, as their studies had always known, the continent had been significantly eroded by horrible storms and crushing ice sheets. The entire landscape had been changed.

He was genuinely astonished to find anything of the old world left standing in any condition.

However, as curious as he was, he did not draw too near to them.

Skeletons of buildings and other structures, highly eroded and decayed, lay beneath the soft green of some kind of clinging plant growth. A road, arched by an overpass, seemed to go nowhere, and Jay drew his invisible Rover underneath the ruin of the bridge.

The green leafy growth was nothing he'd seen before. It appeared to resemble the kudzu in its tenaciousness. But it was a denser growth, more like lichen or moss. It seemed to be in the process of slowly crushing whatever it surrounded. This included steel girders. The plant—clearly a mutated life of some indescribable sort—seemed to possess the ability to secrete strong acids which dissolved metals and glass. Perhaps even plastics. However, nowhere could he see smaller shards of debris, and this naturally would include discarded plastic.

Weren't the ancient Americans the masters of throwaway artifacts?

"Throwaway wives, throwaway lives . . ." he sang to himself as he drifted through the ruins.

But none of this he found tragic. Life went on. All of their holy books said this, although few people understood its true import. It was as an old Native American once said—an ancestor of Bill Laughing's?—Only the mountains and stars last forever.

*Indeed they do, indeed they do*, he thought to himself.

He looked around him. The ruins disappeared beneath the carpet of leafy green plant growth. He had thought that he'd reached Topeka, but the map showed him that he was some distance away.

The meager quality of the ruins made him wonder what might have been here that the nasty old Russians felt it necessary to flatten with a ten-kilo-ton warhead.

Or perhaps he actually was on the outskirts of Topeka, but time, wind, ice, and fluffy green plants had erased whatever had sprung into existence here.

"So where are the unicorn kingdoms?" he asked aloud. "Where the black empires full of mutants and dragons?" He pounded on the Rover's dashboard, rattling the lights. "Where, where, where!"

He laughed. There were no special kingdoms after the Last War. A certain kind of literature from the old world had survived with them down in the Meadow that suggested—in book after book after book—that not only would man survive, but also a kind of fantasyland where the rules of science would be held in abeyance. The true horrors of nuclear war were almost universally ignored, and history had shown, tragically, that those writers had been fools to believe that anything but the worst could happen.

Still, to find a unicorn wouldn't be half-bad, Jay thought to himself.

He did, however, find a dragon. Of sorts.

He had been noticing just how debris-free much of the terrain was, both within the small ruin he'd just passed through, and beyond it. No paper, no plastic, very little scrap metal was to be found anywhere.

Leaving the ruin, he came across a lichen-encrusted mound that seemed rather artificially constructed. He stopped the Rover and stepped out to examine it closer.

He opaqued out, just to make sure.

The mound definitely was a structure made of bits of metal and plastic, with daubs of paper and other flexibles used as a kind of mortar in the cracks.

A hole near the bottom flashed with movement, and Jay leaned over to look inside.

Suddenly a twelve-inch-long metal rod—sharpened at one end—came sailing out, followed by a crisp hiss of anger.

"*Whoa!*" Jay shouted, leaping back.

He drew out his assessor gun almost as an instinct. He'd abandoned his Russian farmer's clothes shortly after leaving Anytown the night before, and had donned his Appleseed tunic, with the assessor gunbelt as an afterthought.

Too bad it didn't work, he suddenly realized.

The creature which came out was something the size of an otter, but was definitely reptilian. It seemed to be a pebble-skinned salamander of some kind, and it worked its fingers in a peculiarly mammalian way. Those were fingers adapted for survival.

The creature, though, was not afraid of Jay. It merely did not want to be disturbed. It snarled at Jay as the *duende* backed off.

"I get the idea, little one," Jay said.

The creature eyed him warily and drew up another long spike. Something amber-colored dripped at its tip, and Jay suspected that it might have been a poison of some kind.

Jay stood up his full height as the creature's wide eyes stared at him.

"Top o' the mornin' to you!" he said loudly.

Then deopaqued.

For a moment the beast was thoroughly confused. It looked around briefly, finally coming out to see where Jay had vanished to. It even used the long steel spike as it jabbed the ground, perhaps thinking that a trapdoor had opened up and swallowed the biochemist.

Jay laughed at its antics.

However, the creature tired of this and withdrew to its hovel. A door of some kind was slid into place and that was that.

Jay returned to the Rover and ghosted away, happy that he hadn't spoiled the little one's morning. And equally happy that it hadn't spoiled *his* morning. He didn't know what that goo was on the tip of its spear, but he privately suspected that had it gouged into him, he probably wouldn't have had a lot of time to analyze it.

"Live and learn," he said.

The closer he got to the Missouri River—at least the place where he assumed it to be—the more he anticipated seeing bigger ruins. But these were not forthcoming.

He rechecked his Rover's map and compass.

Everything seemed to be in order. Perhaps he just wasn't

used to surface travel. Or perhaps he was just veering off in a wrong direction. Still, he persisted in his journeying.

An object on the horizon caught his attention and he turned the Rover toward it.

"Holy of holies," he muttered to himself. "What have we got here?"

Nothing lizardlike had built *this*.

It was a Soviet lander, but of a design he'd never seen in any of their files down in the Meadow. The thing was a bright, uneroded crimson, and squatted on legs that gave it an almost human appearance. A bright orange sickle and hammer was decaled on its side, and several gaping holes were in evidence at its base.

And underneath it was a virtual wilderness of wild wheat.

"An Appleseed," Jay suddenly recognized.

The ship had set down gently some time ago and dumped its cargo right upon the ground. Holes higher up its side might have been vents for birds—or insects or bees—to escape. Indeed, as he approached it in his ghostly Rover, several odd-looking ravens dove out of the upper reaches of the lander and scattered themselves across the countryside, presumably in search of breakfast.

Jay stopped his Rover and climbed out.

"Well, I'll be damned," he said, opaquing out.

The lander stood above him like a bronze conqueror, proud in its rule over so much solitude. The leafy green growth had begun its tortuous climb up the lander's sturdy legs, and Jay could now see just how long the iron leviathan had been sitting there. The wheat had proliferated, and drifted far and wide upon the wind. Its purpose had long since been served.

The Soviet lander stood before him as if it belonged there. And far in the distance to the north, Jay could see another machine just like it. Lone sentinels, they were the solitary reminders of the works of man.

"So?" Jay held his arms out questioningly. "What's the big deal?"

Then, almost as if in answer to his rhetorical question, a noise sounded directly behind him in some low-slung, moss-covered ruins. He spun around, his assessor gun out once more.

He did not pull the trigger—as if it would have done any good.

It didn't matter. He was scared stiff.

In the quiet ruins danced an occasional green wisp of spectral light. Several of them came into sight from wherever they had been hiding; then they vanished in the bright sunshine. Small sleek-furred rodents fled the ruins because of them.

Jay, following their apparent common sense, did the same.

# 14

The languorous journey to the place the Russians had called Missouri Landing took them all night. The powerful train engine dutifully bore its cargo along at a comfortable speed, but it never pushed itself beyond a mild twenty-five miles an hour, as if it had to tiptoe across the countryside, careful not to wake what might be sleeping there.

Preston tried to gauge the progress of the train, but the darkness—and the Russians' insistence that the dura-plastic shutters be kept down all night—made such evaluation difficult, if not impossible. The trip, if he recalled Kansas topography correctly, should not have taken them the whole night, but it had. Inwardly he suspected that the sluggishness of the journey had been due to the incursions of the *prevedenir*, the ghosts, in the distant ruins, rather than any particular difficulty in the land itself, such as broken highways in the way or small rivers which required fording on rickety, uncertain bridges.

Yet, the Russians were a brave lot, and while they had exhibited a great deal of emotion as they gazed at the distant lights on the horizon, they were also not foolhardy. It was still a dangerous world—all farmers live with nature's unpredictability—but these Russians filled their lives with equal proportions of courage and caution.

On the other hand, there was, to Preston, a certain indescribable ambience to their journey—and the Russians themselves—which suggested that there wasn't that much of a hurry anyway. It was in this fashion that Preston managed to get several hours of a restful sleep—so much so that when he awoke the next morning he almost felt transformed, so comfortable was he.

He rose to the rasping sound of the window shutters being automatically opened by some hidden command from elsewhere in the train. The other passengers in his particular car awoke as well.

Outside, a feather-light dawn mist had blanketed the gray fields. Preston could almost feel the closeness of the ancient Missouri River nearby, and he thrilled to the sensation. His very skin tingled. He almost felt like a child once more as his mother turned page after page of a new story-book: Each mile they traversed was another page, another chapter in the mystery unfolding before him.

However, as the Magins and Yuri Kreutin roused themselves from their night's sleep, Preston stared out the window. He noticed that there were no ruins to be seen from his side of the train. A large pasture of statuesque brown cattle passed by them unfenced and unbounded, and the creeks over which they rumbled on sturdy steel bridges thrived with green, unfettered life. But there were no ruins, no chemical spills, no "brown spots" of irradiated moonscapes. In fact, he could not even find a single melted-down high-tension-wire tower. And if there were the cement foundations of former houses or businesses falling into decay, he could not find them.

Even the fields themselves seemed altered by the wide stretch of time. Undulations in the landscape became small hills, and between some of those hills were clusters of autumn-washed trees that probably had not been there when America had been busy and industrious. He knew from his university studies that the entire Plains had once been covered with forests of a wide variety of trees, and that it had only been the advent of man that had caused them to disappear. Now, it was almost as if pre-Columbian America was returning. Preston was merely at a loss to explain *how*.

The train had begun to slow as they pressed through lands which were obviously in the process of being farmed. Most of the furrowed fields had been harvested, but off in the distance appeared farmhouses, barns, and the unusually massive grain silos similar to the ones he had come across just south of Anytown.

Then the train made a wide curve to the northeast, entering a long, flat area which possessed a colorful riot of maple trees and oaks. They plunged through them, sucking red and yellow hand-shaped leaves behind the train, much to the delight of little Irina, who crouched at the window anticipating their arrival.

Swinging out across the sleepy meadow, the train then passed three enormous objects which Kitteridge had not expected to see—but they accounted for the forests, the fields, and the Russians themselves.

They were landers. Russian space landers.

They stood in obvious ruin, almost like monuments. But they glistened in the morning dew and they made Preston gasp in absolute astonishment. They stood on spidery tripodal legs which appeared to be entwined with vines of one sort or another, and one space lander careened at an awkward angle. They each were forty feet high and were a bright, though rusty, crimson. Some of their paint had begun to flake, especially around the encrusted yellow initials that said CCCP.

There were no roads—dirt or asphalt—leading toward the abandoned landers that Preston could see, and the train quickly passed them by, as if they were to be forgotten or ignored.

*Arks*, Preston thought suddenly. They had been lobbed into orbit by diligent Russian scientists to be dropped back down into an injured biosphere long after the dust and ash of the nuclear winter subsided. He recalled how persistent the Soviets had been in the twenty-first century in maintaining their space platforms, some of which were in very high north orbit. Perhaps those rotting behemoths had come from one of those lofty platforms which NASA and the Pentagon had assumed to be full of Soviet technicians.

Now the truth was known.

But just when they had been brought back down, he might never know. But clearly all the life he had seen, from the pond scum in the creeks to the very trees hugging the railroad tracks out in the middle of nowhere, had come from each of those landers. The Russians may have themselves come from Hives—or "cubbies"—somewhere beneath the choppy waves of the Atlantic, but the life which was necessary for their total survival had been kept safely aloft in the high reaches of space.

\*     \*     \*

Missouri Landing, like Anytown, seemed to have been built as far away as possible from the desolate reminders of the nuclear holocaust. The train's whistle hooted sharply several times, announcing its arrival, and the engine pulled its gathering of cars into a train station which was already abustle with activity.

The community of Missouri Landing, much to Preston's surprise, was easily five times the size of Anytown. Even at eight o'clock in the morning, he couldn't imagine so many people being out and going about their chores—but there they were: farmers, ranchers, merchants, even wives and mothers doing their part.

The three congenial Russians invited him to accompany them to breakfast in a small café nearby which catered to a crowd of mostly rail passengers, with some farmers added here and there for relief. Yuri Kreutin, however, merely had coffee, and with a kiss for little Irina, he quickly disappeared into a crowd of shoppers, off on a mission of his own. But not before a fast shave in the café's restroom. Preston caught a mention of someone named Karla whom he had to "see" before he went about his real business in Missouri Landing. Irina said her uncle was silly.

Lev Magin finished his coffee after consuming a large platter of pancakes and eggs and crisp bacon. He looked up at Preston, who was relishing every single bite of his meal as if he were a connoisseur of exotic foods.

"And when do you expect to return to Centerville?" he asked as he set his coffee cup down.

Preston considered this for a moment. He then said, "If there is a train out today, I'll probably take it. I have a few things I have to do here in town, but I don't suspect that they'll take me too long."

Lev nodded, and didn't press him further.

His daughter, still in the midst of her syrupy pancakes, turned to Lev. "Can we stay for two or three days, Poppa? I want to stay here for a week!"

Lev frowned, but only slightly. "There is still much work for us to do at home. There is an afternoon train back to Anytown and we must be on it. Once I locate the part for the harvester and that ignition switch which I should have gotten long ago, we will have to return."

"Is Uncle Yuri coming with us?"

Lev managed a laugh and a wink. "Not unless he wants to walk home."

So Preston asked, "Just when is the train leaving?"

Lev Magin considered his watch. "Two-thirty, unless they've changed their regular schedule on us. Which I doubt. An empty freight train will head back south an hour before, but we don't want to be on that. We can wait the extra hour."

"I want to see a movie," little Irina sang.

"No movies," Lev countered. But his daughter smiled up at Preston as if somewhere in their day a movie might be forthcoming despite what her father said.

Preston hefted his secretive tote bag, preparing to leave the café. He had approximately six hours to investigate the entire town and he already knew from its size that it was going to be extremely difficult. He fumbled in his pocket for money, hoping that he had enough.

"I will meet you here for the return trip," Preston said. "If that's all right with you."

Lev lifted a hand in a friendly gesture. "We shall enjoy the pleasure of your company. And I hope that your business goes well in the Landing."

"I hope so too," Kitteridge confessed as he tugged out the money he had found hidden away in the baggage compartment.

Lev's eyes widened somewhat upon seeing the denominations.

Preston, though, missed this. He tossed down several crumpled bills. "Will this cover my share of breakfast?"

Little Irina's bright blue eyes widened with incredulousness. Lev Magin laughed. "Not unless you wish to buy breakfast for everyone here."

He reached over and separated a bill of apparently lesser denomination from the wad.

Preston blushed, discovering his *faux pas*.

Quickly, to cover up his blunder, he said, "I have no real use for money where I come from. This was all a gift."

As a *duende* he had no real experience with money; it had never crossed his hands. Meadow society traded each other's services in a more equitable manner, having long ago decided that money was the cause of more evils than they really wanted to contend with. He was going to have to watch himself. These people were quite familiar with the ancient American currencies, and they knew the difference between a hundred-dollar bill and a five-dollar bill. He should have looked more closely at the money when he had lifted it from the money box he'd found in the compartment. Indeed, as he thought about it, someone back there was going to be in for a slight disappointment when he found a portion of his savings had disappeared. Preston hadn't thought he'd taken so much.

Lev took up a five-dollar bill. He smiled wryly. "I did not realize that there was so much wealth in Centerville. But this will do."

Preston had never once in his life seen pictures of American money in their Meadow histories. He'd only known that the bills he'd found in the baggage compartment were American because of their writing. Looking closer, he discovered that he was in possession of over four hundred dollars—and some change.

He left the café, because of it, feeling like a criminal.

It was an unnerving sensation to be standing alone in a town inhabited by men and women and children of foreign ancestry. Yet, nowhere did Preston overhear a word of original Russian, and nowhere could he find anything of Russian manufacture.

And as much as he hated to do it, he had to deopaque back out, for there was just too much to see and learn, and there were too many places where he'd have to have access, where he would not normally be able to enter in his corporeal form. He longed to stay out with these people, but there was no way around it.

Preston found a nearby alley, making sure that no children were in the vicinity. He feared now that all of the younger generation of Russians had Irina's same intuitive abilities to sense a person in his m-field form. And he didn't want to be seen by anybody, let alone the children.

As soon as he deopaqued back into invisibility he attached the assessor gun to his m-field belt beneath his clothing. He also tried to raise the Meadow on his radio. He held the thin headset up to his mouth.

"Dr. Wainwright?" he called out in his pin-mike. "Is anyone there? Can you read me, over."

A very large house cat bearing stripes of orange and an iridescent purple rummaged through a garbage can and seemed not to know that a *duende* was close at hand. It made a great deal of noise.

"Is anyone down there listening? Hagerty? Are *you* there?" he called out.

But no one responded.

Had they given up on him as they had his brother? His last communication with the Meadow had been that previous evening. They all had understood that he was going to maintain some sort of contact with the *duendes* down in the War Room, but they also knew that Missouri Landing was at an unknown distance from them.

Something was wrong. All he got on the channel was the silence of static.

But then as soon as he began to assess his first Russian in the river town, he noticed that the readings on the gun appeared normal and that they were being broadcast normally down to the Meadow. The gun worked and the information was received, so he knew that there was some other reason for the communications blackout.

So he ghosted out into the streets of Missouri Landing and continued with his assessing.

The city, like Anytown to the west, was virtually brand-new. The wood of the buildings seemed newly hewn from trees near the river, and the cement of the sidewalks and streets seemed freshly laid down. There did not seem to be an idle Russian about anywhere, and everyone seemed to fill a niche, with work to do or someplace to be.

He picked up snippets of conversation here and there that spoke of concern for the progress of the Great War. He also heard reports of the true nature of this year's harvest. All quotas had exceeded their original estimates, and much more salvageable metal was coming in from the surrounding ruins.

Preston decided that he wanted to see the waters of the Missouri River before he continued to probe the depths of the city itself. Assessing every Russian he passed, he made his ghostly way to the docks. Even the pier seemed brand-new, and the river itself was a wondrous phenomenon. Preston sat down with his assessor gun in his lap and watched a giant paddle-wheeler churn down from the North. It was a boat unlike any he had ever seen from storybook annals of Mark Twain and Robert Fulton. Behind it trailed a barge loaded with bales of hay, bins of wheat, and neatly stacked lumber for wherever the boat was bound.

Citizens on the shore waved at the paddle-wheeler as it passed on by Missouri Landing.

Preston also noticed that the train tracks, for all intents and purposes, ended here at Missouri Landing. There was a special rail siding that led down to the dock, and at the dock hardy longshoremen stacked the crates and boxes and moved the metal ingots back and forth on electric dollies. Wizened cottonwood trees clustered at the water's edge, and some children playing hooky from school were fishing off behind the gnarled boles of the trees in the tall grass.

Preston surveyed all this as if in a daze. He assessed the Russians, feeding the information down into the Meadow, but he did this with complete indifference. The longer he found himself out in the sunshine with the corporeal Russians, the more he longed to join them. Whatever genetic damage or mutagenic drift might exist in these people, he couldn't tell. They seemed normal to him in every respect. In fact, they even seemed *American*.

What the leaders down in the Hive thought they were going to do with their new neighbors topside, he did not know. He only knew that there were many more of them than Colonel Chaney could possibly eliminate in a minor skirmish. He didn't even know if the militarists in the Hive, after six hundred years of purposelessness, would be able to mount any kind of offensive.

But for the obvious lack of military hardware in both Anytown and Missouri Landing, the fact still remained that the Soviets were industriously providing goods for the various wars transpiring on the opposite side of the globe. Something would still have to be done about that.

Returning into the town, he took a route which allowed him to assess a great many people. The readout on the assessor gun indicated that so far he had assessed over five thousand men, women, and children. He kept at a distance whenever he came near a schoolyard or a day-care center, but he was able to assess all the noisy little ones without any problem.

But around noon he found that he was getting tired of walking in and out of buildings, ghosting into the mundane— and surprisingly nonmilitary—affairs of the Russians of Missouri Landing. He wished his brother had been there to help him, or that he had the convenient services of a Rover to make the job a little less tiring. But his true exhaustion came from the simple cavalcade of visual data, the town itself.

However, he did find a library. And in it were the answers to many of his questions.

The Outcome Book down in the Meadow embraced dozens of scenarios which tried to describe how the physical geography of America would look once all of the dams which held back rivers and reservoirs had been demolished. They knew that inland waterways would be profoundly affected, as well as coastal cities, which would have seen vast increases—or decreases—of sea levels after the War.

He ghosted into the town library and found a very large wall map which had evidently been drawn from satellite photographs of quite recent vintage. What he saw shocked him.

Most of the northern hemisphere was uninhabited— despite the thousands of Russians in Kansas.

The greater part of the Soviet Union itself was swathed in a continent-wide frosting of ice. The Baltic Sea was an immense ice shelf and all of Scandinavia was lost beneath glaciers.

From what he could tell, there were only three major cities in Europe, none of which were associated with any city of the European past. England, because of the slight lowering of the sea level worldwide, was now connected with Europe by a land bridge. It, too, was a wilderness of blowing snow and ice.

Dashings of green upon the large map did indicate that forests now thrived throughout the continent, and Preston noticed that there were mighty rivers where rivers did not used to be. The Volga River in southern Russia was now an elongated inland sea; Volgograd had long since lost its radioactive ruins beneath its waves and was nowhere to be seen. If there were major roads or highways in southern Europe, they did not show themselves on the wall map.

The Mediterranean Sea was a mere lake, the Sahara strangely verdant with prairies and newly spread forests.

However, what attracted Preston's attention the most was a large red star beneath the ice shelf which covered the entire Barents Sea north of the Soviet Union deep in Arctic waters.

*Barents City.*

Posters flanking the large public library portrayed the underwater haven which had allowed for the Soviet survival. Asleep in their cubbies underneath the ocean as their landers orbited safely above the earth, they had waited out the devastation of World War Three. It was as simple as that.

And at the far end of the library, framed in a modest picture, was a full-length photograph of the Awakener, standing proudly in a baggy off-white undersea uniform, holding his helmet beneath one arm. He smiled quite compassionately, his mustache and bright, dancing eyes now ever-so-familiar to Preston. *The Awakener!*

Another map showed that America and Canada had also suffered beneath the icy scalpel of the nuclear winter and the Ice Age which had followed it. The Great Lakes had been reformed into a grotesque inland sea which had swallowed Chicago and Detroit: Michigan itself was a tiny island freckled with permanent ice. Hugh finger-lobes of glacial ice reached down from western Canada, clutching the peaks of the Rocky Mountains as far south as northern Mexico. California and the Oregon coast seemed free of ice sheets in the west.

Only the Midwest seemed empty of winter's presence. Smaller stars designated the landfall of the Soviet Arks; these were green in color. The towns were tiny golden stars on the map, and Preston was surprised to find only five of these: Missouri Landing, Anytown, Centerville to the south, River City fifty miles upriver in Iowa somewhere, and Delta Town slightly upstream from the ruins of Baton Rouge to the far south. In fact, the tremendous erosional forces which had followed in the wake of the War had completely bloated the mighty Mississippi River. As such, it had thoroughly wiped out all of lower Louisiana. The Gulf itself reached deep into the state of Texas, and upon the map was a tiny isolated golden star which seemed to indicate that the Soviets had a fledgling colony there. It had no name.

To the east of the Mississippi River were no Russian colonies whatever. There were also no roads or highways linking any of the five established Russian cities; merely the railway line stitched itself between them. Except for the one in central Texas. It seemed all alone.

The Russians had conquered America—but not by much.

What remained of the country was ruled only by sage-brush, forest, and mountain-bound ice. And that was it.

He needed his Rover.

Torn with the desire to opaque out and rip all of the maps from the library wall, he had to fight his instinctive urge to gather all of the information he could. The genetic data going down to the Meadow via his assessor gun was one kind of information. But the library was a more valuable source.

Even as he assessed the old people in the library, he knew that it was the true center of the town. This was where their common history bound them, especially during the colder months of winter. These Russians were rugged souls, and Preston now realized that they must have been among those who had lived through the original migration to America from the underwater fortress of Barents City. These men, and perhaps even the bespectacled librarian, might have known the Awakener personally.

In his assessing of the town, after he had abandoned the library, Preston had noticed that there was no town jail. There hadn't been one in Anytown either. There was a county courthouse where matters of civil bureaucracy were being carried out, such as the issuing of licenses and marriage certificates. But there were no police of any kind—certainly nothing like centurions—to keep the populace in check. What traffic there was moved efficiently and courteously.

It was almost too good to be true.

Missouri Landing and Anytown seemed to defy what Preston knew from human nature. Here, perhaps for their own mutual survival, the Russian farmers had transcended petty disputes and arrogant behavior. How they had done this, Preston did not know. Had they made these seemingly godlike transformations biologically? Were their genes truly altered? What had the Awakener done to them?

He knew one thing for certain. Those were not the same kind of belligerent people, descendants or otherwise, which had once threatened the security of the United States and Europe. True, the original Russians were responsible for the destruction of three-fourths of the human population of the globe, but *these* folks were different.

Preston stood in the afternoon sun of Missouri Landing mesmerized—and exhausted—by all that he saw. He assessed everyone who passed him by, but he no longer went out of his way to cover the entire town. It was just too large and it would take him days or weeks to get those whom he had missed.

As two o'clock approached, Kitteridge began drifting back toward the busy rail depot. Since this was the railhead for the entire Russian line on the continent, the peculiar-looking train engine had been rotated around so that it could head back to the communities south and west of the Landing. Preston followed the chirping sounds of excited children as they were caught up in the excitement of watching the train revolve at the switching yards.

As he stood in their midst—apparently unseen by the new generation of Russian children—he continued to assess everyone he could. Behind him on the large main avenue of the town a thick and restless crowd of adults had formed. An electric touring car of twentieth-century styling was approaching the train station through the crowd, and the cheerful adults were waving at the people within the car. Preston turned and ghosted in its direction.

As he did, he found the Magins—minus Yuri Kreutin—exiting a nearby ice cream parlor. Irina gripped a mountainous double-decker ice cream cone in her hands and was less interested in the old-style touring limousine that was coming their way.

Lev Magin, however, craned his neck to see the individuals who were in the process of disembarking from the touring car.

"It's the *mandali!*" one Soviet woman cried out next to Preston's ethereal form.

The crowd of farmers and farmers' wives at the train station were very respectful and were not at all boisterous or pushy as they tried to capture a glimpse of the two newcomers.

The *mandali*, whoever they were, were so unlike the other Russians that Preston was absolutely taken aback by their appearances. As he assessed them and their driver, he watched as they spoke to the waiting crowd, touching several outstretched hands as they went among them.

One was a man who wore nothing but a white tunic of modest cotton weaves, and the other was an attractive woman of either Pakistani or Indian descent. She may have been a Hindu or a Muslim, and her dress was a rainbow of mostly reds and yellows. Her long hair flowed gracefully down her back.

*These*, Preston suddenly realized, *are not of the same stock as the Russians here.*

From what he had gleaned from the talk throughout the gathering of Russians at the train depot, these particular *mandali* were their provincial rulers, governing *in absentia* for the far-off Awakener. Apparently they had been out of town surveying the outskirts of Missouri Landing while Preston had been about his own duties assessing. But now the *mandali* had a train to catch, and the flock of Soviet well-wishers accompanied them to the depot.

Preston ghosted as close to the Magins as he dared, reminding himself of little Irina's uncanny ability to sense a *duende*'s m-field. The tumult of the crowd helped to distract her as the two *mandali* gained the wide depot platform and secured their tickets from the waiting stationmaster.

"She's pretty," Irina commented happily from above her ice cream cone.

"Her name is Mani," Lev said. "The gentleman is called Gadge. Wave at them."

"That's a funny name," Irina said distractedly.

"Shall I ask him what he thinks of the name 'Irina'?" her father challenged playfully.

Irina said nothing, sidling closer to her father in the tussle of reverential Russians. She continued to lick her multicolored cone.

The driver of the touring car, a burly Russian who ignored just about everyone around him, hefted the *mandali*'s bags up onto an oft-used luggage cart. A porter was about to draw it away toward the baggage car of the now-ready train, when Yuri Kreutin whistled and called out.

"Hey, boy! Not so fast!" he cried, rushing up onto the loading platform.

Kreutin was shouldering what looked like an old-world scuba tank on his back, except that a long snaking hose of spring-coiled black plastic with a flat nozzle was strapped to its side. He dropped the whole affair loudly upon the luggage dolly, the baggage underneath sagging with a sigh under its weight.

"Watch my foam, son," Kreutin said to the young Russian porter, unraveling a few bills for his trouble. "It cost me a lot and I don't want you to lose it—like you did the last time."

The boy blushed and looked down. "Yes, Yuri Kreutin." He took the bills and gingerly pushed the dolly toward the baggage car whose open doors and wooden plank waited for him.

Kreutin then saw the *mandali* getting their tickets and

he called out to them as if they were lifelong friends. Preston was thunderstruck at the man's extroversion.

Kreutin whistled loudly—almost obnoxiously. "Hey, Gadge!" Yuri cried out as Irina and her father made their way up through the milling crowd.

The handsome *mandali* officer, Gadge, turned with his ticket in the firm fingers of his hand. A look of pleasant surprise washed across his face as the exuberant Kreutin—dressed in his ever-present red tunic—rushed up to shake his hand.

"Thought I was going to miss you on this one!" Yuri said, greeting him.

Gadge's brown eyes sparkled. "Yuri Kreutin, you exhaust me sometimes. Good to see you again." He turned to Lev Magin, who had respectfully kept himself and his daughter aside. "And you, Lev. I am surprised to see you both here in the Landing."

Irina hugged close to her father as her ice cream cone began to melt. Mani, the beautiful female *mandali*, came over with her ticket. The train's whistle shrilled loudly and the conductor stepped along the platform and shouted out that it was time for everyone to climb on board.

Yuri said, "We had to come here on business, even though it is in the middle of the harvest."

Lev Margin held out a tightly wrapped package containing the gear he'd broken the day before in the crimson harvester. "A small part to a big machine is always the one that breaks first," he said with a congenial laugh.

"Isn't that the way it always is?" The male *mandali* laughed. "And you, Kreutin. Was your business to do with plutonium sweeping or had it to do with the fairer sex? I seem to recall someone in these parts. A Miss Karla Payno."

It was Yuri's turn to blush. He cleared his throat, and managed a laugh.

Lev Magin smiled stiffly, feeling complicitous, as if he had contributed to Yuri's delinquency in some way.

Then Gadge turned and looked down at the little blond Russian between them. He said, "And your business was with ice cream cones, I see."

Lev introduced his daughter to the *mandali*. "This little one is Irina. I've told you about her."

"Irina," said the woman, Mani. "That is a very nice name."

Irina looked back up at her father, wide-eyed and astonished. Lev tousled her hair.

On this particular train returning to the southwest, there were many more people. The conductor began helping the Russians on board, and Mani led little Irina toward their chosen car.

Lev said to Gadge, "We are waiting for a friend of ours. You go on ahead. We will find you."

Gadge stepped over to the train with the others as Preston bolted with panic.

"Nemesis!" he swore to himself.

He searched around for a place—any place—within which he'd be able to opaque back out. He had been so caught up in the excitement around the *mandali* that he had forgotten that he, too, was supposed to be on board the train in corporeal form. Otherwise, it would be a long overnight wait for another train back to Anytown.

Swiftly he ghosted through the walls of the ticket house, finding a closet within which to shift his m-field frequencies.

However, he had to abandon the assessor gun. He had left his tote bag in its *duende* form back in the alley in which he had originally returned to his ghostly state, and there wasn't any time now to try to find it. He'd done what he could anyhow.

With ticket in hand—a ticket lifted from the teller's cage—he ran out to where the two Russian brothers-in-law waited.

"Almost missed you!" Kitteridge breathed.

They guided him toward the rail car. Kreutin said, "And you almost missed the *mandali*."

"Are they traveling with us?" Preston asked, playing his part.

"They are indeed," Kreutin said happily.

"Unless Irina has pestered them into staying away from us," Lev then added with a smile.

Preston found himself laughing with them. But so far, no one had suspected a thing.

They found their proper compartment several cars back as the mighty engine pulled away from the station in the bright autumn afternoon. The *mandali* were taking their time making their way through the various cars of the train, speaking in turn to the other Russians on board. Preston didn't know if they were simply politicking or just simply interested in the lives of the people over whom they held jurisdiction. However, they seemed friendly enough.

Preston sat with Irina as Lev and Yuri fought with their assorted parcels, trying to get them in the overhead rack. Irina looked at Preston quizzically.

"Where's your bag?" she asked innocently.

Yuri and Lev found their seats, opening the dura-plastic shutters to view the train's daylight passage.

Preston turned bright red. "I . . . I had something to deliver in town. It was in the bag."

Irina nodded, seemingly content for the moment, but Preston knew that for someone capable of driving a harvester alone all day, there was a very wary adult deep within the little Russian.

Yuri and Lev, though, did not question him. As adults, they understood propriety and kept their business to themselves. They both knew, as little girls did not, that grown-up men sometimes had *other* concerns.

However, few people on the train were in the mood for much conversation once the train got under way. Preston found that he, too, was totally drained of energy and that his feet hurt from all his surveying. His mind fairly seethed with all the things he had seen and learned about their world. He was dog-tired.

The two adult Russians across from him were also tired, but each for differing reasons. Yuri Kreutin leaned back with a blissful smile, no doubt thinking of someone named Karla back in the suburban haunts of the Landing, and Lev seemed preoccupied with whatever maintenance chores awaited him on his harvester back home. In fact, he cradled the new metal gear in his lap as if it were a talisman. Irina, perpetually full of energy, watched the countryside go by, and when this bored her, turned to study the various other passengers on the train.

It was just when Preston was feeling comfortable in their midst that the *mandali* appeared at the other end of the car. They had apparently finished their tour, and Yuri Kreutin hailed them over.

The train, by then, had wended its way well into the Kansas country. Missouri Landing was half an hour behind them, and it was their last sign of human habitation. They were back coursing through the prairie wildernesses.

Preston had nearly fallen asleep in the train's gentle

rocking motion. He was getting tired of playing his role of the solitary traveler from Centerville.

The woman, Mani, with a friendly smile said to Preston, "I do not believe I have ever met you before."

All eyes fixed upon him.

He came wide-awake. She continued, "I had thought that I knew most everyone in the settlements. The Awakener has a great interest in everyone who serves him. What is your name again?"

Lev and Yuri looked at Kitteridge. All of their conversations had been conducted at a polite level and not once had Preston told them his name.

What should he do? Make one up? He'd read several pre-War Russian novels which they'd had in the Meadow library, but he was at a loss to recall any of the minor characters' names.

He said, "My name is Preston Kitteridge." It was all he could think of.

Mani, though, without faltering said, "That is an American name. I did not realize that they were taking on their new names in Centerville already."

Irina then looked at her father. "That was the name of the sighting in Gregor's tavern, Momma said."

Kitteridge could feel the sweat trickle nervously down the hollows of his spine. He very carefully inched his hand ever so slowly toward his m-field belt underneath his farmers' clothing. With just a flick of a finger up against it, he would be able to deopaque back into his *duende* form, but it would be at the cost of any element of surprise which the *duendes* down in the Meadow might ultimately have.

But little Irina's comment let it be known that all of the Russians—with the exception of the *mandali* who had been far away in Missouri Landing at the time—were all too aware of Jay Kitteridge's incursion into their quiet lives.

Everyone stared at Preston as if waiting for some kind of adequate response. They weren't hostile, merely interested.

That was when Preston received one of the greatest shocks of his life.

The *mandali* vanished.

Lev Magin jerked around violently as dust motes pushed by a gentle breeze rushed to fill in the spaces which the handsome proxy rulers had occupied.

Irina screamed as the other passengers in their particular rail car also vanished.

Only Lev and Yuri and Preston and Irina remained as the train itself, devoid of passengers and crew, ground to a halt.

The deep silence of the Kansas countryside came at them almost thunderously.

# 15

"Great heavens!" Yuri Kreutin burst out, rising in his plush seat, away from the window.

"Poppa!" cried little Irina, huddling near.

Lev Magin rose from the aisle and stared up and down the compartment like a surprised animal, not knowing what to think.

"What happened to them?" Lev asked, turning to his traveling companions.

"I've never seen anything like it," Kreutin said, stepping out into the wide, empty aisle.

Preston was just as astonished, and traded equal expressions of surprise and confusion with the Russians.

But little Irina was looking around the passenger car with a different gaze. Her eyes focused narrowly as if she were seeing into the hazy halls of dreams.

"Ghosts," she whimpered just then, her fist to her mouth. "Poppa, they're ghosts!"

Preston leapt out into the aisle, his own heart beating fiercely in his chest. *Ghosts? How could they be ghosts? Where did they go?*

Nothing whatever remained of any of the Soviet passengers. Even their overhead luggage had vanished somehow, leaving the rail car entirely barren. Kitteridge glanced out of the window, but he could see nothing in the countryside beyond that might somehow account for the disappearance of the Russians.

And what was he looking for?

He knew.

Members of the Hive and their modified B-10 Stealth bomber. Or one of the advanced Apache attack helicopters. Even centurions parachuting in from the skies . . .

And yet, that didn't make any sense despite the established nefariousness of the Hive personnel.

No one in the Meadow knew what he was going through. They had no way to track him; they had no visuals, no audio link. Their only true link was through the assessor gun, which was far too small to do any damage to anyone. And *it* was back in the station.

It certainly wasn't capable of something like this.

*Or was it?*

He swallowed hard, not wanting to admit to himself what his mind was concluding about their sudden situation.

"Let's check on the other compartments," Lev suggested, steering his daughter out into the aisle ahead of him.

"Right," Yuri Kreutin said grimly.

The train had brought itself to a halt in an area of gently rounded, humpbacked hills with a grassy meadow and a stream to their right and a copse of wind-chattering maples to their left. The train's engine still vibrated powerfully, its gears having been thrown into the idling position.

But other than the breeze in the autumn-tinged maples beyond, the only sound which they could hear came from the tremendous steam compressors beneath the engine a hundred yards out ahead of them.

Irina jumped and skittered after her father and her crimson-clad uncle. Preston quickly followed in pursuit, just as anxious as they were to find out what was happening to them.

At least they had forgotten that "Kitteridge" was the name of the ghost sighting back in the tavern in Anytown.

The three adults and one child plunged through the coupling section between their car and the one ahead of them. Piling into the fore compartment, they discovered—to their horror—that it was also empty.

It was almost as if no one had boarded the train in the first place.

There were no traveling cases, no bags of needlepoint, no games laid out on vacant seats for fidgety children to amuse themselves with. *Nothing*.

The train lay upon its silver tracks as if it were a stunned reptile of some kind, out in the wide reaches of nowhere, far from Missouri Landing on one hand and Anytown on the other.

They ran all the way to the engine, and as they did, little Irina clutched to her father.

"Poppa!" she persisted. "Can't you *see* them? They're here! They're all ghosts!"

Yuri Kreutin, without his usual humor, said, "There can't be any ghosts here, child. That's why they built the rail line in this part of the country."

Lev turned to him. "Well, Yuri, they had to go somewhere." He pondered his daughter's desperate expression. "You say you can see them?"

But evidently Irina's metaphysical abilities were not so certain. Perhaps her sudden fright had interfered.

She scanned the car in which they stood—the one directly behind the rumbling engine—and squinted.

She started to respond, then hesitated. She was suddenly unsure of herself, as if the ghosts had transcended their own unseen dimension. She looked at her father hopelessly.

Yuri found that the door which led to the large engine ahead of them was locked shut. He turned to them.

"It's a precaution," he informed them. "We're going to have to go around." He pointed to the outside of the train.

"Let's go," Lev said.

Preston followed as they slid aside the folding door and jumped down onto the crumbling asphalt stones of the rail bed. Lev helped his daughter down as Preston swung out behind her. They jogged toward the huge beast that was the train's magnificent engine.

Yuri Kreutin shouted up to the engineers in the driver's compartment, but no one responded.

"Damn!" he swore to himself. "I don't understand this at all!" And with that, he began to mount the rungs that led to the engineers' cranny. He cranked aside the door and pulled himself within.

Out in the open, with the wind in the maples to his back, Preston desperately yearned for a private space in which to call the Meadow. While he didn't have his assessor gun any longer, he did have his pin-mike radio strapped to his m-field belt.

But he wasn't in a position to sneak off; that would alarm the already alarmed Russians for sure.

He followed them up to the mammoth, rumbling engine, trying to expel from his mind what little Irina might have witnessed: Dozens of suddenly deopaqued Russian travelers, now trapped in the m-field which composed the train. If that's indeed what happened to them, then Preston knew that the Russians would be right there with them in full panic, crying out like the poltergeists they'd now become.

As they feared, the two engineers and other train personnel had all disappeared.

The engine itself had come to a halt when the chief engineer had vanished. His foot had been on the deadman's pedal, and when the foot's pressure had ceased, the pedal shut down the engine, as it was designed to do.

Everything else about the train's functions, though, was in normal working condition.

"What are we going to do now?" Preston asked the Russians, having followed them into the engineers' compartment. He had no experience whatsoever with trains. On the other hand, he had no experience with disappearing people, either.

Lev Magin began going over the controls with an expert eye. Before them were dials, pressure gauges and valves, and several computer screens which gave the engineers' compartment an unusually sophisticated character. Lev seemed familiar with much of what was before them.

"Irina and I can get this thing moving, I think." Magin nodded.

Irina was already perched upon one of the engineer's chairs.

Magin said to them, "But we've got to get word back to the Landing. They've got to know about this."

Preston volunteered: "Well, isn't there some communications equipment in the last car, the caboose?"

"There is," Yuri Kreutin acknowledged. "Good idea. I might be able to raise the authorities there. I might even be able to raise Anytown, if we're within range."

Then little Irina glanced over at her father, her face torn with adult worry. She said, "Is it the War, Poppa? Are they attacking us?"

Lev and Yuri traded looks with each other, wondering what to say to her that wouldn't frighten her.

Lev said, "The War is very far away, sweetheart. No one is attacking us."

She looked out of the front window plates. "Ghosts," was all she seemed able to say. Clearly, the child was riddled with fright.

Yuri pulled his cap down resolutely. "See if you can get the train going. There's no use in us staying out here. Night will fall soon and I don't want to be stranded alone with the . . . lights." He said this with a cautious glance at Irina. "I'll see if I can contact Missouri Landing."

Kreutin swung himself down the guardrail and landed outside in the black gravel of the asphalt. Preston heard him dash back down the line toward the communications caboose.

Lev Magin stepped over beside his daughter. He put an arm around her shoulders. "Do you know how to run something like this? How well did your instructors teach you?"

For a moment Preston thought that Lev was merely being fatherly, trying to comfort or distract his scared youngster with talk about school or her lessons. But when Irina examined the dials in front of her, Preston suddenly realized that Irina—like six-year-old Barrie Ressler down in the Meadow—was more than capable of running a machine as big as this.

And it would also act as therapy: It would get her mind off the ghosts she had seen created around her.

That instantly led Preston to consider the possibility that the *real* engineers might still be with them in the small compartment. He shuddered, realizing that the train was now genuinely haunted. There could be no other explanation.

Were the two engineers in their ghostly condition shouting out instructions, shouting for help? Or were they somehow drifting away helplessly in the surface m-field, confused and doomed?

Even worse, had some of them stepped down from the train and were now running around in panic? What would happen when they started up the engine and left?

What *was* going on?

Irina pointed to a particular pressure valve. "It says here that the forward containment gears have shut down. This valve opens it. Once we do that, we can go," she said solemnly, no longer the girl interested in movies and ice cream. "At least, I think we can," she concluded.

Lev nodded and smiled. He patted his bright child on her curly blond head. "That's right. They've taught you well."

Together, they made the proper adjustments, allowing Irina to lower her chair so that she could reach her feet to the deadman's pedal.

Lev was going to let her be the engineer.

Preston was not entirely out of place here. He located the radio intercom for the whole train, and he patched them in to Yuri Kreutin in the rear caboose.

"Kreutin?" Preston signaled into the microphone as Lev watched.

Steam hissed below them from the hydraulics.

"Yuri, can you read me?" Gears meshed and Preston managed a smile for the two Magins near to him. He said, "I wouldn't want to leave our friend out here with his lights."

Lev said, "We are fifty miles away from the Landing. It would be too far to walk before nightfall."

Irina moved her deft fingers over the controls as Lev assisted her. "I don't like the ghosts," she mumbled. "They're everywhere."

Preston continued to blush. He hoped that Lev Magin would not notice, hoped that Kreutin would reach the caboose and plug into the intercom.

Lev confessed in a low voice to him, "Our village has reported more sightings than usual. Our daughter here saw one only the night before and I must admit it is beginning to bother me."

"Ura saw him too," Irina stated, never taking her blue eyes from the dials as oil and steam pressure built up to their proper levels.

Lev, though, managed a smile at Kitteridge. "I do not know how it is in Centerville, but our children are quite peculiar. They see much that we do not."

But Irina was not looking at Preston now. He could almost feel his skin prickle with her fear of him. He was a stranger, and as such almost equal to a *prevedenir*, a Russian ghost.

Yet, he tried to radiate friendliness. There was nothing for them to fear from him.

He said, "I know a six-year-old girl who can drive an engine like this. She works on it every week when her mother and father let her. You would like her."

Irina smiled slightly, but chose to lose herself in her preparations.

Lev Magin, knowing only too well his daughter's ways, seemed embarrassed for her rudeness. He shrugged and smiled thinly. There was no hint of accusation here. They were all living in unusual times, and none of their lives were ordinary in any regard. Ghosts were everywhere; especially ghosts of the past.

Yuri Kreutin's voice suddenly sprouted from the intercom speaker. "Are you there? Does this thing work? *Hello*—"

Quickly Preston grabbed the mike. "We're here. Irina's almost ready to get us moving."

Lev leaned over the intercom mike. "I've been thinking. Should we move onward, toward home, or do you think we should return to the Landing? They might know more. What is your opinion?"

There was a moment filled with an unhealthy silence. The Yuri Kreutin's voice returned. He said, "There may not be anyone to return to in the Landing."

"What do you mean?" Lev asked.

Irina glanced sideways at them both.

"Yes," Preston blurted out. "What are you talking about?"

"I cannot raise them at all," Kreutin said. "The equipment is working, but I've just been signaling the Landing authorities and there is no response from anyone."

Lev looked grim. Irina turned away in her engineer's chair, hands on the controls, ready.

"Do you think that it's happened to them as well?" Magin had a difficult time voicing those words.

Kreutin returned with, "I do not know what to think. No one I know has any experience with something like this."

Preston considered Irina's father. The man was Jay's age, if perhaps slightly more affected by time and hard work in the fields which surrounded his home.

Preston said to him, "Lev, this may have happened to Anytown as well. We'd better not rule out any possibility. I think we should go onward."

"Momma!" Irina gasped. "What about Momma and Ura?"

A pang of sorrow soared through Preston's heart. Had he assessed Yelena?

He couldn't recall.

Obviously, he hadn't assessed the three other Russians

in his company. It had never occurred to him to do so. His mouth was suddenly dry. No, he then remembered. He hadn't assessed Yelena Magin.

He clenched his fists, suddenly thinking about Second Lieutenant Sebastian Monaco and his goddamn assessor gun. His gut instinct told him that Monaco was behind this. But how they had managed to deopaque so many Russians—and so far from the Meadow itself—was totally beyond him. He hadn't even known that such technology had existed down in the Hive.

Irina threw several switches at her father's nod, then began easing back on a single lever. Her foot held to the deadman's pedal and the massive hydraulics which propelled the engine engaged themselves. Slowly, ponderously the train moved out as Lev went over the dials, double-checking that they hadn't done something which might jeopardize the engine itself. They hadn't.

They were off.

Wind rushed at them as Irina increased the train's speed. Lev found a seat next to the opposite window as Preston crouched at the radio set, keeping in contact with Yuri Kreutin several cars behind them in the caboose.

He noticed that within half an hour Irina was accelerating the train to speeds they had not experienced the night previous. They were cruising at a hefty eighty-five miles per hour.

He looked over at Lev. Shouting above the wind and interior roar of the gigantic engine, he asked, "Why so fast? I thought that the train was supposed to go slow!"

Lev pointed out at the pastoral landscape beyond. "Only at night do the lights come out." His voice was loud and strong. "We go slow so as not to disturb them. They give us much trouble."

Then he gave Preston a quizzical look. Strands of brown hair tousled in the wind. He said, "You sound like a man who has never traveled much."

Irina was not looking at Preston. There was only so much she could handle, and the world of the grown-ups was not one of them.

"I have never traveled on a train before," Preston said truthfully. "My work has not required it until now."

Lev Magin eyed him suspiciously, but not so much that there was overt hostility in his voice. Out of curiosity he asked Preston, "Then how did you arrive at Centerville? Not many of us were born here, you know."

Preston's eyes could not lie. "A great number of my people were born here," he said.

"The ruins near Centerville are many," Magin then said. "The Awakener specifically has told us not to raise our children near them."

"There are ruins everywhere," Kitteridge then said, almost wistfully, wondering where his brother, Jay, was about now. Kansas City? Topeka? Further into Missouri? Or was he just Wandering the face of the earth?

Jay himself had once told him that everyone had his own burdens of karma, his own trials. So, too, had these Russians. Even Lev Magin. Preston could see just how difficult their lives truly were.

Magin then said, "The ruins act as reminders of the kind of people we once were. We wouldn't be here if it had not been for the Awakener."

Preston nodded, echoing the words his own brother had spoken the day before: "I would like to meet the Awakener someday."

"You would like him," Lev said.

"You've met him?"

Magin turned in his chair, the wind whistling everywhere about them. "Of course I've met him. He founded Anytown. He founded Centerville as well. Surely you know the many things he has done. All of the Soviets live because of him."

Preston faked a smile and nodded his head to indicate that he did indeed know of the Awakener's importance to them. There was little else he could do.

"Without him," Lev said, "we would not be in heaven right now."

The fields of heaven passed them by on either side as the train's speed neared ninety miles per hour under Irina's influence. In the distance, Preston thought he could see the melted forms of high-tension wires bending to the ground, weighted by time and erosion, but he couldn't be too sure. A ruined highway or two passed beneath the rail tracks, but weeds and trees grew in their midst, the concrete long since broken and crushed. He also tried to find those places along the horizon where he had witnessed the lights of the night

before. But there were no visible signs of civilization anywhere. All cities and towns had been obliterated by the War
and the horrible winter which had followed. He gave up looking for them entirely.

He did, though, see animals. Deer and some elk could
be seen browsing in the meadows which they passed. He also
thought he saw something that might have been a wild boar.
If it was, the beast was the size of a Bengal tiger, its long
tusks harking back to images of the Eocene.

But the land began to flatten out more as they approached the environs of Anytown. Yuri Kreutin was silent
far behind them in the caboose, but they knew that he was
busy trying to raise the authorities in Anytown.

Irina raced the engine toward her home. They had an
hour of daylight left to them as they drew near. Each one of
them could feel the excitement and the dread mounting
within as the fields and scattered forests became familiar to
them.

At this point, Lev wisely took the throttle away from his
daughter, carefully slipping onto the deadman's pedal as they
traded places.

He pointed to the west. "Look! There are the Smeryanski
silos! We're getting close now."

Preston and Irina glanced out of the window as several
very tall grain silos hovered distantly at the far horizon.
Kitteridge hadn't noticed them before, but suspected that
they were very close to Anytown. He knew now that none of
the Russian farmers lived too far away from the security of
town.

Lev began braking the train as they rounded a bend on
the horizon. Smaller outlying buildings of Anytown began to
heave into view.

Magin pressed the horn button and the cry of the train's
engine raced out ahead of them over the wheat fields.

Irina and Lev both began to throw switches, slowing
down the train. Hydraulics went into place as the brakes
were engaged. It was not an easy process, apparently, and
Preston marveled at their competence. It seemed that the
Awakener and his legions had trained these Russian farmers
well.

But something was wrong.

A bitter lump had formed in Preston's throat as he
watched the town come closer into view.

Brakes squealed and steam hissed as the engine pulled the rest of the train into the station.

There was no one there to greet them.

No trucks in the street.

No farmers around and about.

There was nothing but wind, which chased a tumbleweed across the main avenue.

The Russians of Anytown, USA, had vanished utterly.

# 16

"What is this?" Yuri Kreutin stammered as they all stood about the deserted railway platform of the Anytown train depot. "What's happened to everyone?"

There was a slight afternoon wind drifting through the empty town. A scrap of newspaper fluttered across the main street and off in the distance a dog barked, its voice forlorn in the vacant alleys.

Behind them at the station, idling thunderously and hissing pressurized steam, the train's engine waited. They could feel its impatient vibrations.

"I think we'd better find out," Preston said to them. "And fast."

He knew that his Rover was nearby, but he couldn't see it. If he could find a private space away from the Russians, he might be able to deopaque and reestablish communications with the Meadow. But at the moment he was feeling as if the problems of the Russians were very much his own. He felt betrayed by his own kind, forced to participate in something he opposed both emotionally and philosophically. He didn't even know if the Russians who had disappeared were still alive. While six hundred years of ghostly concealment deep within the earth's sea-level m-field had allowed their generators to circulate out enough oxygen-nitrogen mixture to keep them alive, no one had done any studies to show how much of it hovered topside. He hoped that there was enough surface atmosphere to sustain the newly deopaqued *duendes* of Missouri Landing so far away, because he had no idea how

194

long an individual could survive without an m-field belt at his
or her waist.

He couldn't forget the almost divine light in the eyes of
the *mandali* back on the train. Mani was not an evil woman,
nor was Gadge an evil man. They may have been provincial
governors, but they definitely were not part of the Soviet
military machine.

Nor were the Magins or Yuri Kreutin.

Preston bounded into the street and ran to the tavern,
which was the nearest establishment. He crashed through the
open door with Yuri Kreutin close by.

The two of them looked around frantically, allowing their
eyes to adjust to the sudden darkness within.

"Fyodor! Chevensky! Show yourselves!" Yuri Kreutin
called out.

Irina and Lev came up behind them. The tavern was as
empty as empty could be. Glass shone in an amber afternoon
light upon the bar, reflected from the open door. Card games
had been abandoned in progress. But the smoke from the
many cigars and pipes had long since dissipated, leaving
behind an acrid aroma which, to Preston, smelled of death.

Lev said, "It's the whole town. It's touched everything."

Then Irina looked up at her father. "What about Momma?
What's happened to Momma?"

"Let's hurry home," Lev Magin said, and they all stepped
from the deserted tavern.

Yuri Kreutin dashed back to the depot for his truck,
which he had left there the night before. He fired it up and
brought it around and Irina was helped inside by her father.
Preston rode on the running board on the passenger side.

Kreutin drove madly through the small streets and around
the tree-lined corners until they reached the farmhouse in
which the Magins lived. The strange dog, Ura, with his full
coat extended in fear, was there to greet them.

"Ura!" Little Irina pointed.

The dog barked as the truck rode up into the gravel
driveway and parked next to the giant crimson harvester.

Preston stepped down and Irina and Lev piled out of
their side of the vehicle. Yuri was out of his door and the
three adults bounded noisily up to the porch. Irina stayed
behind with Ura, who jumped at her with an almost furious
relief.

"Yelena!" Lev shouted, removing his cap.

Preston was right behind him.

The inner door to the Magin home suddenly flew open and out stepped centurion Brian Busch, in full Hive regalia, with a deadly machine rifle in his hands instead of a paralyzing stinger.

He meant business.

"Right on time, friends," the centurion said.

The Russians were physically shocked and Lev Magin's eyes went wide with surprise and not a little bit of fear. The machine rifle clicked ominously.

"Busch!" snapped Kitteridge as he and Yuri Kreutin froze on the porch steps.

Little Irina screamed from the front yard and the adults turned from the porch to see other Hive soldiers rush from behind the house where they had concealed themselves, waiting.

Not a single man did Preston recognize. The deception had been complete.

"*Lazari!*" he gasped, his heart fluttered with betrayal.

Unfortunately, the lazari from the Hive 'combs did not recognize Preston Kitteridge either, and they treated him as just another Russian farmer. However, they took their orders from centurion Brian Busch and held their distance.

Busch prodded Lev Magin back away from the porch steps and out into the open.

"Who are you?" Magin demanded, indignant that anyone uninvited would be in his home. "What have you done with my wife? Where is she?"

Irina hugged Ura as the soldiers surrounded them.

Centurion Busch ignored Magin. Instead, he grinned sourly at Preston. "You did your job on these people too well, Kitteridge. We were hoping that you wouldn't come back. You would've saved us some trouble."

"What is the meaning of this, Busch?" Preston demanded, stepping around the startled Kreutin, who was staring into the ugly snouts of the shiny machine-gun barrels.

From inside the house Yelena Magin, frazzled and scared, appeared in the grasp of a uniformed and helmeted Tom Winehall. He carried a machine pistol in one hand and Irina's mother firmly in the other.

"Momma!" Irina cried, and jumped up, running to her side.

The soldiers let the little Russian girl through and Yelena swept her up into her arms.

Tom Winehall, the Armory supervisor, pointed his gun at Preston.

"Now, Preston," he began slowly, "remember that we're on the same team. This is part of the plan. The Colonel's orders, you know."

"What plan?" Preston demanded. "This isn't part of any plan, Tom, and you know it. What the hell are you talking about?"

He tried to ignore the expressions of surprise and confusion his new Russian friends were giving him just then, but clearly they were beginning to understand what his strangeness had betrayed all along: He was different.

Centurion Busch sneered. He said, "We're still at war, Kitteridge. Or have you just conveniently forgotten that fact?"

Yuri Kreutin faced the arrogant centurion. "War? What war? You are not our people. Where did you come from? And where did you get these weapons?"

"We're the people you wiped off the earth!" centurion Busch growled. "We're the Americans who belong here in the first place. And we're taking all of our land back!"

Captain Tom Winehall waved his gun at the Hive soldier. "Go easy there, centurion. Play it by the rules."

Brian Busch was livid with righteousness. His eyes were bloody maps of anger and revenge.

Kitteridge glanced back at the contingent of lazari soldiers surrounding them. Their uniforms were neatly pressed, their guns freshly oiled. But the men themselves seemed barely able to comprehend what was happening, although undoubtedly they'd all been briefed.

*Freshly hatched*, Preston thought to himself. *Like spring chickens . . .*

"And them?" Preston pointed to the soldiers. "What are they doing here?"

"We need them," Winehall said, holstering his gun, clearly in control of the situation.

"The lazari? How many of them did you unfreeze?" he then asked.

"All of them," Winehall said casually.

"*All of them?*" Preston was almost yelling. "There are over three hundred people sleeping down in the 'combs!"

Both Captain Winehall and centurion Busch—as well as half the soldiers themselves—wore telling smiles.

"Not anymore, there aren't," Busch said. "Let's move it."

A large convoy carrier truck rumbled on diesel fumes down the street, coming toward the Magin home. The soldiers, numbering about a dozen, dutifully ran over to meet it, their job having been done.

"They aren't from the *mandali*, Poppa," little Irina said in a small voice. "They're the ghosts."

"One good turn deserves another," centurion Busch said down to the child, light gleaming off his helmet.

"You keep away from her, Busch," Kitteridge said. "I want to talk to Dr. Wainwright *and* the Colonel about this. I don't give a damn who's giving orders here."

Busch prodded Preston with his gun. "You know the plan, Kitteridge. The Hive gives the orders on Resurrection Day if there's a war still going on."

"There is no war! Don't you understand?" Preston found himself shouting. "These people are just farmers! They're as American as you and I!"

"I don't think so," Brian Busch said.

"Just open your eyes!"

"That's enough, Preston," Captain Winehall said, waving them over to the waiting convoy truck. "We're going back to the Hive. The first part of our mission's done."

Busch prodded Kitteridge with the end of his gun and Preston spun around, suddenly angered, and crashed his fist into the proud centurion's face with a knuckled Sunday punch.

"Don't you *ever* do that to me!" Kitteridge shouted.

The centurion came up, fire in his eyes, and one of the lazari commanders ran over and held Busch back. "Not now," the man said calmly. "We've got our orders, just as Captain Winehall said."

The centurion shook himself away. "I've got your number, Kitteridge. I swear that when this is over—"

Preston faced him off. "What? You swear what? I'll take you apart right now!" His fists were clenched and ready.

Winehall fired his gun in the air, shattering the moment. "All right! Everyone into the truck! *Now!*"

Lev Magin held onto his wife, suddenly resembling more a young farmer and his family, rather than stolid Russian conquerors, part of the master race conceived in a Marxist nightmare.

Magin turned to Preston. "Friend," he began slowly. "Can you tell us who are these men? Can you tell us what is happening?"

Preston said, "I'm afraid it's a little complicated. But one thing I can tell you—" And here he broke off to scowl at all of the soldiers. "is that none of these people are friends of mine," he concluded.

Held captive in the back of the large convoy carrier, they rode back through the empty town, presumably heading toward the harvested wheat fields to the south of Anytown. They were flanked by the watchful lazari, some of whom were still blinking back the cobwebs of their age-old sleep. Brian Busch guarded them with his ever-present machine gun, never once taking his eyes away from Preston.

Preston sat the whole trip with the Russians, shaking with so much rage that it was all he could do to prevent himself from strangling the centurion.

From the open door at the rear of the convoy carrier, they could see that Anytown had now become infested with other uniformed lazari and occasional centurions to command them. Several of the convoy carriers rumbled hither and yon through the town, dropping off soldiers at strategic locations. Overhead, a restored Apache attack helicopter from the Armory fluttered past them. Irina gasped upon seeing it, and clutched tighter to her father's side.

Lev stared at the centurion. "Are you the real Americans? We were told that there weren't any Americans left."

"Only the ghosts," Yelena said with worried eyes.

"Ghosts . . .," whimpered little Irina.

Brian Busch drew a thin smile across his face. He said, "Ghosts is about it. The ghosts of Christmas Past."

The Russians missed the association.

But Busch continued, "We're going to get even for what your leaders did to us. We're bringing the war back home."

Lev and Yuri Kreutin looked at one another. Lev then said, "There is no war. You keep talking as if there were."

Busch bounced with the rocky motion of the convoy carrier. He had an audience and he was loving every minute of it. Even the lazari—men from the twenty-first century—were listening to his recital with great interest.

The armed and dangerous Hive centurion leaned over to

make sure the Russian understood. "We know what's going on in your town, Magin. You have enough harvested plutonium and uranium to make dozens of atomic bombs. All for your Great War in Africa and Indonesia. You can't fool us anymore. We've been watching and we know all that we need to know."

He glowed triumphantly. A nod of his head indicated that he now considered Preston to be part of the Russians.

Yuri Kreutin then said, "You are mistaken, friend. The Awakener has forbidden us to manufacture bombs of any sort. We bury the radioactive monazite nodules deep in the ocean—"

"Just can it," the centurion said. "The fact of the matter is that you're living on *our* land. And we mean to remove you and your precious little town from it."

The ride to the barren wheat valley south of town seemed nearly interminable to Preston. He wanted so desperately to get at centurion Busch, but he knew that such an action would be extremely ill-advised. He needed to find out what was going on first. More helicopters filled the sky and more troop carriers passed them by on the dusty road. He needed more facts.

What facts he did have told him that they had declared war upon the Russians in some extrajudicial way, no doubt without the consent of the Appleseeds in Saxifrage.

The truck made a bouncy turn in the road, leaving it completely. A Hive tractor had graded a newer path sometime earlier that day, and the convoy carrier followed this.

After about ten minutes on the new road, they came upon the Hive itself.

Kitteridge gasped upon seeing it when he climbed from the rear of the armored convoy carrier.

The whole Hive administration building, complete with the Armory underneath it and the 'combs off to one side, had been fully resurrected, opaqued out and locked into place upon the surface of the earth. He could see where the Meadow locks had been blown, for there were large patches of kudzu, torn into shreds, still remaining on the Hive's half of the concourse.

Behind the Hive, the huge B-10 VTOL attack bomber had been wheeled out into a circular area the engineers had hastily carved for it just east of the building. Mounds and pyramids of arms lay piled neatly underneath the aircraft, including what looked to be actual nuclear bombs.

"Oh, my God," Yelena Magin choked.

The vision of the B-10 VTOL was a bad dream for them all. Lazari in overalls were hoisting air-to-air missiles underneath its wing fans. Fuel tanks were also being wheeled out.

On the top of the Hive were several other lazari setting up two microwave antenna dishes. The hammering of nails could be heard, even the snarl of a buzz saw.

Yuri Kreutin was absolutely aghast at the sight of so much military industry.

"I don't understand. How . . . how did it get here? All of this . . ." He turned to Preston. "Who *are* you people?"

He spoke as if he were referring to gods. Gods from a horrible and distant mythic past. Gods they all wanted to forget.

But Preston had other matters to ponder.

He turned to Captain Winehall, who came toward him from where he had been sitting in the front of the convoy carrier.

"Where's Saxifrage?" he demanded. "Where's the rest of the Mall and the Arks?"

The only thing which stood in the wheat field was the building of the Hive.

The Mall was nowhere above the earth.

Winehall ushered them toward the Hive building, followed by the lazari guards. He said, "Let's just say that they elected not to resurrect just yet."

"That's absurd!" Preston argued. "They have as much right as anybody to resurrect. Dammit, we're a *city*!"

"I don't think so," centurion Busch said. And in saying this, he jabbed Preston once again with his gun. "Whatever the case, you don't have any say in this."

Stifling his anger, he entered the Hive administration building along with the Russian captives. The lazari, though, went about their duties outside. Only Captain Tom Winehall and the centurion escorted them within.

Like the Russians, Preston was astounded by all the sheer activity inside the Hive. Nothing like it had ever been seen before. Men and women—formerly *duendes*—were now going about their long-programmed duties as resurrected soldiers of the United States Air Force, going through drills and procedures which most of them had been practicing underneath the earth for twenty or thirty years. *This* is what they had lived for. Computers were awakened. Television screens came alive. Antennas scanned the skies for any surviving satellites—American or Soviet—into which they might plug or probe for information.

They reached the War Room and all of the military leaders of the Hive had long since been assembled.

But none of the Appleseeds were there.

Abe Koch, the 'combs supervisor, stood beside Sid Rankin, and both men were dressed in their full Hive combat fatigues. They were also armed with service revolvers.

Second Lieutenant Sebastian Monaco was also present, along with Colonel Chaney. Both officers seemed to effervesce with victoriousness, now that the Russians had been finally captured—and the Appleseeds had been temporarily removed from the action.

The Russians huddled in a group but Preston stood before the Hive leaders, clearly siding with his new friends.

"All right, Colonel," he said flatly. "What is going on here? What's the meaning of all this?"

"Calm down, Kitteridge," the Colonel began in an almost patronizing tone. "You don't know the full story."

"I know more than you give me credit for."

"Do you know that we are at war?" Sebastian Monaco sauntered over to him. He took in each one of the Russians, sniffing slightly as if they were distasteful to him.

Yelena and her scared daughter had found a place upon a long couch in the War Room. The two men, however, stood and watched.

"Hogwash," Preston retorted. "There is no war. Haven't you people been watching and listening?"

Monaco then said, "Indeed, we have. But you've forgotten about why the Meadow was created. It was designed to defeat the ancestors of *these* people." He gestured aside to the Russian family. "The Soviets had planned it all along. And now they're using our country for their own purposes, which is world domination. It isn't any more simple than that, Kitteridge."

Lev Magin glanced around them all with the wonder expected of a captive thrust into a situation which he neither anticipated nor understood.

He said to them, "Wait, wait! None of this is true! We are just farmers . . . harvesters!"

Monaco snorted his disgust and Kitteridge stepped before him, allying himself with the Magins and Yuri Kreutin. He stared the second lieutenant right in the eye.

"I want to know what you did to all of the Russians in town, Monaco," he demanded. "That's first."

The lazarus smiled ruefully. "It's not what *I* did to them, Kitteridge, but what *you* did to them. They're *duendes* by now, one and all. Wandering around in limbo like lost souls."

Preston closed his eyes, stunned, confirming what he had inwardly suspected.

He then said, "You had no right to do that. No right at all."

"There are no rights in war, Kitteridge," Monaco said.

Lev Magin stepped over to Preston and softly touched him on the arm. "Explain, please, what your countrymen are saying. We don't understand."

Preston's neck burned hotly—but not at the Russian. Monaco had done this to him, and now he was caught in the middle of the conspiracy.

Preston looked at the Russian farmer. "I'm afraid that for the time being your people have been made invisible and intangible. They've been converted into ghosts."

"What is this?" Yuri Kreutin asked. "Ghosts?"

Irina cowered in her mother's lap. "*Prevedenir . . .*"

Yelena said nothing, watching her husband closely. Her fingers twitched as she held her daughter.

Preston told them, "We have the ability to convert people and things into ghosts. We are ghosts ourselves, or at least we were."

Colonel Chaney glared at him. "Don't tell them too much, Kitteridge. They're officially prisoners of war."

"And what am I?" Preston then asked. "You betrayed me. You lied to me. I've unwittingly made hundreds of innocent people into temporary *duendes*."

Monaco crossed his arms. "Not temporarily, Kitteridge."

Preston's heart almost ceased. "What do you mean?"

The Colonel stepped over to one of the busy computer technicians and spoke. "They're out on the upper m-field and most are probably getting hungry by now."

Preston dashed over to the glowing computer board, pleading with the Colonel. "Then opaque them back out. They're harmless, absolutely harmless. They're just farmers and ranchers. *Good* people."

Monaco's gaze was hollow, resolute. He said, "They've really taken you in, haven't they, Kitteridge? In my day, we called goons like you Communist sympathizers."

The expressions was so anachronistic that, for a moment, he didn't know its six-hundred-year-old implication.

"What?" he stared with disbelief. "A Communist sympathizer? What kind of government do you think *we* have in the Meadow?" With a laugh of startled surprise, he waved about them in the Hive War Room. "We rule ourselves by committee, we contribute to the general well-being of the *commune*, we live as an organism for our mutual survival. That's Communism, Monaco. The definition hasn't changed in six hundred years. Only *we* have."

But Yuri Kreutin, just as puzzled as anyone, broke in even as several hostile machine guns turned in his direction.

He said, "But we are not Communists. They are long dead."

"Then what are you?" Sebastian Monaco addressed the plutonium harvester for the first time. He now rested his right hand upon the butt of his holstered gun.

"We are the Americans," Kreutin said. "Russia no longer exists for us . . . or anyone. It's uninhabitable, or so we're told."

Kitteridge faced the Colonel, concurring. "What he says is true. I saw several maps when I was in Missouri Landing, in their town library. All of northern Europe is covered with ice or snow or tundra. There are no major cities whatever. It's a completely different world over there."

Yuri Kreutin then said, "Even if it were possible for us to return, there would be too much plutonium for us to sweep up. It was horribly bombed during the war."

Captain Tom Winehall, over in a protective corner, said across to the Colonel, "Supposedly they dump the plutonium monazite stones somewhere in the ocean."

"Or they use it for bombs," Monaco insisted. "Are we going to take their word for what they do with the usable materials they find over here?"

"Why not?" Kitteridge countered. "Have you seen signs of any other kind of war industry or munitions manufacturing? I haven't, and I've been places the last couple of days none of you have."

"It doesn't matter," Monaco reasserted his authority. "There is still a war going on—" And he pointed to the

Russians, Lev and Yelena Magin. "And that's all they talk about in their home. We've got hours of it on tape. Hell, they've got a son who's a soldier over in Africa."

It was little Irina who spoke out just then. She jumped up. "Mikhail is a doctor! He's not a soldier!" She turned quickly to her mother. "Momma, tell them! Tell them about Mikhail!"

Yelena, worried and scared, and unable to keep it from her daughter, turned her brown eyes to her captors. "Yes, Mikhail is a doctor only. There are no soldiers that we know of in Africa."

Monaco turned on her like a mongoose on a cobra.

He snapped, "Well, then, just who is this Awakener person you so fondly worship? We know he's leading your troops in your so-called Great War in Africa and Indonesia. Those two countries could have survived most of a nuclear exchange between the superpowers. So who is he?"

Little Irina looked questioningly at her father, then at her mother. "Baba?" she cried. "Are they going to hurt Baba?"

Lev Magin firmly squeezed her shoulder, and Yelena took her back under wing.

Lev Magin stood between Monaco and his family, standing as close to Kitteridge as he dared. He said, "He is the one who awoke us. Without him we would have slept on forever underneath the sea."

"What?" Monaco looked at Preston as if he were surrounded by idiots. "Just how many of these fairy tales do you expect us to believe?"

Preston said, "If you had studied the tapes I originally sent down to you when I scanned their living room, you would've seen that they survived the war beneath the ocean. They had an underwater storage facility, like the 'combs, located underneath the Arctic ice cap in the Barents Sea. They're lazari, Monaco. Just like you. My guess is that they were children when they were frozen in their 'cubbies,' as they call them. You and Lev Magin, if you look close enough, Monaco, are almost the same age."

Monaco shook visibly with his indignation at being compared to these Soviet usurpers.

Preston, seeing that his words were making sense, if disagreeably, quickly continued, "And they're not Russian soldiers, either. They're descendants of scientists and technicians—*Appleseeds*, Monaco—of Russians who knew that there was only one way to survive a nuclear holocaust and that was to hide. Just as we did. They had Arks orbiting in space stations and they were eventually brought down when it was thought that the life within them had a fighting chance in the changed biosphere."

"That's ridiculous," Monaco said. "NASA would've known of such operations in space. So would have NORAD—"

"The fact is," Preston pressed on, "that they didn't. Nobody knew anything."

Yuri Kreutin then interrupted them. "Yes, but you see, it was the Awakener who brought the spacecraft down. They are all over the globe. Many years later, he brought us up from our chambers. You must understand, it is not a war we fight. It is hunger and disease."

Blank expressions pervaded the War Room as they all stared at Kreutin. The metal harvester said, "The Awakener is directing all foods and metals harvested from the ruins to go to those lands which continue to suffer from the nuclear fires of the past. You must believe us!"

"Mass starvations and plagues," Preston said in a low voice. He pointed over to the counter where the Outcome Book lay with its leaves closed. "You know what the scenarios have projected. Once the major bread-basket countries collapsed, all of the countries of the Third World would be thrown into complete disorder. Even if the biosphere survived, the War's secondary effects would still have caused untold millions of deaths each year when food and medicine became scarce. These people here are providing all of those things now."

Monaco pulled out his gun and pointed it squarely at Kitteridge. "Just whose side are you on, anyway? They destroyed America! Think about it. New York is gone. Los Angeles is wiped out. The whole country's a wilderness because of them!"

Preston then said, "And what about *their* country? You think they're any less human? You think they don't have any feelings about who they are, what their own history was like?" He glared at the lazarus. "I *am* on their side, friend. It took me a while to realize it fully, but we're goddamn lucky that we even *have* a planet to live on. They're partially to thank because of it!"

Colonel Chaney walked around them. "Kitteridge, you're

not an expert in these matters, regardless of what you've seen or what you think is the truth. There are other important issues at work here."

Preston, though, was continuing to stare at Monaco. He was the real enemy. "Such as?" he asked.

"The rebellion below in the Meadow," the Colonel said glibly, almost plainly.

"The rebellion?" Preston turned to him. "What rebellion?"

The Colonel fingered the Outcome Book. "I take it that you haven't read the Outcome Book lately."

"Not lately, no," he confessed.

"Well, we ran all the data through the computers, following the closest approximation of one of the more favorable Outcomes, and what it came up with was a recommendation that the Hive establish martial law. The Mall personnel in Saxifrage didn't like that idea."

"Martial law? There's nothing about martial law in any of the Outcome recommendations. We're all in this together," Preston contended.

Monaco, still with his gun leveled at him, said, "Not quite. The computer confirmed our belief that we were still at war, and it recommended that we raise the Hive only, once we deopaqued the Russians in the vicinity. The Mall will come up later. Much later. As you can imagine, Dr. Wainwright didn't much like that notion."

"Is he still down there?" Preston turned inquiringly to the Colonel.

But the Colonel and Sebastian Monaco exchanged knowing looks.

"You tell him," Monaco said to the Colonel.

"Tell me what?"

The Colonel sighed heavily—not because he regretted the Appleseed's fate, but that it was a mere inconvenience. He said, "Dr. Wainwright was under a great deal of strain, I'm afraid. He had a heart attack when the computer came up with its recommendations."

Preston jerked as if bitten. *"What?"*

Monaco held up his free hand. "Don't be alarmed, Kitteridge. I know how much the old guy means to you. Hagerty and a couple of loose Appleseeds took him to the Mall hospital."

"But right after that," the Colonel continued, "we decided to engage the lift engines and blow the concourse locks.

That was when the Russians were . . . disengaged from their world."

"Damn you people!" Kitteridge shouted. "Damn your stupidity! You're murderers! You're going to kill everybody!"

"Not everybody," Monaco said with stern features upon his face. "Just the Russians. Look, pal, you think you know everything, but you don't." The lazarus pointed at Yelena Magin. "We watched them while you were gone. That camera you left in the kitchen told us a lot about their Awakener. He's some sort of bozo religious leader, or so they believe. All they talk about is how he and his *mandali* made this heroic trek up to the goddamn north pole and unfroze a couple hundred of their countrymen. So what if he brought down satellites full of seeds and bees? It's just a fairy tale that you want to believe in. The Awakener and his men have gotten these people to believe it, and you've been sucked in with them. This is war, and these are very dangerous people, Kitteridge."

Preston paced back and forth, waving his arms about. "I can't believe that this is happening." He faced Monaco. "What about the Arks? What about the rest of Saxifrage?"

"They elected to stay below," Monaco said quickly.

"I can't believe they'd do that."

"Let's just say that we 'elected' for them," the lazarus stated.

"That's why they rebelled," the Colonel followed up with.

"But you should've brought them up with you."

"Not when they refuse to obey our orders, we're not," the Colonel said flatly.

"You mean that you're holding them *hostage*?"

Preston practically flew at the Colonel, but centurion Brian Busch brought up his gun and clicked it into firing position.

"We had to do something to establish order. It's all in the new Outcome Book chapter and they knew they had to expect something like this. But they don't have too much longer to think about it," the Colonel said grimly.

"Wait, wait," Preston began. "What do you mean?" He didn't like the sound of that at all.

Monaco spoke for the Colonel. "You've got to remember that this is an emergency military situation. We told them that if they didn't yield to our authority in all matters, the computers would automatically opaque out the Meadow *where it was.*"

There was no emotion in his voice, the executioner who'd just thrown the switch.

"*What?*" Preston almost screamed.

"The new chapter in the Outcome Book calls for a hostage program and we locked it into their Mall computers. They can't break it in time." The Colonel *almost* laughed, but didn't. He said, "If your brother, Jay, was down there, he'd probably be able to tapeworm it out. But there's no way now. I'm sorry, Preston. But it had to be done."

"You would sacrifice two hundred people and all of the Arks just because they wouldn't participate in the slaughter of these . . . these *farmers?*"

Monaco motioned his gun at Yuri Kreutin, who was now standing beside Preston.

He shouted, "They are *Russians.* They are responsible for the deaths of over three *billion* human beings. They even sacrificed their own kind. They're worse than Stalin during his purges in 1945. But what the fuck do *you* know about history? These people have no sanctity for human life whatsoever." He prodded Preston on the chest and Kitteridge's anger rose in his throat. He continued, "You forget that I know these people. My kind lived with them. They wanted every nation of the world in their power. Well, now it's over. It ends here."

Little Irina was whimpering, backing away from the arguing adults. Her eyes began roving about the large room

"Momma," the little Russian cried.

But Yelena and Lev were too caught up with their captors to pay her any mind.

Preston tried to calm himself. He said, "What about the Mall? What about the Arks? Tell me."

Monaco and Colonel Chaney looked once again at each other. It was the second lieutenant who spoke. He said, "They're almost out of time. If they don't give in, then the computer keeps the Saxifrage lift engines from working. They'll opaque out where they're at—inside solid rock. That's the bottom line, I'm afraid."

"How much time have they got?" Preston demanded.

"About an hour."

"An *hour?*" Preston exclaimed. "It takes more time than that just to warm up the lift engines!"

The Colonel and Sebastian Monaco wore their executioners' masks quite well. None of the other Hive personnel gathered in the War Room were looking at them.

"And all those deopaqued Russians," Kitteridge began. "I suppose that they'll be dead soon, too."

"They're the first of many casualties, Kitteridge. Face it. We're at war now," the Colonel said. "And there's nothing you can do about it but follow orders."

"Or join them," Monaco said, pulling out what looked to be another assessor gun, aiming it at him.

*Another lie*, he realized, seeing the gun. *Another military lie*. Deceit and betrayal were in the very air he breathed.

But Preston now knew what he had to do.

He leapt sideways to his right and elbowed centurion Brian Busch in the solar plexus. The centurion caved in with a sudden groan, and Kitteridge had his machine gun.

But Yuri Kreutin had acted first.

He crashed to his left, surprising his guard, fighting for the machine gun. Thunder caromed around them as bullets danced along the ceiling.

"You have no right—" shouted Kreutin.

"Yuri!" his sister cried out.

Monaco dropped the assessor gun and brought up his service revolver, tired of fooling around with technological tricks.

He fired point-blank at Kreutin.

The Russian metal harvester's body rebounded off the opposite wall violently, splattering crimson bloodstars everywhere.

Lev Magin grabbed his wife and together they tumbled backward out of range. Yelena Magin fell to the floor with a scream.

Preston spun around as a guard brought up his machine gun. He aimed at the Magins, but Kitteridge tugged off a dull spurt of fiery lead. The guard fell forward, trying to plug the sudden leaks in his stomach.

Monaco's steely eyes turned on Preston as the service revolver came up at him.

*Click, click, click* . . .

Monaco's eyes went wide as he stared at the gun. Empty. It took all nine rounds to kill Kreutin, and it had all happened so fast. Kitteridge had him.

The computer personnel had plunged underneath their

desk consoles for safety, and the Colonel was up on his feet shouting.

*"Guards!"*

Through the glass doors which separated the War Room from the outer hallway, half a dozen centurions came crashing.

Preston dropped his machine gun and instead dove at the little Russian. *Someone had to survive.* . . .

"Guards!" shouted Monaco, quickly reloading his gun.

Preston grabbed little Irina Magin—and just as suddenly deopaqued out. The frightened nine-year-old went with him.

"Momma!" cried the girl in Kitteridge's arms.

With a glance over his shoulder he saw that the Magins—though under the gun—were safe. The incoming centurions had not fired upon them, startled by Preston's initial vanishing.

"Stop him!" the Colonel ordered to the technicians at the computers who were scrambling back into their chairs.

But Preston was gone by then.

He ghosted through the walls of the War Room and adjusted his m-field downward, passing through to the first floor of the Hive.

He then bolted outside the administration building into the wan afternoon light. Irina cried and screamed in his arms.

"Honey," he tried to assure her. "It's all right! It's okay!"

He struggled with her as he put as much distance as he could between himself and the technicians who might be able to track him.

"I'm on your side!" he continued to say. "I had to get you out of the way!"

A klaxon of alarms sounded throughout the Hive grounds, and some of the soldiers posted outside the building began looking around for them, in touch with the War Room by radio.

But Preston had long since disconnected the unit on his m-field belt which would affect a trace, just as his brother had done the previous day. They wouldn't be able to find him unless they came after him as *duendes*.

He put Irina down onto the surface and held her. He looked deep into her ghostly blue eyes. "Sweetheart, I'm going to go for help. But I don't want you to be frightened. Everything's going to be all right. You've got to trust me on this one."

She whimpered and stared about her in the wheat field

which only a couple of days before this she had so efficiently harvested all on her own. Everywhere about them were scattering soldiers, sirens of urgent alarm, and a weird greenish light which Preston had not noticed before this. It frightened even him. He thought he saw other ghostly shapes in the distance moving in their haphazard way toward the monolithic Hive building, but he didn't have time to hang around and find out what they were for certain. He suspected that he already knew.

Many of those spectres were coming from the direction of Anytown.

The two of them made for the small creek a hundred yards away in which Jay had frolicked upon his original opaquing. The creek was below the real surface of the stubbly wheat field, and it was enough to keep the little Russian hidden from the many eyes of the Hive.

Preston said to her, "I want you to wait for me here and I don't want you to worry, baby. Okay?" He held her close for a moment.

That seemed to help. Irina nodded, trying to be brave.

With a swift adjustment to his m-field belt, he opaqued Irina out. A gust of wind silently accompanied her appearance back into the real world. She quickly dove for the rushes and reeds of the gentle creek.

"Good girl," Preston said proudly. The little Russian was safe—for a while.

He then made for the ladder with its automated camera locked on top of it. With a final glance to make sure, he noted that there were no soldiers coming in their direction from the Hive, although many of them were still running about.

He had less than an hour. He didn't know if he could make it.

# 17

Even though the robot camera was still attached to the top rungs of the ladder, it had apparently been switched off. Even so, Preston didn't want to be seen in his *duende* state in case some Hive technician in the War Room had the television remote sensors still connected. It might come alive if he was seen.

Carefully he crawled beneath it and adjusted his m-field belt to the m-field of the ladder—and the lower m-field where Saxifrage lay.

Swinging down into the darkness, he began his descent once again.

This time he had no safety lines to hold him in place in case he lost his grip. Moreover, he had no climb-lights dangling beneath him from his belt to guide him down the dangerous ladder. All he had to guide him was his own strength and resolve to make it down to the Meadow in time.

However, there was plenty of light to see by, cascading up at him from far below. The whole of Saxifrage Mall was haloed with the fevered luminescence of the lift engines.

He could even feel their distant vibratory growl as he held onto the plastic rungs of the ladder.

"Nemesis!" he swore, setting his feet down faster and faster.

Somehow the Mall engineers had managed to engage the starting mechanisms of the lift engines themselves. But the Mall wasn't rising. Something was still wrong. They had yet to break whatever computer code that Sebastian Monaco had treacherously thrown into the system.

But they wisely were in the process of warming up the engines. They could go nowhere without them.

Down and down he went, faster and faster, the ladder shaking impatiently as he went.

He got himself into an easy, rocking rhythm, swaying from side to side as hand went under hand and foot under foot, taking each rung carefully and precisely. The descent needed his whole attention.

Within several minutes, however, he happened to glance up into the eternally dark night.

He noticed that all of the ghost constellations to the east of the Meadow had shifted and warped. They were all wrong, scrambled somehow.

The Lute was horribly contorted and the Three Bells now seemed to be one giant Bell with a comet's tail of misty ocher light hazing off toward the southwest. The Spider's Lair, the largest accretion of the lights, had made the most significant changes of all. The Spider herself was an elephantine jumble of lime-colored sparkles; the Lair was pulled thin, elongating toward the apex of the ladder above the Mall.

And they seemed to be moving. Slowly they drifted around each other and as Preston went further and further into the underworld he seemed to sense some connection between the lights and the firing of the lift engines underneath the Mall. But he didn't know why the constellations were behaving the way they were. For thirty years or so they had never moved. And now there was a whole "sky" full of new shapes, new creatures to be imagined. Gone was their old familiar firmament.

But then, gone was their whole familiar world.

*Down and down.*

*One, two, three, four . . .*

His arms were beginning to get tired, constantly needing blood, and his hands persisted in getting sweaty, making each grip upon the rungs of the ladder more precarious than the one before it. But he couldn't stop.

He didn't dare stop.

He kept the vision of frightened little Irina all alone in the reeds of the creek to sustain him. Nor could he forget

Yuri Kreutin being thrown against the wall of the War Room, struck by bullets from Monaco's gun.

The constellations shifted above him and he thought about his brother. About his raven-haired mother. His father. And Dr. Wainwright.

And he thought about all of his years as a *duende*. No one had thought that Resurrection Day would be anything like this. . . .

He had to reach the Mall and find a way to break that computer code. He had to. Otherwise, Monaco and the Colonel would only continue to wage a war that no longer needed to be fought. The Awakener, whoever he was, had given the planet a second chance. And he had already seen the fruits of that second chance: He'd smelled the air, tasted its food, heard its natural sounds.

It seemed to him that the whole world had gone insane and that each rung that he took downward into the darkness was a step closer to sanity. *If* he could make it in time.

Then the ladder jolted.

"Holy Nemesis!" he shouted out, hugging the rungs. He glanced down far below.

The light from the lift engines was getting brighter, but he knew that the shock which burst up through the ladder had nothing to do with the possible elevating of the Mall.

He was about four hundred feet from the bottom concourse, bathed in sweat, chafed by the awkward farmer's clothes he still wore.

Then he noticed that the ladder was suddenly—and ever so slightly—beginning to sway.

The m-field ladder-locks, spaced every hundred feet upon the ladder, were starting to glow. The ladder was being allowed to disengage itself from its anchorage in the rock!

"*Whoa!*" Preston shouted.

It jumped again, only this time he didn't malinger. Holding to as best as he could, he started down. The ladder was starting to move laterally and he felt it start to lean.

However, the Mall itself wasn't moving upward.

*It was moving sideways.*

"Hey!" Preston shouted.

But no one could hear him.

While he could now see a few *duendes* running about the concourse preparing the Mall for lift, there was such a din rising from the powerful lift engines that there was no way anyone would have an occasion to look up and see him coming at them on the ladder.

"Shit!" he cursed.

This time he put his feet on the outside of the rungs and began sliding down the ladder, using his hands to lower himself. It was as fast as he could manage.

The ladder took another lateral jerk and Preston could see the Meadow inch to the southwest.

Now he could see how it was happening.

It was being towed.

Far at the opposite end of Saxifrage Mall, linked to the hitch at the base of the Sonoran Ark, the giant trawler was throwing down its ponderous glowing tread-plates, slowly lugging the whole Meadow in its wake.

But in order for the Mall to be pulled along the lower m-field, it had to have the lift engines to buoy it, and it had to have all other *duende* artifacts, such as the ladder, disengaged from the m-field surface. The ladder had come loose from its m-field anchors and was swaying dangerously in place, as any structure of its kind might. And he was attached to it.

Just *why* the Mall was being towed, he couldn't understand. There was no real reason for it.

He reached the kudzu. Tiny, leafy vines still clung to the horizontal rungs even though the rest of the creepers had been shorn from the sides of the ladder when the camera had been sent aloft an eternity ago.

He finally came within fifteen feet of the concourse and dropped the rest of the way, rolling in the soft, cool kudzu.

He scrabbled to his feet, surrounded by a white sea of intense illumination from the lift engines. There, at the very east end of the Mall, now that the Hive was gone, the engines were at their brightest and loudest. He was almost blinded and deafened by them.

He started for the Mall.

Just as he did, he came across Ike and Tina.

"Jesus, you guys!" he shouted, falling into a roll to avoid crashing into them.

Ike was strapped into his cart, and Tina was sitting on the flat platform. Together, they were towing their own precious store of goodies. During all of the chaos among the *duendes* they had apparently come all this way on their own.

"We're going up!" Tina sang in kitty-trill. "Here we go!"

Preston shouted down to Tina so she'd understand. "Don't go beyond the kudzu, Tina! Don't do it! I don't want you out on the m-field!"

The two cats stared off into the wall of blinding, mesmerizing light.

"Stupid cats," he said to himself.

He took off for the Mall administration building.

It was so strange to see utter darkness fill the eastern half of the Meadow where the Hive was supposed to be. All the locks had been expertly blown and there was concrete rubble strewn throughout the kudzu and the rest of the concourse.

Preston entered the Mall, crashing across their artificial creek that ran down the center of Saxifrage. Appleseeds and other Mall technicians were running everywhere and alarms were sounding off, echoing loudly throughout the facility.

He burst into the administration building, nearly stumbling as the Meadow jerked once more. He could hear the heavy lock-treads of the trawler slamming into place upon the blank m-field as the giant craft hauled the Mall after it.

"Preston!" someone shouted.

It was Stu Hagerty sitting at a row of computers along with the Appleseed technicians.

The Appleseeds were frantically going over the computers and their faces glowed with a devilish light from the screens.

Hagerty, looking apologetic and relieved, waved Kitteridge over.

Preston, breathing heavily, said, "Monaco told me that there was a lock on the lift engines—" He tried gasping for breath, but Hagerty interrupted.

The former Hive technician said, "I broke it. Monaco thought that he could override the Mall computers and m-field generators, but he needed me to do it." The diminutive technician looked as if he had just about endured all that he was going to. He continued, saying, "They threw me out when Travis had his heart attack."

"Dr. Wainwright, is he—?"

Lee Williams came around the row of computers, having been notified that Preston had arrived. The Ark computer-integrator was also glad to see him.

He said, "I took him to the hospital, Preston. He's alive but he's in bad shape."

"We're all in bad shape," Hagerty said as the Meadow took another lateral jolt, shaking some of the equipment in their moorings. Some lights even dimmed.

"The trawler," Preston started, grasping a console edge. "Who's operating the damn trawler?"

Hagerty looked up, ripping the earphones from his head. "I don't know, but we can't elevate unless that trawler is disconnected. It'll weigh us down."

"Shit!" Preston said, turning. "I'll put a stop to this nonsense right now!"

Hagerty was out of his chair as if shot from it. He grabbed Kitteridge quickly. "Preston, wait! You don't understand! I've broken the lock program and the lift engines are ready."

Preston stared at him. "Then what's the problem?"

"The problem is that we've only got seven minutes to elevate," the technician said.

"What?"

The other Appleseeds and technicians stared at them.

"Part of Monaco's program was not only to keep us down here, but to opaque us out. And I can't stop the opaquing program. We're trying to circumvent it, but it doesn't look like we're going to make it in time."

"The trawler—" Preston began, but he knew that he was wasting time. "Start lift in *five* minutes. Regardless!"

"But, Preston . . . !" Hagerty called after him.

Kitteridge turned and crashed through the door.

The whole Mall trembled as the trawler continued. Trees down beside the creek shook and the kudzu sang its leafy song as the concussions shuddered sickeningly throughout the six-century-old structure.

Preston sprinted down the wide lower level of the Mall and stampeded over a footbridge which crossed the creek. People were running everywhere, some screaming, some shouting orders. And a great deal of the *duendes* had gathered at the entrance to the Sonoran Ark.

Deep within the crowd, Preston found his second-in-command, Besty Morrissey. Despite her cold, she was scared almost senseless.

"Betsy!" Preston shouted above the roar of the trawler's colossal engines outside.

Betsy turned and grabbed him as the *duendes* let him through.

"It's little Barrie!" she said. "She's inside the cabin of the trawler!"

Betsy ran with him through the crowded Ark. She said to him, "We all saw the Hive lift off and she got scared, I guess. She won't come out."

"Oh, Christ," Preston said, running out into the darkness before the Ark.

Several *duende* technicians were high above him in the upper reaches of the Sonoran Ark, shouting down instructions, trying to get the frightened six-year-old's attention.

Down at the side of the huge trawler, her older sister, Holly, was jumping up and down, waving, but the tyke high in the cabin of the trawler wasn't interested.

The long superalloy hitch between the trawler and the Ark was bolted solidly to the Mall and there Preston saw Barrie's father, Hugh Ressler.

He looked like he'd been through a lot.

"Hugh!" shouted Preston. He gestured frantically at the hitch. "Blow the hitch when I say! I'll get Barrie!"

Hugh Ressler had been trying to figure out what to do, but he didn't know of their deadline. Preston did and he shouted to the *duendes*, both in the Ark and out upon the m-field.

"Everyone back!" he directed.

The light from the lift engines which ringed the Meadow cast up a frightful brilliance. The trawler itself glowed as if it were a metal artifact newly pulled from its die.

Holly ran up to Preston. "We've got to do something!" she shouted above the clamor of the lift engines and the locking treads of the trawler.

He grabbed her suddenly. "Get back into the Ark! Do as I say! We're almost out of time!"

He shoved her a little harder than he intended, but the other *duendes* scrambled out to retrieve her and help her into the Ark. Her father, Hugh Ressler, waved from the top of the hitch where he balanced like a trapeze artist. He was ready.

Preston ran around in front of the gigantic machine.

The treads were individual m-field units, each of which was designed to lock the trawler onto the floor of the lower m-field as it moved along. They were as bright as the lift engines. Shielding himself from their glow, he shouted up at the cockpit of the trawler.

"Barrie!"

Goggled and helmeted, little Barrie Ressler was crying. She gripped the huge steering wheel as she guided the craft to what she thought was safety, away from the bad men of their world.

"Damn!" Preston cursed.

He waited tensely as another tread came down and slammed itself firmly into place, then he ran around to the side. There, he swung himself up onto the housing above the mono-tread that ran underneath the leviathan. Swiftly, like a monkey, he climbed up the complicated structure and reached the closed door of the cockpit.

"Hey, kid! It's me!" he shouted in through the plastic window.

The terrified six-year-old—child of six hundred years of darkness and superstitition—grappled with the steering wheel, thoroughly lost in her nightmare vision of the world. Her little feet fought to reach the pedals beneath her.

Preston gnarled up his fist and bashed it through the brittle plastic window of the door. He toggled the door handle and swung the metal door outward.

Barrie, crying pitifully, clutched the big wheel. She could only barely see where she was taking the trawler, for the seat—the whole cockpit—was designed for a grown-up. All she knew was that she had to get away. . . .

"Come on, pest," Preston said gently, prying her from the controls. She didn't struggle and he held her tightly.

He jumped down behind the trawler's cowling, reaching the dark m-field floor. Up above them, at the Ark, he could see Barrie's father standing at the coupling and Betsy Morrissey with her headset linking her to Lee Williams, waiting for orders.

To Betsy he shouted, "Tell them to *go!*"

Then to Hugh he said, "Catch!"

And running up to the hitch, he shunted the hysterical six-year-old into her father's arms.

"I'll get it!" he said to him. Preston turned to the hitch.

The mighty lift engines began to whine and the Appleseeds, looking out of the windows of the Ark above, leapt back inside. Preston wrestled with the hitch coupling and threw it. It hissed apart as its main bolt dropped to the m-field floor, disengaging it from the Mall and from the powerful trawler.

The instant the hitch fell to the surface of the m-field, he heard Betsy cry out, "We have Resurrection!"

She stuck her fingers in her mouth and whistled for all she was worth.

Hugh Ressler, at the edge of the Ark, handed Barrie to waiting hands at the exit and reached down to pull Preston to safety. The trawler, shining in the tremendous light cast down from the lift engines, stamped its single-minded way off into oblivion. Even Jay's deserted observatory dome was visible to them now as it dropped beneath the Meadow.

Cheers from the Appleseeds and other technicians went up throughout the Mall as the Meadow slowly rose skyward.

Preston clambered up into the Ark and Holly was there to hug him.

"We did it!" she shouted above the roar of the lift engines outside. "I didn't think we were going to make it, but we did!"

Hugh Ressler held onto his little girl as Barrie's mom, Peggy, found her way through the Sonoran Appleseeds.

"You did us one hell of a favor, Preston," Ressler said.

Then Betsy Morrissey came through the crowd. She yanked off her headset and handed it to him. "It's Lee, Preston," she said with great urgency. "There's something new in the computer program. Something's wrong."

He took the headset and put it on. He started running back through Saxifrage as he did.

"What's going on?" he shouted into the pin-mike, breathing heavily from the excitement. Both Stu Hagerty and Lee Williams were on the line.

Williams said, "Preston, there's another program set into the computer."

Kitteridge burst out into the Mall causeway, speaking as he ran. "It's not an override, is it? Don't tell me we're not going to make it!"

Then came Hagerty's frantic voice. "Yes, we're going to make it, but there's something else. It's Monaco's doing!"

Williams: "We just found it. The upper m-field is programmed on our signal from here in the Mall to give way entirely."

"What do you mean?" Preston shouted. The technician's voice was nearly inaudible above the roar of lift engines.

Williams said, "The upper m-field is programmed to drop down all those people you deopaqued, Preston. We just came across it. Monaco must have put it in long ago. It was apparently part of the assessor gun's capacities."

"Oh, my God, no," Kitteridge stammered.

Hagerty said, "They mean to eliminate those Russians made into *duendes*, and they mean to eliminate us."

"Son of a bitch!" Preston shouted, running down the concourse. "It just never stops!"

Williams came over the line. "We can't sustain them in their *duende* form, Preston. That's the idea. It's either them or us. And it was locked into whether or not we achieved lift. There's nothing we can do. Nothing."

Preston stumbled across the artificial stream of the Mall, plunging through the vines of dangling kudzu. He darted out onto the exposed concourse and stared up into their forever-dark sky.

The ladder, he saw, was passing swiftly down into its hole in the concourse, being left behind as the Meadow threaded its way to the surface. It crashed and wobbled as it went.

He found his two cats near the ladder. Ike, out of his cart and hunched in the leafy kudzu, watched the ladder whiz downward with great curiosity. Tina, bored by the spectacle, turned when Preston came up to them. She suddenly looked upward.

"Look at the stars!" she sang to him in her primitive kitty-trill.

Holly Ressler and several of her Sonoran colleagues came out onto the concourse behind Preston to witness the full light of Resurrection. They gasped, looking up.

"*No!*" Preston cried, staring into their dark sky.

Like falling stars, silent in their awful beauty, the deopaqued Russians fell from the security of the vanished m-field above them. The Meadow rose and the individual ghostly lights passed on all sides of the Mall, on their way to the center of the earth, now that both the upper and lower m-fields had been disengaged by the lift engines.

There was nothing he could do.

Preston fell to his knees in the kudzu as the glittering shower of Russian *duendes* sparkled in their descent about the rising form of the Meadow. Within seconds they were gone deep into the earth's bowels.

Then Resurrection!

The Mall broke out into full daylight with Lee Williams

shouting into Preston's earphones, "Seconds to spare! *We're out!*"

In the late-autumn light the Appleseeds who were out on the concourse covered their eyes from the sudden glare of the sun, as the Mall's lift engines locked the Meadow into place. A brief second later, strong gusts of wind—and very fresh air!—swirled around them in fierce eddies as the whole of Saxifrage opaqued out onto the wheat field.

The Appleseeds shouted in their excitement as they ran from their stations in the Arks and other Mall buildings.

As they did, there came a garbled rumble from deep beneath them, far below them in the earth. The Appleseeds were thrown to their knees.

Preston fell into the remains of the kudzu. Into his pin-mike he shouted, "What was that?"

"The trawler, probably," Stu Hagerty returned with. "And the observatory and the ladder and everything else we left out on the m-field. They were tied into our m-field generators and they opaqued out when we did, wherever they were. Inside solid rock—" His voice trailed off.

The entire Mall shook briefly, but not violently. It then subsided.

They were out.

Then came their next surprise.

Walking toward the Mall concourse with a grievous expression upon his face came Jay Kitteridge. He carried his assessor gun in his right hand and he seemed profoundly disturbed and shaken.

The wind of Resurrection fanned his brown hair.

"It's Jay!" shouted Tina as she jumped from the kudzu of the concourse and out onto the stubbly wheat field of the real world. Ike ran after her, his tail high in the air.

"Jay!" Preston said, turning to him.

Then he glanced toward the Hive building. The soldiers of the Hive were nowhere to be seen.

Instead, scores of Russian farmers, housewives, and schoolchildren stood about in complete astonishment, not knowing what was going on.

More than that, Preston saw dozens of *other* people standing about.

These individuals he had never seen before. Some were in rumpled nightshirts, others in flannel pajamas, and some were buck naked.

Every one of them was baffled.

"Jay?" Preston began, running over to his brother.

He grabbed him and looked far into his brother's troubled eyes. "What happened here? I don't understand—"

Jay waved the assessor gun, which was still linked to his m-field belt. He pointed toward the empty Hive.

"I'm sorry about Kreutin. I really am. I got the others, though."

His voice drifted off and he swallowed hard. He was quite distant just then.

Out across the wheat field, jumping from her hiding place near the creek, Irina Magin ran for her parents, whom she'd just seen exit the Hive building.

"Momma! Poppa!" she cried out.

The others—the newcomers in pajamas—looked upon them all with expressions of immense perplexity.

In the light of Resurrection Day, Preston Kitteridge glanced around the people-filled wheat field.

"Jay," Preston began, "just who *are* these people?"

The look in Jay's eyes almost broke his brother's heart.

# Epilogue

In the October light of Kansas five years later, Preston Kitteridge stood on the very spot where he had faced the truth of Resurrection Day with his older brother.

Saxifrage Mall, disassembled and bereft of its Arks, was now a windswept, wildflower-haunted ruin. The kudzu had not survived the savage climate. The Hive, a hundred or so yards away, was in no better shape. The tall obsidian obelisk made entirely of monazite, erected in Yuri Kreutin's memory, shone in the amber afternoon light. In the heart of the monazite cenotaph was a cubic centimer of harvested waste plutonium as a reminder of Yuri Kreutin's work upon this earth.

Preston smiled as he considered it. Little Irina Magin, now a blossoming fifteen-year-old beauty, had designed it and built it. It was a fitting monument for what had transpired here so long ago.

When Jay had taken off from Anytown in his Rover, he never got any farther than the ruins of Topeka. His natural curiosity had kept him there until he had made an unusual discovery. Within the ruins of the city, the greenish lights he had originally seen that morning were actually everywhere. These were identical, as they later found out, to those Preston and the other Russians had witnessed during their train trip to Missouri Landing.

The lights were mostly located in the suburbs and were the morphogenetic forms of the thousands of Americans who were deeply asleep on that Christmas morning of the Third

World War. They were ghosts, real *duendes*. They were those particular individuals who just happened to be dreaming, traveling in their astral bodies, when the bombs had fallen.

It had long been suspected that ghosts were the souls or spirits of people who had died violently in their sleep and who were wandering the locale of their untimely deaths, searching for their bodies so that they could complete their natural lives. Jay had entered the ruins and with his assessor gun assessed them, not knowing what else to do.

As was later learned from the Magins, the ghost-lights—the *prevedenir*—had only appeared when the Russians, at the urgings of the Awakener, had begun to harvest the American heartland. This coincided with the appearances of the ghost-light constellations as seen by the *duendes* down in the Meadow. The constellations were merely the gatherings of lost souls radiating down from the surface. They had been disturbed into literal existence when the Russians sent in their first colonies to lay the railway system.

And like lost little lambs, they followed Jay back to the vicinity of the wheat field.

When he arrived, however, the Hive had already been locked into place and opaqued out.

Ghosting into the Hive, he unearthed the true nature of the militarists' plans. He "tapewormed" the assessing program in the computer right under their noses, and then assessed the entire Hive military personnel, reversing the process.

Unfortunately, Jay had thought that when the computers instigated Resurrection the military would be temporarily held hostage on the upper m-field when they were suddenly deopaqued back into their *duende* form. But this was not the case. Monaco had tied the switch-over into the Mall computers, not those of the Hive. So when Resurrection Day was brought about, it wasn't the villagers from Anytown who plummeted to the center of the earth. It was the full contingent of the Hive military, one and all.

The few Russian *duendes* within range of the Meadow computers were opaqued out, although it would take the Appleseeds days to locate and retrieve all of the other Russians, particularly those in far-off Missouri Landing. They had been out of range, but survived. When they were found, most were scared and hungry. Especially the two *mandali*.

What the Appleseeds also had on their hands that day were the new corporeal forms—bodies returned to them by the natural m-field conversion—of several hundred former citizens of Topeka, Kansas, who were suffering from a kind of transition shock. They would eventually have to undergo many months of debriefing and therapy before they would fully comprehend all that had happened in the ensuing six hundred years.

Preston pondered the desolation of the Meadow and the elegant obelisk between Saxifrage and the Hive. In the intervening months following Resurrection Day, Jay had gone with the *mandali* to the mountains of Africa, and then on to Indonesia, to meet with the Awakener. Everything that Yuri Kreutin had told them in the War Room that fatal day had been true. The Awakener was not some obsessive Communist general fighting a distant, troublesome war. He was indeed a spiritual leader that part of the world needed.

Preston glanced into the Mall ruins. From deep within the nearest building came a clattering noise. Then, bursting out into the open air, past the brittle husks of the once proliferating kudzu, came two felines. But these cats were not Ike and Tina, who now lived back in a restored Salina, where the Ark had eventually been towed.

These cats were named Poncho and Cisco, and they both could talk.

Poncho, a tubby marmalade tom, mewled, "We found a *squirrel!*"

And Cisco, a wiry and sleek pitch-black male with many scars, growled, "Help us catch him!"

Preston laughed at the cats, who had been exploring the empty Mall. They came dancing toward him.

Then from the deserted building came someone else.

Gingerly picking her way through the ruins, four-year-old Carly Kitteridge pushed aside fragile strings of dead kudzu. Smiling, she said to her father, "They scared a big squirrel, but I stopped them. Silly cats."

She beamed proudly, blinking in the afternoon sun, having moved, as her father had done so long ago, from darkness to light.

## ABOUT THE AUTHOR

PAUL COOK is a native of Arizona, and currently is a Lecturer in the English Department at Arizona State University. He received his Ph.D. in English in 1981 from the University of Utah, and has two previous science fiction novels to his credit, *Tintagel* and *The Alejandra Variations*. He has published over 150 poems in such journals as *The Georgia Review*, *The Seattle Review*, *Quarterly West* and *The Southern Poetry Review*. He has also done some occasional script writing.

**In the Tradition of**
*Alas, Babylon* and *A Canticle for Liebowitz*

BANTAM SPECTRA
Proudly Presents
DAVID BRIN'S Breakout Novel

## THE POSTMAN

An urgently compelling fable for our times—a chronicle of violence, brutality and fear but also of hope, humanity and love. It is a moving, triumphant story of an individual's dream to lift mankind from a new dark age.

# THE POSTMAN
## by David Brin

On Sale October 10, 1985

\* \* \*

Other books by David Brin:

THE PRACTICE EFFECT
STARTIDE RISING
SUNDIVER